AMERICAN DREAM

Kirby V. Nielsen

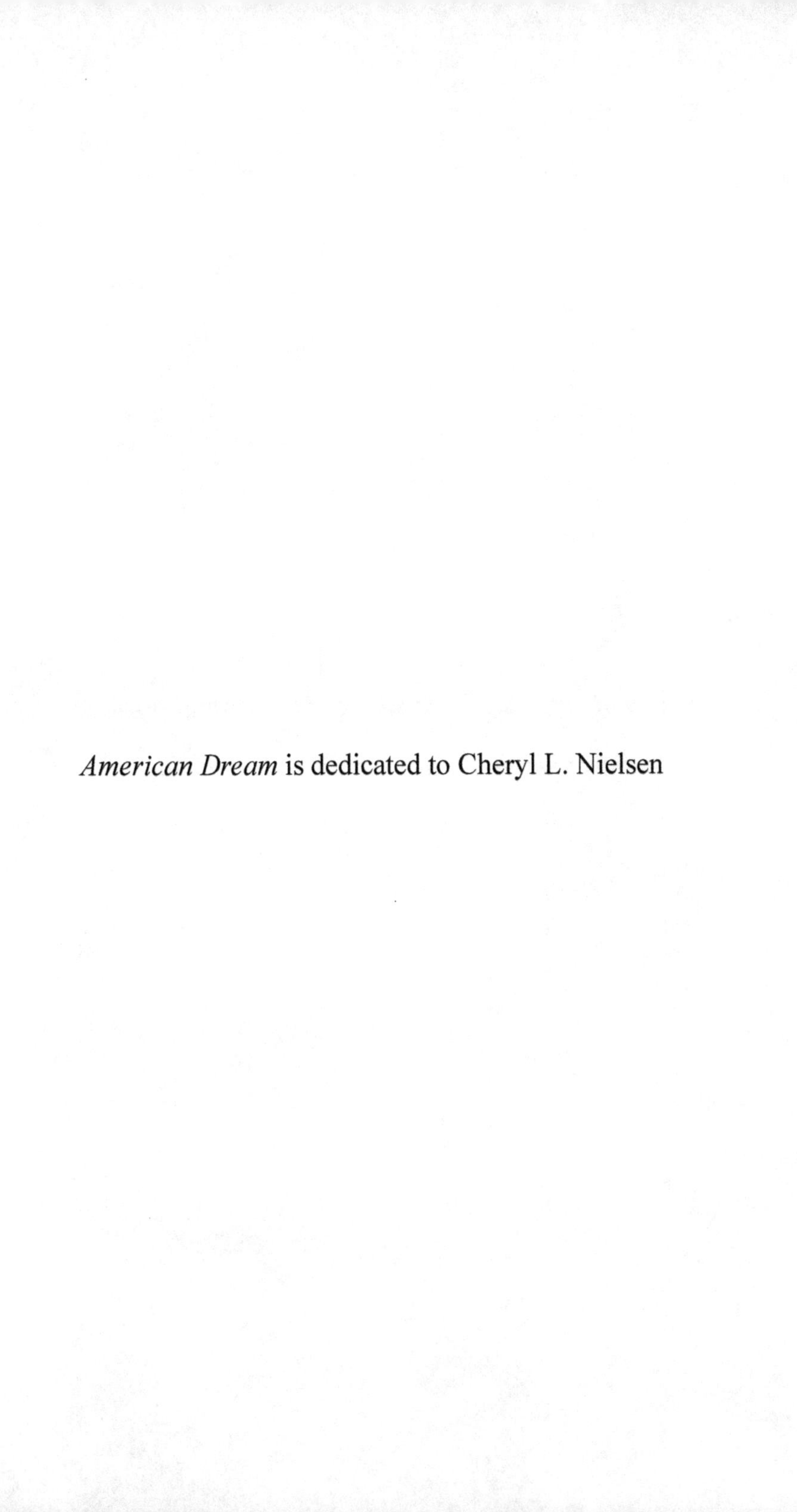

American Dream is dedicated to Cheryl L. Nielsen

Out of suffering have emerged the strongest souls;

the most massive characters are seared with scars.

Khalil Gibran

CHAPTER 1

FREEDOM DAY ONE

"Think of it as crossing the river of hope into the new land of green grass, welcoming people and opportunities you never dreamed you would have."

Beth Smith

1975

The howling of the car's snow tires filled the void in Anna's mind until the noise gradually faded into the background. Slowly, she focused on her life and what was happening at that moment. She was in the front seat, and Beth Smith, the social worker who arranged the community placement, was driving. Anna's precious wooden locker, suitcase, and a big bag of sewing materials were in the trunk. She sat up straight and turned to look at Miss Smith.

Miss Smith noticed Anna's stare and broke into what remained of her dark, quiet space.

"I imagine you're pretty excited, finally leaving Helmhurst after all those years."

"*Excited?* Is that what you think I'm feeling? I'd say terrified is more like it." Anna's tone bordered on caustic.

"You're a smart person. You'll adjust. All you need is a little time."

"I don't know. I've seen many people leave that place only to return . . . people so used to institutional life they couldn't live anywhere else. I don't think you know anything about this. You haven't lived in some shitty asylum like Helmhurst for over forty years with someone constantly telling you what you can and can't do. It gets under your skin and becomes who you are."

Miss Smith nodded but added, "True, I haven't lived it, but I've seen many people successfully adjust to a new life."

"Not too far in the past, the staff called us 'patients,' like we had a heart problem. Before that, we were 'inmates' and needed to be 'paroled' as if we were criminals. And now they call us 'residents,' like renters in an apartment complex. But it was a place where some of us could never leave. I don't want to live there, but it might be the only place I fit in."

"You mean you are *thinking* about going back? After all the work we went through to arrange your discharge?" Now, Miss Smith had a sharp tone.

Anna shrugged. "Maybe, I don't know. But I have to figure out what it means to be free."

"Anna, that's easy. Freedom means going where and doing what you want. Stuff like that."

"That's easy to say, but I think it will be hard to figure out in real life. I mean, where am I going in life? How will I get there? My list of questions is a mile long and still growing."

"Sarah Jensen and her staff will teach you what you need to know. You'll soon have most of your questions answered."

"Maybe, but this is harder than anything I've ever had to do. I don't remember much about my sadness and grief when my parents died. I was young then. I remember the pain of the harsh things they did to me and others at Helmhurst. I still carry the aching I felt when people I loved died. All that was very hard to endure, yet somehow, this seems harder."

Anna turned away from Miss Smith and drifted back into her private world of fear, where freedom did not yet have meaning. The music on the radio replaced the howling snow tires, but Anna soon lost interest. For a while, she thought about loneliness . . . she was lonely. Tears formed around her eyes and trickled down her face. When the social worker turned onto the main road to Minneapolis, Anna asked if they could stop at the next gas station or rest stop. Miss Smith soon found a small rest area and pulled over. Anna walked as far away from the car as possible and lit a cigarette. *What would Rhonda, her mentor and friend at Blue Sky Cottage tell her if she were here?*

She took a couple of drags. The brief, sharp sting of smoke hitting her lungs diverted her self-absorbing thoughts. She stood beside an old fence, staring at nothing but dirt and patches of snow, which reminded her of the nothingness she felt inside. She stubbed her cigarette on the fence post, realizing she was wasting Miss Smith's valuable time. The short break had allowed her to compose herself and it solidified her resolve to go back to Helmhurst.

As soon as Anna closed the car door, she said, "Please take me back to Helmhurst. I don't think I can do this. At least there, I know how to get along."

Miss Smith ignored Anna and continued driving to Minneapolis.

"I said I wanted to go back!" Anna angrily repeated.

"You can get someone else to take you back if that's what you truly want. You are not thinking clearly right now. Your emotions are running too high. You don't believe anyone in your new world will help and be good to you? Well, they will be all around you. You act like it's the end of the road when it's only the beginning of a whole new future. Think of it as crossing the river of hope into the new land of green grass, welcoming people and opportunities you never dreamed you would have.

"If you go back, you'll shrivel up and die. They won't let you stay in that Blue Sky program which has helped you so much. That's a training program for people with potential to go live in the community. No, you'd get sent to a ward with low-functioning people. People die young in those wards, Anna. You know that. Is that what you want, to go back and shrivel up and die? I think you'd better at least sample the new world before making up your mind. That's all I'm asking."

Anna was shocked at how Miss Smith had turned so terse. No one except maybe Rhonda had been that brutally honest with her. Ironically, her angry exchange with Miss Smith drove away some of the fear, and she felt at least some peace as they moved toward her new life.

Anna found it too hard to imagine what her new life would be like and soon gave up trying. Instead, she imagined living out her life at Helmhurst, rocking away the days on the veranda at the backside of the administration building. *Why couldn't I stay in Blue Sky Cottage? Maybe they would make an exception for me. Or, possibly, I could become an assistant to the staff in Blue Sky Cottage? Aside from Rhonda being the staff in charge of me, Rhonda and I could continue to enjoy a friendship.* All the other alternatives she saw for her future ran like an endless loop of questions on an eight-track tape player.

§§§

"Hi, I'm Sarah Jensen, and I'm so glad you're finally at Community Bound. Come, put your things down over along that wall." Sarah pointed to the only open space in her small office. Her smile was warm, and Anna liked something about her voice and mannerisms. A peace sign poster, family pictures, and a Khalil Gibran poem were prominent on three walls. The fourth was an observation window that looked out onto a room with small groups of two to three people.

Sarah's blonde ponytail and blue eyes betrayed her Scandinavian roots. *She looks like a kid,* Anna thought. Despite her youthful appearance, Sarah had a presence that filled the small office with warmth. Anna's first impression of her was that she was genuine—a truth-teller.

"Can I get either of you coffee?"

Anna said, "Yes, black."

Miss Smith replied, "No, thank you."

Anna saw an ashtray on Sarah's desk and asked. "Is it okay if I smoke?"

"Sure. I smoke a bit here at work, but my boyfriend is in medical school, and he is giving me a hard time about quitting completely."

She returned to her desk with coffee for Anna and herself. She continued, "Anna, you've waited a long time to get here. Hopefully, you will find our services are just what you need. We designed this program to help previously institutionalized people become independent citizens. We've worked with quite a few people like you."

"How is that? I mean, how are they like me?"

"It means they spent decades committed to institutions for no known or valid reason. A few had average intelligence but needed help getting up to speed on modern American life. Some are less capable and never reach complete independence. But they do very well with only occasional supervision. Others live in group homes because they need more help getting from one day to the next. The main thing you should keep in mind is that this program is for *you*. We customize programs for each individual. Our goal is to help them overcome the many significant hurdles that arise when moving from living in an institution for many years to living in the community. And there are hurdles.

"The longer people have been inside institutions, the higher the barriers. It would be normal to have fears and reservations about your future. It would be normal to be lonely and afraid. At one time or another, everyone feels like they are put in the wrong place or feel angry. We'll help you deal with those emotions if and when they happen to you. You will find that emotions are the most significant part of making the transition. They are challenging. It can take years for some people to adjust fully."

She's talking about me like she understands me, Anna thought.

"Do you have any questions, Anna?" Sarah took a drag from her cigarette and a sip of coffee.

"Everything is a question. I'll be honest with you. On the way over, I got so anxious I asked Miss Smith to take me back to Helmhurst. As you can see, she refused, and I know this is for my own good. *Questions?* My whole life is in question, that's all."

"You're completely normal, Anna. I'll wager everyone in our program has had mixed emotions about their discharge."

Sarah continued, "I thought I'd discuss business matters with Miss Smith, then we could do a quick tour of our facility and go to lunch. This afternoon, Anna, you and I will get you settled into your new home and meet your landlady. Is everyone good with that?"

Miss Smith responded immediately. "That sounds good to me. I'll start. Even though Anna doesn't qualify for Medicaid, Redwood County, where she was born, will pay three hundred dollars monthly for her room and board for the first six months after her discharge. We feel this is the correct way to interpret the state's new financial support guidelines."

"Why no Medicaid?" Sarah looked surprised.

"To answer that, I have some big news for Anna. As I prepared the paperwork for her discharge, the probate court clerk gave me this paper." She handed it over to Anna and waited.

As Anna looked at the paper, Beth Smith turned to Sarah to explain. "Anna doesn't qualify for Medicaid due to her finances. Sarah, I know from our correspondence that the state of Minnesota will pay for the cost of your program. Is that still correct?"

Sarah nodded.

Anna's eyes moved over the page, then scanned it again. She looked up, gazing at a spot far behind Miss Smith. There was silence while Anna gathered her thoughts. "What does this mean?" she asked.

Miss Smith answered without hesitation, "It means you have a lot of money. I consider that information confidential and not directly affecting Sarah's program, so you can tell her how much money you have if you wish, but you don't have to."

Great! This was Anna's first big decision post-freedom, and she couldn't determine if she should disclose her finances. What other decisions would paralyze her? Miss Smith continued speaking.

"Here is how you got this money. When your father died, he left the farm to your mother. When she died, she left the farm to your brother and you. In 1935, when Peter quit farming, they sold your parents' farm. The probate court judge put your half, which amounted to one thousand, nine hundred forty-two dollars and fifty cents, into a custodial account for safekeeping until you were declared competent, which is now. The amount you see there is all yours and in an account in Mankato. The Redwood County probate clerk informed them that you are now the sole owner of that account. You must call the brokerage company to establish your identity and complete a signature card. Sarah will help you do this."

Anna looked down at the paper. "It says here one hundred and twenty-two thousand, eight hundred and ninety-nine dollars and ninety-five cents. Can that possibly be right?"

Miss Smith replied, "I don't know, Anna, I'm not a financial expert."

Anna exploded. "You mean I have all this money? Money that has always been legally mine, and I've had it all these years? And no one has told me a thing about it? Christ, that's wrong, just like everything they have done to me."

Miss Smith added clarification. "That's the amount the brokerage firm says your account was worth as of January 1, of this year. Look, I don't know anything about these money things, but you need to recall that you were committed to the state of Minnesota's care. During that time, you didn't have the legal right to access your money. They took away your rights when they committed you, but they did protect your assets. You now have a lot of money. You aren't rich, but you have a very comfortable financial cushion. In your discharge instructions, Judge Lundquist reminds you not to tell anyone about this money. 'Keep it private, and you will keep it,' as the old saying goes."

Anna said, "Good Lord, here I thought my savings account in Helmhurst was a big deal."

"Savings account?" Miss Smith was curious.

"Yes, do tell us about that," Sarah chimed in.

"Only my best friend knows about my secret savings account, and I intend to keep it that way."

"Okay, but I'm required to record all your assets to finalize my report. The Minnesota Department of Welfare requires me to get a complete and accurate financial assessment. Don't worry; neither of us will say anything about it," Miss Smith said.

Anna relented. "Put down eleven thousand dollars, although I think it's a little more. It's in an account at a bank in downtown Helmhurst."

"How did this savings account come about?" Miss Smith asked.

"I've had it for a long time. It's money I earned in my little mending business. I saved almost all the fees I charged staff for doing their personal mending."

"Wow, you have a lot of money." Miss Smith smiled, enjoying the story of this supposedly feebleminded woman having a secret savings account for decades.

Anna continued. "I have much to learn about what stuff costs to understand how much money this is."

Sarah smiled. "We're going to teach you how much things cost and a lot more. But all in due time. Beth, do you have anything else we must cover with Anna?"

"Oh, yes, and here is the check for three hundred and sixty-five dollars and twelve cents, the balance in Anna's canteen account at Helmhurst."

§§§

Sarah Jensen toured Anna and Miss Smith through the Community Bound facility. She described the building as an old vegetable warehouse now divided into learning stations, each dedicated to one skill. Brick walls replaced roll-up doors, and large panes of glass completely circled the top of the four walls, giving the giant room a bright, open feeling.

Each learning station was where men and women honed a different transition skill. Anna watched two individuals, a lot younger than herself, learning about money. They were trying to calculate how much change they would get if they gave the clerk five dollars to pay a one-dollar and thirty-four-cent bill. *I need help with that, all right*, Anna thought. Then, there was an area where a person was simply reading a paper, and another was learning how to fold clothes. Community Bound even had a basic kitchen with an old refrigerator and stove. Two people were pulling out a batch of cookies that looked and smelled delicious.

Finally, Sarah said the magic words. "I bet you two are tired and hungry. What do you say we go to lunch, and then I'll take you to your apartment?"

Miss Smith excused herself, saying she needed to get home to a birthday party for one of her children. She turned to Anna." It's such a pleasure to help you start a new life. I think you are intelligent, and there's no reason you won't succeed in whatever you decide to undertake. Please, never give up on yourself. Good luck, Anna."

"I won't. I'm sorry about this morning. I was very nervous."

"It's fine, Anna. I've helped others who have had the same anxieties."

After telling her staff their plans, Miss Jensen took Anna to a small restaurant about a half-mile from Community Bound. Anna saw a waitress put down a hot roast beef sandwich at a nearby table and ordered it. It was her father's favorite, and it had been decades since she'd eaten one.

Sarah explained, "We use this place to practice eating in a restaurant. You know, learning how to order, matching the cost of the food you order with how much money you have. Also, everyone comes here to celebrate when one of our students is ready to graduate.

"After lunch, we're going to your apartment, and you'll meet your landlady. Hilda is a nice older woman who is set in her ways, but deep down, she cares about people and wants to help. She may be crabby at first, but you'll like her once you get to know her."

On their way to her apartment, Anna listened silently

as Sarah talked. She said a van would pick up Anna every weekday morning for the next two weeks. "Then, you'll ride the city bus to Community Bound. So, you'll have to learn fast!"

The comment jarred Anna, once again increasing her anxiety. *Learn what exactly? What happens if I don't learn?*

In five minutes, they arrived at 4132 South 23rd Street, and Sarah said they'd arrived. All the homes on the street and in the neighborhood were plain but well-kept. When Sarah pointed to Mrs. Brown's house, Anna had difficulty understanding where an apartment would be. Her mind was blank as she followed Sarah up the steps and onto the porch. Sarah knocked.

"Hi there, Hilda." She chirped in her cheery voice.

"Come in out of the cold," Hilda said.

They stepped past an older, pleasant-looking woman and into the living room.

"Hilda, this is Anna, Anna Olson, the client I told you about."

"Anna, this is Hilda Brown, your landlord."

The two stared at each other before simultaneously greeting one another, a phenomenon that startled them both. "I imagine you are here for the keys," Hilda said as she walked to a China cabinet near the door. She picked them up and handed them to Sarah. "As usual, there are two keys, one for Miss Olson and one for you. Sarah, I want yours back when Miss Olson becomes independent."

"Of course, Hilda. I have the first month's rent here somewhere." Sarah found a check in her papers and turned it over to Hilda.

"Thank you, as always," Hilda replied.

"Did you follow all of that, Anna?" Sarah asked.

"No, it sounds like someone pays Miss Brown the rent each month. Do I do that?"

Sarah replied. "Yes, you will get the check from Redwood County and deposit it into a new account we'll open for you. Then you'll pay Miss Brown the rent, which is eighty dollars per month."

"I don't know a thing about having a checking account. It's like a new life suddenly plopped down in front of me. I don't know if I can do it. Sorry, Miss Brown, it's not you."

Letting the comment slide, Hilda looked at Sarah and said, "You know where to go."

Turning back to Anna, "It was nice to meet you. Today, I want you to come down at five p.m. sharp. I will have supper ready." She looked at Hilda. "You know what we do here. Anna must learn to fend for herself. I don't want you spoiling her."

Hilda looked disgusted as though she'd received this reminder from Sarah every time a new person from Sarah's program came. "I know, I know, but one little meal here and there won't hurt anyone."

Sarah and Anna thanked Hilda. They returned to the car to get Anna's belongings. Retracing their path to the house, they veered to the right and around the porch. On the side of the house was a stairway. The stairs were an obstacle course in and of themselves, narrow and steep. *Made for a young person*, Anna thought. The small landing at the top provided just enough space to turn and face the door to the apartment.

Sarah commented, "Well, here we are, Anna, your first apartment. Your independent life starts here!"

The apartment was small but at least twice the size of any room Anna ever had in Helmhurst. The entrance led to a small kitchen, flooded with light streaming through a window framed by thin white curtains. A small stove, an old GE refrigerator, and a two-person dining table filled the small room. Open shelves, which served as a pantry, were barely adequate for one person. The pantry shelves included cooking utensils, silverware, a canister set for coffee, sugar, and flour, and mixing bowls.

Straight ahead was a sparsely decorated living room. A well-worn couch, an easy chair, a floor lamp, and a bookcase took up the whole room. Anna set her suitcase, her giant bag of finished needlepoint pieces and supplies, and her locker in the middle of the living room floor. She stood still for a moment with nothing registering with her, no emotions, thoughts, nothing. Anna felt empty, already overwhelmed by everything that had happened that day. Plus, she was tired. Anna spent the prior evening tossing, turning, and worrying about what today would bring.

The last room was a small bedroom with a single bed, a small chest of drawers, and a metal storage cabinet. On the bed were clean towels and one set of linens. The bathroom was adjacent to the bedroom and was as sparse as the rest of the apartment.

Anna had no idea if this apartment was good or bad. She had nothing to judge it by. It was like someone trying to judge wine who had never tasted it. "I hope there aren't bugs here," was the first thing she could conjure up.

"Oh, no." Sarah put her hand to her chest in amusement. "Hilda wouldn't tolerate that. She is the type of person who would never have even one bug in her house."

"Sarah, I guess it will be okay," Anna said.

"I thought you would be thrilled with it," Sarah replied.

"I am, I guess. I don't know. I've never seen an apartment before. Sure, it's great."

"I would call it cozy," Sarah answered in a cheery, upbeat tone, finally understanding Anna's point. "Okay then, let's get you unpacked, then discuss what you need to buy to start your new life."

She received a terse retort from Anna. "I can unpack my things, so let's check that off your list. What else is there?"

"Anna, I'm not used to having such a capable person enter my program. Many of my people need help getting started on things you may consider simple. So bear with me. I need to be sure I don't miss any steps and cause you to suffer any hardships.

For the next hour, Sarah went through a series of checklists that assessed everything from making a bed to personal care skills. Anna didn't do well on four of the lists. Shopping, cooking, handling money, and transportation were all things Anna knew she needed to learn.

When they finished, Sarah and Anna made a grocery list. Anna's first food list included basics such as milk, bread, and eggs. Then, there were personal care items such as soap, shampoo, and toothpaste. Anna looked at her lists, and it dawned on her how much work starting a new life would be.

Sarah stood up and said, "We better get going. The day's not getting any younger." Once at the store, she rattled off instructions about selecting items. There were more sizes, prices, and brands than Anna had imagined. Sarah tried to give Anna grocery shopping tips, but everything Sarah said went in one ear and out the other. Anna's mind was too preoccupied, gazing in amazement at all the choices. The store was another place that made her feel like an immigrant.

With the groceries put away, Sarah gave Anna her final instructions for the day, "Remember, the van will pick you up in front of Hilda's house at eight tomorrow morning. We will review your night when you get to Community Bound."

"Thanks, Sarah. I mean, Miss Jensen."

Anna wanted to collapse as soon as the door closed, but she had to be awake and alert for dinner with Hilda. There was nothing left to do but start unpacking.

Dinner was vastly different than eating at Helmhurst. There were attractive China plates and real silverware, not the cheap institutional spoons and forks, many of which were bent. The tablecloth returned her to her mother's Grant Grove dinners in their dining room.

Anna's eyes quickly scanned the living room. To the left was an oversized, overstuffed couch with doilies on the armrests and a crochet blanket draped over the back. An old Persian-style rug looked worn and tired. Mid-1940s style end tables, lamps, and a coffee table made the room feel comfortable.

Hilda had a barrage of questions for Anna about her past life and hopes for the future. Anna's fatigue and the stress of a new life shaped her short answers. She helped carry the dishes to the kitchen when the meal ended, feeling its warmth and charm. After coffee and a piece of cobbler, Anna said goodnight, explaining that she was tired and wanted to finish unpacking.

She was exhausted. She started her day in a large institution, and here she was, sitting in her dark apartment. *Funny, all those years, I wanted out of Helmhurst to be free, and now I don't know what that means.* It was difficult to sort through her feelings.

Leaning back into the softness of the well-worn couch, Anna immediately fell asleep. She didn't wake up until the clock on the wall read ten-thirty. Minneapolis' newest resident listened for sounds coming down a hall or a distant scream . . . the usual noises of Helmhurst. Instead, she heard a siren, far away and fading into the night, along with the steady hum of the old refrigerator.

Anna's heart ached for Jimmy Dale, her boss at Helmhurst. He was the one who looked out for her, gave her the only room she ever had to herself at Helmhurst, and was the person who killed a man to save her life. He was the one she loved more than anything. She longed for him to wrap his big arms around her and protect her. Anna saw herself whispering into his ear, *Jimmy, I'm scared.*

CHAPTER 2

HILDA BROWN

"Here I am. My body is in Minneapolis, where I always wanted to live, but it feels like my soul is still back in Helmhurst."

Anna Olson

1975

On January 8, 1975, the second day of freedom from Helmhurst, Anna was waiting for Sarah to get her so they could go to a bank and open her accounts. By chance, she was sitting in the section of the Community Bound program where she had seen two people learning about how much change they should get from a five-dollar bill. Play money, old receipts, and an old bank statement were lying on the table in front of her.

She was alone, slouching over, staring at the floor. Lost in a sea of memories, she imagined hearing a familiar voice. *"Anna Olson, there you are, moping around, staring at the floor. Sit up. You have a great life to lead. Get your shoulders back. Stop looking like a crabby old lady."*

Anna was stunned to hear her friend and supervisor from Helmhurst, Rhonda. It sparked two equal reactions. It warmed her heart to know her mentor was still nearby. But she was sad that none of this was real. Her only thought was letting her former mentor down, *I'm sorry, Rhonda, that crabby old lady followed me here.*

Suddenly conscious of her demeanor, Anna sat straight and looked around the room. There was a quiet buzz about the place, and other participants seemed intent on learning new skills.

Anna glanced at the two checks she held. One was from Helmhurst; the other was from Redwood County. Soon, Sarah appeared with a big smile on her face. That smile and Sarah's upbeat, cheery personality reminded Anna of Rhonda.

"Good morning, Anna."

"Good morning, I guess."

"Today, we will do something that usually comes much later in our program. However, we need to be sure your two checks get deposited in a bank, so your money is safe. You already have a savings account in Helmhurst, but you need a local checking and savings account. You may not know how a checking account works, but we will learn all about it after you have been in our program for a while.

"I will be your guide to getting everything set up. Okay?"

Anna nodded. With the help of an attentive staff member at the bank, they set Anna up with a checking and savings account using the two checks she brought. Sarah started Anna's checking account with one hundred fifty of the three-hundred-dollar check Miss Smith gave her yesterday. One hundred and fifty dollars in cash would be used by Anna to buy groceries and incidental items. They used her canteen money to start a new savings account. Finally, with a nod and a signature from Anna, they transferred the Helmhurst Bank savings account to the local bank. Soon, Anna and Sarah were returning to Community Bound.

When they got back and settled into Sarah's office, they reviewed Anna's four checklists and how the prior night went. Had she thought of anything else she needed to start her new life? Anna joined a routine that was established for all program participants. Each day, they would get their folder from a plastic crate and sit down with whomever was available to review how things had gone the day before. Mastered new skills were checked off, and problems were reviewed for what to do to resolve them.

§§§

The Community Bound staff slowly but surely began introducing Anna to Minneapolis living. Within a few days of starting the program, a staff member took Anna and two others for a ride on the Metro bus. He showed them how to pay for their fare and, after a short ride, how to pull the cord at the top of the bus to signal they wanted to get off. He took them across the street and repeated the process, returning them to Community Bound. The instructor asked his students, "What did you think of your bus ride?"

"It doesn't look very hard," Anna shot back.

"No, it isn't tough, but it takes some practice. Next time, you each can pay your way."

One of Anna's companions said he didn't think he could learn the steps. The other student sat in total silence.

Their teacher was patient and knew how to guide his students. In one week, he had each of them identify which bus they needed to take by looking at the number on the front and side of the bus. They also learned to pay their fares and get off at the right stop. Their instructor said, "You all are doing well. We'll learn how to transfer buses next week."

§§§

Anna knew she had the best of two worlds by the end of her first week with Hilda. Privacy when she wanted it and Hilda when she was in the mood for a companion. Both women were alike in many ways. Each had a surly side and a degree of warmth and caring. It was often hard to predict which version would show up at any given time.

Anna knew nothing about cooking, which appalled Hilda. "How can you be a fifty-eight-year-old woman and not know a thing about cooking?"

Anna crossed her arms and sulked. "Well, cooking is far from the only thing I've never learned. Try living in an institution and see how many chances you get to bake cookies."

Hilda resolved to teach Anna how to make simple meals, starting with the basics. Anna wasn't too happy with the idea initially, but when she realized how often she would have to cook for herself, she accepted the instructions more cheerfully. Basic cooking lessons turned into shared evening meals at least twice a week. Hilda's cooking skills were like Anna's sewing. They came to her easily and with wonderful results.

Anna was surprised that she was no longer interested in needlepointing in her new home. What's more, she had difficulty even looking at her old work. She thought needlepointing was something in her past, like Helmhurst. In its place was a creative void, waiting to be filled by something meaningful.

Besides sharing meals, Anna liked to sit in Hilda's living room, where the walls and furniture displayed Hilda's cherished memories. On a bookshelf were old brown, hardbound books. On the top was a picture of Hilda and her husband. Mr. Brown wore his Army uniform, and Hilda wore patriotic pins, ribbons, and a Statue of Liberty hat. They were the picture of happiness. Their country had won the war, and he returned to her alive. Anna wondered what it must have been like for Hilda to have the love of her life go away to war and never know if he would return.

There was another old picture of someone's parents, an end table from another era covered with old, crocheted doilies, and figurines of a cardinal and a blue jay. The whole house could have been one where Anna's parents might have lived. Perhaps that's why she felt comfortable here. In some ways, Hilda took on the role of a mother figure. Anna liked it, but whenever Hilda scolded her for not getting something right, she would sass back as if she were still a teenager.

"What happens after you finish this program Sarah has you in?" asked Hilda.

Anna stared back at her. "I don't have a clue."

"I bet she'll help you get a job. Sarah is a good lady, and she'll look after you. She likes you."

"How do you know that?"

"I just do. Understanding comes with age, Anna."

Being around Hilda didn't put everything in order in Anna's life. She had wild mood swings that Hilda believed were caused by a "change of life." Anna knew there was a lot more to it than that. She often had regrets and doubts about leaving Helmhurst. Despite all efforts to the contrary, her mind sometimes popped back into the worst days of her life, dragging her mood with it. But always, it swung around toward the positive. *I used to be happy all the time. Maybe I can feel that way again. I need to keep trying.*

§§§

On March 2, 1975, Anna borrowed a piece of stationery and an envelope from Hilda to write a letter to Janice Haggedorn, her best friend from the Big House days, and the woman responsible for getting her out of Helmhurst.

Dear Janice,

Hello, I've finally gotten myself oriented enough in my new world that I can write you a sensible letter. First, I promised my new address:

Anna Olson c/o Hilda Brown

4132 S. 23rd Street

Minneapolis, Minnesota 55405

Here I am. My body is in Minneapolis, where I always wanted to live, but it feels like my soul is still back in Helmhurst. I compare everything I do here with my life there. That is like comparing apples to oranges. Everything here is an adjustment. Even brushing my teeth seems to be a reason for me to reflect. After using a community bathroom for all those years, having a bathroom to yourself seems so lonely and quiet. And nice.

I may sound unhappy or disappointed, but I'm also determined to make a go of this new life. I have so much to learn! Do you know how to ride a city bus? It's more complicated than I thought. You have known how to do a checking account for years. I started my first account two months ago, and I'm always afraid I'll screw it up.

I rent a small one-bedroom apartment on the second floor of a house. My landlady is old. She is like me, lonely and sometimes grumpy. But she's a great cook and has made it her mission in life to teach me some of her cooking skills. Of course, she had to start with boiling water. Ha.

What's new at Helmhurst? Are you still working for Madsen and doing good for the people stuck living there? Hopefully, your health is good.

I would like to come to see you. Give me another month or two to adjust, and I'll figure out how to take the bus to Helmhurst.
Your friend,
Anna

Eight days later, Hilda told Anna someone had called for her.

"Who was it?" Anna asked.

"Margaret Pattersen, but she didn't say where she was from. Here, I took down her number. You're supposed to call her back." Hilda handed Anna a piece of paper with the name and number.

Anna paid no attention to the phone call, putting the slip of paper on top of her dresser.

§§§

Good Friday was on March 28, 1975. Paul Swensen pulled into the Helmhurst State Hospital and parked behind the Blue Sky Cottage. He and his wife were looking forward to having their son John home for the Easter weekend. John always liked coming home. Besides being close to his mother, his older sisters always doted on him. Mr. Swensen was an hour late as he ran up the steps onto the main floor, then down another set of stairs to the garden-level classroom.

Seeing the empty classroom, he thought he was too late. *John must be up in his room already.* Then, he heard a scream from behind a partition. Every parent knows their child's cry, and Paul was no exception. He flew across the classroom. When he reached the divider, he was horrified by what he saw. The classroom teacher, Trace Martin, stood over John, holding his hands behind his back and lifting him off the floor. The result was tremendous pressure on the boy's shoulder, causing extreme pain.

Not knowing Mr. Swensen was there, he cursed the boy. "I know you are as fucking smart as any normal person. You are just too lazy to act right. Well, I'm sick of it."

Mr. Swensen ran to the scene and pulled Martin off his son by grabbing the back of his shirt. He immediately stepped over John, protecting him from further harm.

"Listen, you son-of-a-bitch, get away from my son. *And stay away!* You are going to get your ass fired for this. And if I can, I'm filing criminal assault charges. You can't torture another human being that way, let alone a helpless retarded person. If I were you, I'd leave this minute, or I'll take you down, so help me, God."

Trace Martin turned away, then turned back, "This isn't what you think. And I'd be careful if I were you. if you go blabbing about this to anyone else, you will pay the price." He scrambled to find his jacket and left.

A red-faced and winded father took his shaken son upstairs to the staff office and asked that a nurse check him out. He explained what he saw to the Blue Sky staff who were present. As she listened, the color drained from the face of Rhonda Jones, one of the residential care staff members.

Rhonda thought. *I've got it now. Trace Martin is why Anna had all those scrapes and bruises from falling headfirst down the stairs. Why has it taken me so long to put this together?*

Rhonda phoned the administration building to see if she could contact any of the institution's officials, but everyone had left. She next tried the "on-call" staff member who came and took a full report, promising Mr. Swensen a call Monday morning.

"That won't be necessary. I'll be back here Monday at eight a.m. without John. He's never coming back here again."

The Monday morning meeting was tense. Mr. Swensen had cooled some, but the sight of his son's torture kept running through his mind all weekend. *What else did he do to John or other people in that classroom?*

The Helmhurst director of personnel, Harry Thompson; Jim Madsen, director of professional services; and James Granholm, director of mental retardation services, met with him. The meeting was short.

Jim Madsen spoke first. "Mr. Swensen, I'm Martin's supervisor, and I placed him on indefinite suspension while we investigate what you saw. There was nothing but good things in his background when we hired him. So far, I haven't even had time to investigate your allegation."

Mr. Swensen didn't accept the explanation. "I would say you haven't tried hard enough. If you all don't fire him now, on the spot, you'll never fire him. You have a reliable first-hand eyewitness, for God's sake!"

Greg Thompson replied to Mr. Swensen. "As Jim said, we've suspended him until we verify some things. Plus, Trace Martin is a union employee entitled to a hearing before we terminate his employment. Obviously, we still need to arrange that. And, of course, we need your written statement about the incident. Then, we'll interview all the staff who worked with him to understand his work behavior better. Most likely, this is not the only incident of abuse. But we will not let this slide. And we will follow up quickly. Let me assure you, based on your story alone, this man will never work with any of our residents again. We agree with you. We want Martin gone ASAP. I'm afraid that's all we can say for now."

Paul Swensen was still visibly upset. "Your assurances don't mean shit to me. Let me be clear. This meeting is not the end of this from my point of view. I want someone with real authority to look into how you all run these places and find out why you allow this type of thing to happen."

§§§

Anna had been so busy that she was unaware she had moved past Easter further into spring. Each day, she felt less like an alien and a little more like what she assumed an average person felt. Sarah and Anna were growing closer thanks to the weekly home visits Sarah made to Anna. During these visits, she reviewed all her original checklist items. *"How is the shopping going? Are you doing alright with your cooking?"*

But Sarah also became more fascinated with Anna's needlepoint collection. In them, Sarah saw a troubled life and beautiful reprieves. "You're not making any new ones?" Sarah asked.

"Nope, I've got all I can handle, figuring out what it means to be free. That, plus learning all this stuff I missed while living my life sheltered away in an institution."

If Anna didn't know any better, she'd guess that Sarah was Helmhurst Rhonda's younger sister because they sounded alike and kept an eye on her every move. She'd say, *"Anna, you're scowling too much. You're not back in Helmhurst. You're getting ready to take on the world!"* Leaving no room for argument, Sarah went to take a new prospect on a tour.

When the first graduation lunch for another Community Bound participant came, Anna was displeased.

"Do I have to go to this lunch thing?" Anna sounded like a whiney teenager.

"Yes, you do. It's high time you start thinking of others. You won't get anywhere groveling in your misery." Sarah smiled at Anna as she patted her on the back. Anna was confused because she could make a command sound so caring.

It turned out she enjoyed the lunch. She discovered

another Community Bound person born near Redwood Falls, Minnesota. The two talked about where they lived and shared their memories of the region. The two people who sat across the booth from them couldn't communicate well, but Anna understood them enough to help them order. She felt good about assisting them. Anna topped off the enjoyable lunch with her favorite dessert, warm cherry pie, and a scoop of vanilla ice cream. Later that night, while thinking about lunch, Anna couldn't help but think, *Sarah was right . . . again.*

On May 21, 1975, Sarah presented Anna with her first significant post-discharge crisis. "Anna, I want to let you know you are way ahead of our average participants. You will be ready to graduate soon. We need to start thinking about your future. Do you have any plans for when you finish here?"

"Plans? No, I have no plans. I'm just getting used to your program, and you're telling me I must move on?"

Sarah clarified her question. "Do you plan to return to Grant Grove when you finish here? Perhaps you have some family or friends there."

"Sarah, you must be joking. After all this time, there is no one left for me. I don't even know if my brother is still there or if he lives two houses down the street from Hilda. He abandoned me back in my early Helmhurst days. His attitude towards me was to lock the door and throw away the key."

"Well, I'm not joking, and I worry about your attitude. You get so negative and sharp sometimes. That will hurt you when you go out there to find a job. Nobody owes you a thing. You'll have to figure out how you will make ends meet. I know you have a nice savings account and some inheritance, but those Redwood County support checks stop next month. You need to pick your chin up off the floor and get busy with living."

"If you say so." Anna stared at the floor.

"I do, and stop staring at the floor!" Sarah walked away, leaving Anna to simmer in a new round of fear and uncertainty.

Anna didn't see Sarah again until one afternoon when she visited Anna's apartment for one of her regular home visits. Sarah found an increasingly diverse supply of food, home decorations, and more piles of needlepoint pieces. She deduced that increased food in Anna's pantry meant Hilda's cooking lessons were producing more meal options.

Sarah continued to be fascinated with Anna's needlepoint. "I still think these are so beautiful. Every time I look at them, I wonder how you make a piece of cloth look like an artist's painting. Have you started doing them again?"

"Nope. As I told you before, I stopped when I came here, and I feel no urge to start again. I don't understand it, either. Something inside me broke. Maybe the trauma of leaving Helmhurst has something to do with it."

"How long have you been needlepointing?" Sarah asked.

"Since I was a little girl." Wanting to change the subject, Anna asked, "Do I pass inspection this time?"

"Yes, you pass inspection. Pretty soon, I'll have you come to clean my apartment. You still get along with Hilda?"

"Sure. We're like two peas in a pod. We're grumpy even though we don't mean to be. She is still teaching me to cook, and I do some sewing for her. She should work for you teaching cooking because she's a good cook and a patient teacher."

"So, how often does she cook for you?"

"You always ask that, and I always say she doesn't cook for me. We make things together, with me learning how to prepare the meal. I never realized what was involved with cooking. Anyhow, I probably eat with her two or three evenings a week."

"Excellent, Anna. I'm amazed at everything you're learning. You have come so far. You will be just fine on your own. Of that, I am sure."

§§§

By late April 1975, Hilda felt she knew Anna enough to ask her more personal questions. Over dinner, she let her curiosity loose.

"Anna, you've never talked about your childhood or your family. What kind of upbringing did you have?"

"You never asked," Anna shot back, looking at her potatoes. She soon raised her face to look at Hilda. "I had a good childhood. I lived with my mom and dad on a farm by Grant Grove. We had a typical small farm—cows, chickens, oats, and corn. I went to a one-room school and walked down a dusty dirt road to get there. Funny, I remember the ruts the cars and farm wagons made. They were deep and hard as clay when dry and gooey when it rained.

"Then, I had a seizure. I recovered from it okay." Anna took a deep breath. "Then came the second seizure while I was in school, and I recovered from it. But a terrible thing happened. My father died in a freak snowstorm. He froze to death in a whiteout about a mile from our house. That was a hard blow because I loved him so much."

Anna looked away again before continuing. "Long story short, some friends stepped in to help us because my mom couldn't handle my father's death very well. She suffered from depression all her life, as far as I know. Then, my mom died from influenza, leaving my brother and me orphaned. In 1933, being an orphan and having seizures was a one-way ticket to an institution. So, I went to Helmhurst when I was sixteen, and they kept me there for all these years."

"Oh, my, what a story! I had no idea that's how you

29

ended up there. Did you ever have any more seizures?"

"One, about a year after I got to Helmhurst. But they kept me there anyway, saying I was feebleminded. Do you remember that word?"

"Barely."

Anna explained. "If you were feebleminded, supposedly you could not manage your own life. But for me, it was a false label, another reason they used to keep me locked up. Later, I realized they kept me and thousands like me in institutions to do the laundry, clean the buildings, care for the weaker residents, and cook the food in the institutions. So now, what about you?"

Hilda sighed. "That's so sad. I never heard about that until now."

Anna replied, "Hilda, don't feel bad. Most people have no idea what went on. What's your story?"

"Not much to tell. I was born and raised right here in Minneapolis. My dad worked as a rail yard manager for the Northern Pacific Railroad. He was the one who determined which train went to each track. It was complicated, but he managed all those trains because he knew each one and what time they arrived and when they left.

"So, I married me a railroad man when I was just nineteen years old. Can you imagine? That was in 1913." Hilda paused. "He went off to the Great War in 1919 and, thankfully, returned to me in 1920 all in one piece. Two of his buddies didn't even make it to France. They died of influenza on the ship going over. That was so sad. People today don't remember how bad those two things were."

"1919, that's the year I was born," Anna observed.

"We couldn't have children, but we loved each other and continued our life together. Eventually, I went to work at the downtown Daytons department store. That was a good job. I liked the people I worked with and made my own spending money. Not every woman got to do that back then. During World War II, I switched to Pillsbury Flour to help the war effort. I sewed shut twenty-five-pound bags of flour destined for kitchens in Europe. After the war, I went back to Daytons. From there, not much to tell. I lost him ten years ago, and that's when I started renting the upstairs."

"What was his name," Anna asked?"

"Robert. Robert Harold Brown. I still miss him. Sometimes, I look at that brown chair and see him reading the newspaper. I know that sounds ridiculous, but he still seems so alive."

The conversation died there, but Hilda had opened old wounds for Anna. Many of the more hurtful parts of her life flashed before her in an endless parade. The racing thoughts kept her awake until the early morning hours. Her demeanor at Community Bound and Hilda's house changed for the worse. Most of the time, she was surly, speaking as seldom as possible. A sadness hung over her like a mourner's sackcloth.

Later, at Community Bound, Sarah's cheery voice broke into her private world. "Anna, cheer up. You look like you lost your best friend!" But Anna plodded on, learning the lessons of adapting to modern life quicker than any program participant before her.

Even though Anna knew her graduation was near, it felt like a lightning bolt out of a clear blue sky when Sarah said, "Anna, I have wonderful news! You are ready to graduate. You have mastered every skill we teach. Of course, there is much more to learn, but you know what you need to get by. All the other things you will learn along the way."

"But what am I going to do? Like, where do I go?"

"Don't worry, Anna. I have a plan to get the next phase of your life kickstarted."

June 10, 1975, was graduation day. Anna invited Hilda

to be her guest at her noon celebration meal. Despite the fun nature of the meal, a fire was still burning inside Anna, one kindled by too many sad memories and too few good ones. But as she sat in the booth with Hilda and Sarah, Anna thought about Rhonda. "I have a friend back at Helmhurst," Anna observed. "She was the staff person assigned to help me at the end of my stay there. Her name was Rhonda, and she would really enjoy this. I wish she could be here."

Sarah reached across the booth and took Anna's hand. "I'm sure she would be very proud."

"Yes, she would."

CHAPTER 3

CROSSROADS

"I will not go backward; I'm a survivor, I'm strong, and I have talents."

Anna Olson

1975

In June of 1975, when Anna completed the Community Bound program, she had learned to master basic independent living skills such as grocery shopping, handling money, using public transportation, and basic cooking skills. Her problem-solving abilities seemed as intact as that of an average adult, which helped her use common sense to solve most problems. However, Anna had not yet discovered what she wanted to do with the rest of her life. Nor had she learned to deal with her anger and depression. Making matters worse was the stress brought on by culture shock. Mini-skirts, boom boxes, and traffic were just a few of the things that were hard to understand.

It wasn't as if she didn't have something on which to improve. She did. Instead, it was that she lacked something about which she cared. In her opinion, the job Sarah arranged for her immediately after graduation was menial work.

She put working at New Life Industries on the same level as her early months in the laundry. Sorting bin after bin of donated clothes, toys, and household items simply replaced Helmhurst's piles of laundry. Her peers were people who had already overcome significant roadblocks but, like her, faced even more. Many had emotional problems or struggled to cope due to the damage caused by a chemical dependency.

"I have no idea why Sarah put me in a job like this," Anna complained to Hilda.

"She must have had her reasons," Hilda replied. "At least you have a job doing something. Besides, what else have you got lined up?"

"I don't know. All I know is I didn't agree to leave Helmhurst, only to work beside all the same people I used to live with." Anna's reply contained a heavy dose of bitterness and superiority.

Hilda shot back, "Patience. I think you lack patience."

Anna continued in her institutional persona. It was a comfortable place, blanketed in her misery. The calmness and solitude it provided weren't all that bad. She didn't understand her behavior. Was she angry because of the injustice of the last forty-plus years? Or was she blindsided by the insecurity that came with freedom? She tried to resolve the two possibilities as she lay in bed, trying to go to sleep. Her conclusion was always that both were big contributors to her unhappiness.

To deal with her work frustrations, she began to take long walks. Minneapolis had several lakes, and one of the nicest and largest was just two blocks from Hilda's house. She spent long weekend hours walking the trails where she could watch the geese, ducks, and frogs sun themselves by the water's edge. Plus, it allowed her to smoke again. Not being able to smoke in Hilda's house was hard. But now, she found she could get through a day better if she smoked while walking.

She wrote letters to Janice more regularly. Once a week, she would sit down and tell Janice what was good and not so good in her life.

§§§

By far, Hilda was the person who absorbed the brunt of Anna's ups and downs during the long, hot summer of 1975. "Anna, I'm wondering if you would please help me clean out my bedroom closet?" Ann understood it as more like a command than a question.

"Sure, I guess." Anna shot back with a shrug of her shoulders.

"I'm not asking for you to donate your right arm. Goodness! All I need is a little help reaching the top shelf. There is absolutely no need to get all huffy about that." Anna winced whenever Hilda scolded her. It made her feel like a kid again, and she resented it.

Hilda was disappointed with Anna's unhappiness and sour demeanor. Instead of progressing in her adjustment, she saw Anna regressing. Her sagging shoulders, self-isolating in her apartment for prolonged periods, and terse replies were apparent signs of a struggling person.

Friday evening, August 15, 1975, was hot and humid. The temperature was still eighty-five as the sun was setting. Anna and Hilda were sitting on the porch with Hilda's small fan doing its best to stir the muggy air. They listened to the Minnesota Twins play the Los Angeles Dodgers, who were in town for a three-game series.

Things didn't look good for the home team. All-Star pitcher Bert Blyleven had given up seven runs by the top of the third.

"I don't like Blyleven. He's overrated, always has been."

Anna's sounded disgusted.

"How did you come to know so much about baseball?" Hilda asked.

"I used to listen to games on the radio. I'd ask one of the staff to put a radio where I could hear it, and most of the time, they would accommodate me. Being locked up for so long, you need something of interest that was outside."

When Rod Carew, one of the Twins' power hitters, tapped a shallow pop fly to outfielder Manny Mota, it was all Anna could take. Her short but critical tirade about how badly the team played was too much for Hilda.

"Anna Olson, I've had it with your complaining and crabby, nasty attitude. You seem unhappy with everything, and it's getting on my nerves. I think you need to go back to Helmhurst. The way you've been acting lately, it's where you belong. Or you need to find yourself another apartment where you can bitch to yourself or anyone else who will listen." She stood up, picked up her Ring-A-Word book, and went to bed. As she reached the door, she turned and said, "You can let me know what you decide on Monday."

Anna sat stunned and silent. She had never received such a sharp rebuke from someone she liked and was unprepared for not living with Hilda. Darkness fell on the quiet street, and the sound of crickets was all that remained of the day. Anna picked up the portable radio and the fan and took them inside the house. She shut off all the lights and locked the back and front doors without thinking about what she was doing.

The inside of her apartment was hotter than it was on the porch. She quickly brushed her teeth, splashed cold water on her face, and dampened a washcloth with cold water. For the first time since her rape, she went to bed wearing nothing but a silk slip. She lay on the bedspread and draped the washcloth over her face.

Anna entered a state of mind where she lost awareness of the earthly world. She focused on the psychological part of her existence. In her meditation, she relived the horror of past events, how death came in the middle of a blizzard, taking her father. Then, her poor, broken-down mother slipped away. Although she tried to appear calm when her mother died, she felt her soul break into pieces. She froze with fear about what would happen next. As a teenage girl, she knew she could not do anything about her future.

Living forty-one years at Helmhurst reinforced her feelings of powerlessness. She couldn't get the parole she desired so much. She lived in fear of being raped, and the recollection of that terror was still with her. Helmhurst was a black hole where her hopes and dreams disappeared. But some good people loved her and gave her a sense of belonging. What would all those good people tell her now?

Even in that motionless state, sweat kept beading up on her brow, between her breasts, and on her stomach. She had never felt so estranged from herself and never so unsure of who she was. The simple question, *What am I going to do?* repeated itself on a continuous cycle.

Anna recounted two lines in a letter to Rhonda. *Another big problem is that I feel two things simultaneously. I feel like I do and don't belong here in Minneapolis.* But where would she live? Grant Grove, her childhood home, was a lifetime away. That world was entirely gone, as alien as Paris, France.

All the hurts, disappointments, and love she received and lost were seared into her memory. She desperately needed a way to keep them from ruining her odds of a good restart. *Now, I can decide which world I want to embrace for the rest of my life. But I don't know anything about making choices. Here I am, frozen with fear, afraid of the very thing I've always wanted—a chance to be free.*

§§§

It felt like she was awake the entire forty-eight hours, although she knew that wasn't true. She heard church bells ringing early that morning, but they failed to wake her from her trance. Anna emerged from her soul-searching journey at five pm on Sunday afternoon. Her sweat-soaked slip clung to her body and felt cool on her skin. She brushed her teeth and drew a bath. Soaking in a lukewarm tub, Anna noticed that she felt calmer.

She dried her hair as best she could, then studied the frizzy mess. Anna realized she hadn't gotten her hair styled since the trim and style Rhonda set up before her discharge meeting. She looked into the mirror and said, "Yup, it needs help."

Anna made a small pot of coffee. It was strong, like the coffee in the Helmhurst canteen. But it smelled good, making her hungry for the first time since Friday. She made a peanut butter and jelly sandwich, grabbed a banana, and sat on the little landing. The cool evening breeze was pleasant. *Pleasant?* That was something she noted was missing from her life up to this point. She had forgotten the last time that she just plain felt good.

Everything about life at that moment felt new and fresh. Anna wondered why. She hadn't discovered some unique insight into her life during the previous two days of mental anguish. Yet she was sure that, at this moment, life was good.

She went inside for a refill on her coffee and yielded to temptation, bringing back a pack of cigarettes. She sat in the evening coolness and smoked and drank coffee, feeling more awake and aware of each passing moment. She didn't recall deciding, but the future direction of her life was clear. No going back to the past again—no dwelling on Helmhurst and no wallowing in the hardships in her life. She would do her best to build a wall between today and her painful yesterdays.

One cigarette became two, and two turned into three. Soon, Anna looked down in a tin can turned ashtray to find six butts. Anna realized it was time to go in. She turned on the living room lamp and opened her sewing bag. Even though it had been eight months, Anna picked up her latest needlepoint piece and began making the trim on the last building she lived in at Helmhurst. Anna knew she was finally ready to return to her life's passion. It felt great, the secure feeling of being back doing the thing that kept her sane during her lengthy incarceration.

§§§

Anna slipped out of the house early the following day. She had not yet devised a grand new plan for the rest of her life, but she had a vague idea of what it would involve. When she reached the New Life facility, she knocked on her supervisor's door. "Enter," came a response.

Anna made the announcement, "I've come to give my resignation. I can stay on as long as you need, but I'd like to leave as soon as possible."

"You just started working here. Have you found another job already?" Her boss was surprised.

"No, but I will." Anna offered.

"Are you sure? Does Sarah know about this?"

"No, I'm doing this on my own. I am excellent with sewing and mending, and I plan to put my skills to good use."

"Anna, thanks for telling me. I'll let you know when I find your replacement. I will keep your job open for a few days if you change your mind."

Anna went to her work area with a sense of relief. With

each cart of donations came a better idea of the new Anna. She realized her future centered on traits that she already had. She knew how to work hard, she cared about others, and she had confidence in herself. At a minimum, she knew she could make a living doing mending.

It dawned on her that this was her first taste of freedom. Anna realized she could now make decisions about her own life. She no longer had to rely on someone else to tell her where to go or what to do. This new sensation was exhilarating and lifted her spirits to heights she thought belonged only to young women.

Anna believed one of her most essential tasks was to help Hilda as she aged. She reasoned, *It's time I think of someone other than myself. Poor Hilda is like me; she's alone, and she will need more help in the future. I can be there for her.*

With confidence, she asked herself, *What kind of person am I?* Her answer, *I can be kind to others. I'm older but still attractive, maybe distinguished, and talented.* Her head exploded with possibilities, including new ideas for needlepoint scenes.

Anna felt even better when her shift was over. She had two important things to do. The first was to take the bus to Community Bound to see Sarah. Unfortunately, Sarah wasn't there, so Anna took a slip of paper and wrote a simple message:

> *I quit my job at New Life. I need to start building my future. We'll talk more later. Anna*

Anna caught the next bus southbound on 25th Avenue, getting off at 30th Street, one block from the Fairway store nearest Hilda's house. She went to the meat counter with purpose and certainty. She ordered a two-pound round roast, recalling that Hilda loved leftover roast beef sandwiches. Then came two large baking potatoes, three ears of sweet corn, and a lemon meringue pie. Anna hoped she had enough cash to pay for the groceries because she was still uncomfortable writing checks. She needn't have worried.

Anna entered Hilda's house as if nothing had happened. Before Hilda could start asking questions, she announced, "I'm making dinner. And I think I can do it on my own. It may be a little later than usual. Anna reached for Hilda's Betty Crocker cookbook, set the range to three hundred and twenty-five degrees, washed the roast, salted it, and put it in the oven. With the pie in the refrigerator, there wasn't anything else to do until it was time to bake the potatoes and start the water boiling for the sweet corn.

Taking off her apron, Anna poured herself a glass of water and went to the front room. She sat down in a chair directly across from where Hilda was reading a newspaper. "If you have time, I'd like to talk about my future."

Hilda acted surprised. "I've been wondering what you were up to. You took out of here so fast this morning that I thought maybe I wouldn't see you again."

"Oh, no, just the opposite. I had some things to do. First, I quit my job. I figured I'd been waiting forty-one years to get a chance at freedom. I didn't want to waste one more day to experience it." Anna sat straight up with her head held high.

"What did Sarah say about this?"

"I didn't tell her first. I just went and did it. But I did stop by her office, and since she wasn't there, I left her a note. She'll probably call me soon, upset about what I did."

"It's a pretty big move. Why a lady your age with no experience? How do you plan to support yourself?"

"I think I'll start a mending business. Mending and alterations are services people always need. It just so happens I'm good at both. Hilda, thank you for setting me straight. I am at a loss to describe how horrible my weekend was. It was like sitting between the gates to heaven and hell where the gate to hell would be easy to open, the gate to heaven hard. When Sunday evening came, I realized I had answered the question. I'm going the hard way."

Anna continued. "If you give me another chance, I'd like to stay with you. I like you a lot, and I think you are good for me because you're so honest. Plus, I want to be with you to help you when things get difficult."

"You mean when I get really old and feeble?"

"Exactly. Not that you're so old. You and I still have many years to enjoy each other's company. Nor am I promising you I can change overnight, but maybe I can leave the anger and hatred behind and focus on the good things yet to happen."

Anna hugged Hilda before announcing she needed to change clothes and finish preparing dinner. At a quarter to six, the doorbell rang. It was an angry Sarah, looking for Anna and wanting an explanation of what she had done and why. Anna suggested she stay for supper if it was okay with Hilda. "It's your dinner," Hilda announced as if she were a proud mother.

The three women ate tender, moist roast beef, with Anna and Sarah sharing a baked potato. Anna set the pie in the middle of the table, saying, "I made it all by myself." Pausing momentarily, she smiled and added, "Just kidding."

Anna shared with Sarah the reasoning behind her decisions and how she had Hilda's support. Sarah doubted her plan, noting it was more of a dream.

"Sarah, you don't know me that well yet. I can do things, and I understand a little bit about how the world works. I am also stubborn. I know I can make it work. Don't worry too much about me because you taught me well."

Sarah was too tired to argue with Anna, so she shrugged her shoulders and, for the first time in their relationship, hugged Anna.

As she walked Sarah to the door, Anna asked, "Would

you give me the name of your hairdresser? I mean, your hair is cute, and I'd like her to do mine."

Hilda overheard the question. "Going all lah di dah, are you?"

"No, but I do want to look a little nicer. A small makeover would do me good as I set out on my new business."

Sarah couldn't help but smile as she gave Anna the name and the number of her hairdresser. "You are going to make it, aren't you, Anna? Just like I predicted, but only on your terms."

"I am," pronounced Anna.

After Sarah left, Anna cleared the table, washed the dishes, and put the leftover food in the refrigerator. "Hilda, I'm tired, so I need to sleep. Tomorrow is a new day, and I have more things to do."

§§§

She looked forward to building a new life, whatever that would be. But before doing anything else, she had a call to make.

"My name is Anna Olson, and I'm returning a call to Margaret Pattersen."

"Please hold a moment, Miss Olson." After a short break, the receptionist came back on the line. "She's in a meeting right now. Can she call you back in ten minutes? I'm sure she has your number, but may I have it again for her convenience?"

Thirty minutes later, Margaret Pattersen returned the call. "I don't know if you remember me, Anna, but I was at your discharge meeting at Helmhurst. How are things going?"

"Better." Anna declared. Margaret's voice sounded vaguely familiar. Then she knew where she had heard it. Yes, now she recalled the woman who gave her a business card.

Margaret said, "I'm glad to hear that. Moving from an institution into the community is extremely hard."

Anna tried to be civil. "Believe me, I know about the hard part. But why do you want to talk to me?"

"It would be better to talk in person. I'll explain everything then. Could we have lunch on August 24th? I'll pick you up at eleven-thirty. Is that good with you?"

"Okay, but do you know where I live?"

"Yes, I do. See you soon."

§§§

Anna found that building a new life was hard work. Plus, she had chosen an aggressive path of discovery and rebirth. The epiphany she reached in the heat of her apartment came down to four things—determination, survival, strength, and talent. Anna was sure that, somehow, these assets would be enough for her to have a better life. She would no longer let herself get trapped in roles that others picked for her. Anna was a realist with little to offer the world besides her sewing skills.

After her last day of work at New Life, Anna went to one of the local retail stores they ran, looking for suitable clothing that might need mending or a size adjustment. There wasn't much, but she did pick up a pair of slacks and a lovely blouse that needed minor alterations. *It's a start*, she thought.

Anna planned to buy a new sewing machine, but Hilda offered hers. After looking it over, she said, "Thanks, Hilda. Your machine will do the trick. It has a lot of settings, so that I can take on almost any job. How much can I pay you to borrow it?"

"Oh, I'd settle for you doing a few things for me now and then. Mainly, I'm happy that someone can get some good use out of it. My eyes are so bad anymore that I gave up sewing. I had one too many needles in my fingers."

Anna soon found herself sitting in a stylist's chair. This time, she knew how she wanted her hair cut and curled. Anna was pleased with the stylist's work and asked her for a return appointment. On the bus ride home, she caught a glimpse of herself in the window and liked what she saw.

Later in the same week, Anna went to the Hallmark store and found a large box of their top-of-the-line stationery on sale. She also selected an assortment of greeting cards. As she passed a local drugstore, she stopped to buy makeup. A beautifully aging woman was emerging out of a grumpy old lady.

One of Sarah's employees at Community Bound showed her how to make a simple promotional piece as a handout or to put on bulletin boards. Sarah agreed to make 250 copies of her flyer. Her former instructors were excited to see the new Anna set goals far beyond what any of their students had yet achieved.

Anna was not shy about soliciting customers. She knocked on door after door. "Hi, I'm Anna Olson. I'm starting my own mending business. Do you have any items that need to be repaired or re-sized?"

She could tell from their facial expressions they didn't know what to think of this attractive older lady knocking at their door in the 90-degree heat. "Ah, I can't think of anything right now."

Anna always replied, "That's fine. Let me leave you my flyer with my phone number. If you think of something later, just give me a call. I even offer a pick-up and delivery service."

"Thanks." The surprised homeowners mumbled as they looked down at the flyer.

Many afternoons, she came home discouraged at her slow progress. She only got a few items to mend, but several people did call back and ask for her services. Some weeks, her earnings were less than $25. Still, she stuck with her plan.

§§§

August 24, 1975, Anna immediately recognized Margaret Pattersen, remembering her blue suit and white blouse from her discharge planning meeting in June of 1974.

After introducing Margaret to Hilda, they drove downtown. Finally, she pulled into a place called Mel's Diner. Beside the diner was a large church. "Looks like a Cathedral," Anna observed.

"It sure does. That is St. Paul's Lutheran, one of the biggest congregations in the Minneapolis-St. Paul area. You Lutheran?"

"Yes, but I haven't attended a regular church service since 1933, when they sent me to Helmhurst."

Margaret offered, "I'm one of those strange Scandinavians who is Catholic. Somehow, my parents strayed away from the Lutheran thing."

As they settled into a booth, Margaret took off her sunglasses and ordered them coffee and a menu for Anna.

"I like this place and eat here whenever I can. I know the owner. He looks rough around the edges, but he helps a lot of folks who are down on their luck."

Mel's Diner was a bustling place, full of people moving into and out of booths and tables. Anna heard the clinking of plates and the occasional shout, "Order up." Two waitresses worked the booths and tables, and a third worked the counter and cash register. They moved effortlessly to and from customers and the kitchen window. Margaret drew Anna's attention to the menu, pointing out her favorites.

At first, Anna wasn't sure what to get. There were many delicious-looking choices, but she settled on a club sandwich and fries.

After they both ordered, Margaret removed a cigarette from an expensive soft leather pouch. She offered one to Anna, who accepted, then leaned over for a light. "My landlady doesn't allow smoking in her house, but I still indulge myself when I go for walks," explained Anna. Looking up at Margaret, she asked, "Why am I here?"

"I'll get to that. First, I need to tell you how wonderful you look. You've had your hair done."

"Yes. What's the big deal about that?" As soon as the words left her mouth, Anna realized this was a throwback to the old Anna.

"Nothing, other than it's a pleasant surprise. It's not what one would expect from a recently discharged person. I'm sure you will have many questions, but I would like to give you some background before answering. Don't get too frustrated if I don't answer them right away.

"Let me tell you about me. I'm an attorney for the Disability Advocate Society of Minnesota. This group represents disabled people who do not receive the proper care to which they are entitled and cannot speak for themselves. Most of them live in institutions similar to Helmhurst. We are trying to obtain better care for them and ensure they get it in places more suited to their needs than in an institution."

Margaret explained that in 1971, a group of parents of children who lived in several different institutions complained about terrible care and a lack of services for their children. They complained that conditions in these institutions were poor, even dangerous. They demanded better care. When things didn't improve, they banded together and filed one suit, legally known as a class-action lawsuit against the State of Minnesota.

"These parents are not the first to try this. Parents in other states had also filed lawsuits demanding improvements. The idea is to force the states to improve service. Like the parents in other states, we believe the US Constitution guarantees everyone a safe environment and an appropriate level of services. A good educational program is also guaranteed. Here, again, is an example of something the state of Minnesota doesn't provide for people in institutions."

Anna offered, "I know one thing . . . you don't learn much in institutions other than surviving being attacked or pigeon-holed in some back ward. Or you are being physically abused. That's always a big problem."

Tapping her cigarette on the edge of the ashtray, Anna continued. "So far, I don't understand. I don't see what that has to do with me. I'm out of that whole mess now."

"Good question."

Their waitress suddenly appeared as if out of thin air. Setting down their food and a ketchup bottle, she asked, "Can I get either of you anything else right now?" Both politely declined.

Margaret picked up the conversation. "Here's the thing. I need your help explaining all of this to a judge or maybe a jury. Do you think you could do that?"

Anna's face turned dark as she put out her cigarette and sipped water. She observed, "God, I wish someone like you had come along forty-one years ago. Now, I feel anxious when talking about institutions. I repeatedly told them I didn't need to be there. But they never listened. Instead, they branded me a troublemaker." She sat back, thinking this woman was excited, but all she could think to say was, "These problems were ones I recently promised myself I would leave behind."

The two women began to develop a rapport as the meal continued, and Anna grew more comfortable with Margaret. She listened intently as Miss Pattersen opened a new world where even the most handicapped person had the right to top-quality care and protection from harm. They also had a right to receive these services in what Margaret called the "least restrictive environment." Margaret shocked Anna by putting her personal story in a broader context. She learned there were thousands of people like her, institutionalized supposedly to keep the community safe from their bad genes mixing with those of the good people. But in truth, they were there for the sole purpose of keeping institutions functioning. Anna felt the same way years ago when she first realized why they kept her at Helmhurst. The validation Margaret provided was another epic moment in her life.

As the meal concluded, Anna soon found herself answering questions. "Anna, how did you end up in Helmhurst? What was it like to grow up on a farm? Whatever happened to your brother? How did you survive all those years in Helmhurst with your mind and body intact?"

Anna sensed Margaret knew more about her than she realized because some questions required some prior knowledge of her life. She answered the questions and asked, "How do you seem to know so much about me?"

"As a part of our gathering information about whether we would proceed with our lawsuit, we received permission to review the records of fifty residents in various Minnesota institutions. Jim Madsen suggested I look at yours."

"You know him?" Anna again looked surprised.

"Yes. He and another guy he works with are very innovative, providing services that have never been delivered in institutions before. I like both these guys."

It suddenly all made sense to Anna. Madsen had targeted her as a person who would interest Margaret. She could accurately and clearly describe firsthand what living in an institution for four decades was like. That's why Margaret was at her discharge planning meeting.

"Madsen was the one who got me out of that god-damn

place. He didn't quite understand people like me who were normal in every respect, but we didn't understand the outside world. He thought we could just walk out into the world and get along just fine. I know he meant well. Plus, he gave me a pack of cigarettes before I left." Anna smiled as she sat back to listen to Miss Pattersen.

Finally, Margaret elaborated on what she wanted. "Anna, I need your help. From everything I've heard, you are a person who is exceptionally capable of speaking up and telling the truth. From what you've described, you have been through or seen the worst of the worst. Again, I need you to help me explain how harsh it was to live at Helmhurst. And, to explain that you were never offered a way to get out."

"You want me to stick my neck out and spell out all the shitty things that happened to me? I recently made a pledge that I wouldn't dwell on all that, so no, I'm not willing to take a step back. It's too hard. I'm leaving it all behind."

Margaret ignored her statement and suggested they each have a piece of pie and vanilla ice cream. "Anna, I don't expect an answer right away. Reliving all that bad stuff can be very hard. But others who have come before you overcame their fears and told their stories. There is something I want you to keep in mind. If there is one thing you can do to help others and make sure they don't suffer the way you suffered, this is it. Do you need a refill on the coffee?"

"I'm fine, thank you."

Acting as if Anna's objection didn't matter, she asked, "Let's do this again soon, okay? I can clarify how easy it will be for you to help."

"I'll think about it, and yes, another lunch would be great. I've got to try some of their other pies."

§§§

Anna put another new plan in motion. She studied her schedule for Minneapolis/St. Paul bus routes and learned how to get to the downtown Greyhound bus terminal. Once there, she asked a ticket agent how much it would cost for a trip to Helmhurst and back. The ticket agent wrote the round-trip cost on the schedule and pushed it back to Anna. "Thanks," she said.

Back in her apartment, she sat at her small kitchen table and wrote to Janice.

Dear Janice,

Does that offer to come to see you still stand?

Today, I went to the Greyhound bus terminal and got the schedule and cost for a round-trip ticket. I could arrive at Helmhurst at 3:35 p.m. on Friday and leave Sunday at 1:45 p.m. These times work well for me because I can get there and back in the daylight.

Will you let me know which weekend works best for you?

I am so excited to think I may see you again soon. I look forward to updating you on all that's happened to the new me.

Love,

Your friend, Anna

On Friday, October 12th, Janice greeted Anna at the Murray Super Station. After exchanging a warm hug, they headed to Janice's house for snacks and dinner.

"Anna, I'm so pleased to hear you've made a big change in your life. I'm proud of you for going out and starting your own business. I can't believe how good you look compared to when you left here."

Anna sounded confident, "I'm learning that a positive attitude works wonders. It's so good to see you again and have time to talk without fear of discovery. You did so much for me."

Janice smiled when she spoke. "We don't need to go back down that road. As I said, I'm only sorry I didn't act sooner. But here you are, my long-lost friend is back. Oh, how I have missed you and the others. But mostly you. You were always our leader. Remember trying to catch that Brighton guy?"

"I sure do, and that didn't turn out so well, did it? Do you remember Ida being in that little cemetery? Do you suppose we could see her?"

"Sure, I'll never forget poor Ida. We'll see her tomorrow afternoon," Janice said.

The friends caught up on all that had happened since January. When they finished Janice's excellent dinner, Anna commented, "Wow, that was good".

"I'm always glad to have the chance to cook for two. Especially when one of them is a long-lost friend. Besides, it's kind of lonely cooking and eating by myself."

"I know," Anna said. "I'm just now getting familiar with what that means."

They sipped iced tea as they sat on her front porch, watching the autumn leaves fall. Anna shared her problems with adjusting and her resolve to turn things around. Janice asked about her landlord.

"Oh, I love Hilda. She is sometimes hard on me when I don't do things right. But she cares about me, and I credit her with scaring me into being a better person." After expanding more on her landlord, Anna told Janice about Margaret Pattersen. Janice recognized the name and said she had worked on some memos for Miss Pattersen.

Janice talked about her job and how she thought it was nearing time to retire. Things were changing too fast for her taste, and it was time to let a younger person take over. She talked about her family and how she and her siblings had grown apart after their mother died. Anna felt empathy for Janice as she spoke about her fractured family. She, too, lacked a relative with whom she could build a relationship.

On Saturday afternoon, they went to see Ida. On the way, Janice stopped at a florist so Anna could buy a bouquet. They were soon at the old, rundown apple orchard. They walked down the rows of dilapidated crosses and steel stakes. Eventually, they found Ida, and Anna laid the flowers amid the pile of red and gold autumn leaves.

"Janice, do you think we could find out the names of those buried under each of these stakes?"

"I don't know, maybe. But why would we want to know that?"

"Maybe we can do something, although I don't know what it would be. My heart goes out to them because I've always felt the least capable people at Helmhurst got the worst care. And now, no one even knows their names."

Their visit went by so quickly that when it was over, Anna felt as if no time had passed. She was sure of one thing: they thoroughly enjoyed each other's company.

§§§

Anna returned to Minneapolis full of energy and in good spirits. Each day, it seemed easier for her to live in her new world. She resumed her quest for new customers. As she knocked on doors to pass out flyers, she met some friendly people, and Anna guessed one in ten were rude. A few people gave her items to fix. Others said they would call her if they needed something. All her customers were pleased with her work as well as her fees.

She realized that building her business this way was too time-consuming. She thought she might work with a company where she would do mending and split the fee.

Hilda suggested searching the Yellow Pages for mending, alterations, clothing consignment, and laundries. When she found businesses she thought might work, she asked Hilda how close they were. Anna selected stores to contact. None were interested in her offer. Finally, on November 10, 1975, she found one laundry in a nearby neighborhood with a small Yellow Page ad Anna almost missed.

Feeling like it was time to take a new course of action, and with directions from Hilda, she crossed 25th Avenue, the north-south street she always used to catch the bus. Hilda said her destination was ten blocks east of 25th Avenue. As she walked further east, she noticed the quality of homes changing. Some houses had paint peeling; others had broken windows with cardboard replacing broken glass. Finally, she saw a small sign for a carryout store, and next to it was a business that said Wong's Laundry on the window.

Anna stopped to stare at an old, faded sign that read "Mending and Alterations." It was so sun-bleached that she nearly overlooked it. Anna panicked, no longer having the courage to talk to the people inside. She took a step back and started walking toward her apartment. At the first intersection, she stopped. *There is no time like the present to ask them if they need a seamstress. Why stew about it? Why walk all the way back another time?* Gathering all the courage she could muster, she returned to the store. She opened the laundry door and looked at a young Chinese woman.

"May I help you?"

"Ah, yes, well, I wonder if you have a seamstress to help you with your customers who need mending or alterations? Is it okay to call you Mrs. Wong?"

"Yes, I am Mrs. Wong. But we don't do that anymore. It's been too hard to find reliable help. It's too much trouble and no profit. You need some laundry cleaned?"

"No, sorry, but I am a seamstress looking for someplace

to set up my business. I'm very reliable, and my prices are reasonable. I'm sure that once people know you have a seamstress, they will come in with things that need to be fixed and bring some dry cleaning."

"I'll ask my husband. You can come back next week."

Anna knew she had better try one more approach. "I'll fix three things for free. They can even be things no one else has been able to repair. I'd like to show you that I'm good and fast at what I do. Do you have anything lying around that you'd like me to work on?"

"Okay, wait a minute." The woman left and soon returned with a suit coat, jeans, and a woman's blouse. "See if you can fix these and come back next Monday. I'll ask my husband if he's interested."

"That sounds fine to me. I'll bring these items back to you tomorrow." When she got the words out of her mouth, a customer had entered the store, and Mrs. Wong turned to take care of that person. Anna thought it might be a good time to leave.

On her way home, Anna remembered when she first committed to starting a new life. She repeated her new mantra into the cold November wind: "I will not go backward; I'm a survivor, I'm strong, and I have talents."

CHAPTER 4

WARM COATS FOR CHILDREN

*"Lady, I ain't gonna rob you. I just want to know if you
have enough to pay my friend for a ride home."*

Martin England

1975

Anna returned the mended items to Mrs. Wong the
following day.

Mrs. Wong scolded Anna. "I've not talked to my husband
yet. I told you to come back next Monday."

"I know, but I had these done, so I thought I would bring
them back so you could show them to him when you tell him
about me."

"Okay, but don't come back before next week. Give me
your phone number so I can call you if he has any questions."
Anna took a small notebook out of her purse, looked up
Hilda's number, and gave it to Mrs. Wong.

While she waited for the call back from one of the Wongs,
Anna kept busy going up and down streets, passing out flyers
and trying to drum up business. There was an increase in

orders because Christmas was nearing.

Then came the call she had expected. Mr. Wong said they would give Anna a trial run as their seamstress. Anna went over early the next day, and they worked out a temporary agreement where the Wongs would put up a new sign, set the price for each item repaired, and Anna would get 50% of the fees. After that, they would negotiate a new arrangement. Anna nodded in agreement, thinking at least it was a start.

Anna's income slowly rose with each new and repeat customer from her personal efforts and a gradual increase in new customers at the laundry. Although she wasn't making enough to pay her cost of living, she thought, *I'll keep working at it*.

Sarah continued to visit Anna as much as her work schedule allowed. She was still worried about Anna's plan. Anna could read the doubt on her face and asked, "Sarah, are you still fretting over me?"

"Yes, I am. Most people can't just go out and start a business, let alone someone with your background."

"My background? You mean someone locked up in a state institution for so many years? I think you will find I'm not just anyone. There is one more thing—doing this is one hundred times easier than living in the Helmhurst hell hole."

"You're right, Anna, but I care about you and worry. Call me if things aren't going well. I can find ways to help if you need it. Right?"

"I will," Anna said.

§§§

On Saturday evening, December 12, 1975, Anna looked at Hilda and suggested. "Why don't we both go to church this Sunday? It's the Christmas season, and they'll probably have something special! I saw St. Paul's Lutheran Church when I had lunch with Miss Pattersen. It looked big and cathedral-like, and I'd like to see the inside. We could take a cab and eat lunch at the diner next door!"

"Anna, I'm an old woman. I'm not about to go traipsing off to some church in the middle of winter. You go, enjoy yourself, but count me out."

On Sunday morning, Anna was disappointed to wake up to four inches of snow and ice on the stairs to her apartment. Hilda was in the kitchen and expressed concern. "You're not planning to go, are you? The weather on the radio said there was a winter storm warning, a big blizzard, and all that type of thing."

"Sure, why not? We live in the city, don't we? It's not like we will get stuck in the middle of nowhere. Buses are big, and I imagine they go in any weather. I'll be fine."

Standing cold and shivering at her bus stop, Anna thought of her father dying in a blizzard. She wondered for a moment what it must have been like for him. Did he have any idea of what he was getting into? How much did he suffer? But she soon saw her bus slowly plowing its way through the snowy streets and toward her stop. With his image soon fading into the past, she got on the bus with only a few other passengers. She caught her connecting bus, which lumbered slowly down the street in the ever-accumulating snow. Finally, she reached St. Paul's Lutheran.

Anna quickly entered the church, where she sat near the back. Only a few people moved about the sanctuary. She looked up towards the large stained-glass windows and the arches. Then, her attention focused on the well-lit altar. An oversized white cross took up almost the entire wall behind the altar and commanded her attention. A blanket of brilliant red poinsettias surrounded the communion rail, pulpit, and lectern. They even spilled down the two steps to the church's main floor. Everything here was so big, so beautiful, so different. She had no idea that the inside of a cathedral, even a small one, would make her feel so small.

An usher put a bulletin in her hands and began seating dozens of people around her. Some parts of the service sounded familiar from her childhood; some were new. The Christmas hymns, a sermon, and the choir were all standard parts of Lutheran worship services. None of that was new. However, the pastor was far away, and the liturgy they read was foreign to her. The choir's anthem of joy, handbells, and the pipe organ filled the church with sound. It was different, but she loved it. *I'm coming back*, she thought, *to enjoy more of the majesty of this place.*

No one spoke to Anna when she arrived, nor now as she got up to leave. When she reached the exit, she panicked. She had failed to plan how to get back home. She had no idea when to connect with the 25th Avenue southbound bus, nor could she see a bus going by in either direction. She knew she couldn't stay at the church or stand out on the street for too long.

Anna was becoming distraught. *Hilda was right! I should never have tried to come to this service. Now, what am I going to do?* She recalled Mel's Diner next door, where she and Miss Pattersen had lunch.

The diner was steamy and warm. Only a few people sat in the booths, and a young couple was at the counter. The low hum of patrons talking and clinking cups and plates transfixed Anna. She stood inside the door, not quite knowing what to do next.

The waitress behind the counter said, "Is it just going to be one, honey?"

"I guess so, ah, yes," Anna replied. She hadn't planned on this, eating out.

"Over here, there is a place at the counter. Is that okay, or do you need a table?"

"Counter is fine," Anna replied, resenting the implication that she might be too old to sit there.

"You want coffee, honey?"

"Sure." Anna was out of her element. She tried to remember what Sarah had taught her. Slowly, it came back to her. First thing, *how much money do I have?* She checked her purse and found $5.50 in cash and a check from the Wongs for $7.50. *Plenty to get back home*, she thought. If she only knew the bus schedules.

"Are you ready to order?"

"No, not yet. Ah, do you have a bus schedule handy? I'm new in town and don't know the eastbound bus schedule. I also need to know when the southbound 25th Avenue bus runs."

"I don't know . . . . I might. I'll look when I get a moment. Our Sunday special is a hot roast beef sandwich for $2.25, including your drink. Now, are you ready to order?"

"I better wait. Let me get my bearings first. I'll just stick with coffee for now."

The waitress turned away with a bit of a disgusted look. Anna saw her expression and understood why she would be upset. She was taking up valuable space at the busiest time of the day.

Anna began to get her composure the longer she sat at the counter. She thought through how much she would need for bus fare and coffee. She had plenty. Anna ordered a piece of pie ala mode to help calm her empty stomach. As she waited, she recalled Sarah telling her there was no shame in asking for help because most people liked to do good things for others. As the lunchtime crowd began to filter away and the waitress had a second, she looked under the counter and finally found a bus schedule.

"It's two years old, so I can't tell you it is accurate, but it's all I have."

Anna studied the schedule and tried to make sense of it. She finally found the bus stop and the 25th Avenue southbound weekend schedule. She reviewed her plan to get back home twice to be sure she was doing the right thing when a loud, raspy voice interrupted her thoughts.

"Lady, you got problems gettin' back home?"

"I do. I am new to town and don't know when to get on the eastbound bus."

"Here, gimme that old schedule." He snatched the schedule out of Anna's hands. "It's no good, for Christ's sake." The man looked rough, and unshaven, with a T-shirt and a ball cap turned backward. His apron was dirty and stained with tomato sauce and gravy.

"Where do you live anyway," he continued, his distinctive voice filling her head with sound.

"Down south of here around 26th Street." Anna knew that was not the right street. She didn't want the world to know where she lived.

"How much money you got?"

Anna stared back at him, not wanting to tell a stranger what she had in her purse. The raspy voice again broke into her thoughts, not allowing her much time to figure out what to say.

"Lady, I ain't gonna rob you. I just want to know if you have enough to pay my friend for a ride home. The buses have stopped running, and I doubt the cabs are even out in this. But he has a big pickup that can go through almost anything. You got no business standing out there in this cold 'cuz you haven't dressed warm enough. What do you think this is, October?"

The way he lectured her about not being dressed warm enough initially offended Anna. But something about his voice commanded respect and compliance. She replied as if she were obeying a staff sergeant. "I have $5.50 in cash and a check for $7.50.”

“Okay, we are in business. It will cost you $5.00 for a ride home. My friend helps needy people, and the $5.00 will barely cover his costs. The pie and coffee are on me, with the understanding that the next time you get up here, you gotta come back to eat and leave a big tip for Mary here. Tips are a big part of her income.”

Anna nodded, “I will.”

Anna was finishing her pie when she noticed a big blue four-wheel-drive pickup with a snowplow attached to the front had pulled up next to the diner. “There’s your ride, honey,” Mary announced.

“Are you sure?”

Mary sighed and rolled her eyes. “Yes, I’m sure. Terry will get you home in that truck. But hurry up; he’s ready to start plowing our lot.”

“Thank you,” she yelled to the man at the cash register. He just waved her off, shooing her out the door.

Anna’s adventure that day taught her a lesson. Plan out the whole trip and take plenty of cash in case she needed to take a cab home if some other emergency arose.

The following Sunday, Anna went back to the diner. The weather was milder this time, and she brought enough money to carry out her new plan.

She entered the diner with a clear plan of what she would do. She knew to immediately seat herself at the counter and quickly ordered coffee and the hot roast beef sandwich. On a return trip with more coffee, the waitress recognized her.

“Say, aren’t you the lady in here last week?”

“Yes, I like St. Paul’s Lutheran, so I returned for another service. I was a bit confused then, and the cook paid for my coffee and pie and got me a ride home. I appreciated it very much, so I returned, just like I said I would.”

“Well, it’s nice to see you again.”

When she finished her meal, Anna left Mary twenty dollars. "This should straighten things out for last Sunday and today." She then asked to speak to the man working the grill. He came out, looking angry at being interrupted.

"Thank you for helping me out last week. I didn't think ahead very well. So, ah, here is something extra for your trouble." Anna walked confidently up to the man and offered him twenty-five dollars.

"Lady, you don't owe me nothin'. I just wanted to save you from gettin' frostbite, that's all. You came back; that was all I asked."

"Sir, I would appreciate your using this to help someone else. Get someone a cab ride on me, buy them a meal, or whatever you see fit. I remember now that Margaret Pattersen said you helped her from time to time. Do some more good with it." She grabbed his forearm and practically shoved the money in his hand. The act made her feel like a queen. It was the first time she had helped someone financially and been assertive, all in one fell swoop. It was a small gift, given all the money she had in savings and investments, but it was something given for the benefit of someone she would never meet.

Anna became a regular at Mel's Diner. She liked to sit at the counter and banter with Mary. She learned the man with the raspy voice was Martin England, the owner. He was known as a rough guy on the outside but quick to help someone when they were down. He often fed homeless people before showing them how to get to a shelter. Alcoholics would sleep off their drunkenness in his small storeroom. The constant stream of people with problems passing through his diner received a sympatric ear and a cup of coffee. Anna felt at home here in the diner, as did many others. She appreciated the lack of pretenses and the unconditional acceptance.

Anna believed Martin England was the modern-day

Jimmy Dale, the spirit of goodness in sometimes harsh places. It was Jimmy Dale, her former boss at Helmhurst who served his residents without reservation nor apology. They were poor, destitute and in many cases without a family. Still, Jimmy Dale gave them a hug or a warm touch of his hand that sent the message that he loved them.

On one visit, her waitress, who said her last name was Fortis, explained, "I probably could have found a better job, but I stayed because of Martin. We've been living together for years. He is kind to me, and I think I'm good for him." Anna suspected that, like her, they had survived checkered pasts. They ultimately found their niche in life and had the good sense to stay in it.

Anna also loved the church experience and continued to attend services weekly. At first, it was only rarely that anyone would speak to her, but that was okay with Anna. She enjoyed the music and grew to understand the service. It was also a place to reflect on her life.

§§§

Anna's business with the Wongs continued to pick up, and in June of 1976, Anna approached them.

"I would like to make a proposal. I am now getting five or six things per day from you. That doesn't keep me busy, but I would like to set up a sewing machine in that little space over there." Anna pointed to a small area that had nothing but a bare shelf. "I'll bring my sewing machine to the store, and depending on the work, you can offer some people same-day service. That could be very important to many people, and you can charge them extra for the convenience.

"And, if you'd like, I can help when things get busy. Maybe I can mind the store while Mrs. Wong runs an errand." She stopped to study their reactions, and they were clearly interested. "There is one more thing. I'll do all this, but we need to change my compensation. I want seventy-five percent of what you collect."

Mr. Wong smiled as he stuck out his hand. He recognized Anna as the person they needed. She could attract new customers with her mending and help Mrs. Wong, who was now five months pregnant with their first child. Anna finally purchased a sewing machine, a top-of-the-line Singer with all the settings required to do everything from a delicate blouse to a torn parka. She still did her personal customer's mending on Hilda's dining room table. With her busy schedule, Anna no longer had time to solicit new customers.

Little did Anna realize that Mr. and Mrs. Wong were considering an expansion. A suburban laundry was up for sale, and they believed it was an excellent time to expand.

§§§

On July 3, 1976, Anna boarded a Greyhound bus headed south to Helmhurst. Anna realized she and Janice were becoming like sisters Janice was the sister Anna never had. Once again, Anna asked that they visit the forgotten cemetery.

After a period of silence, Anna said, "My heart aches every time I think of this place. How sad it is, you know, people here who once had a mother and father, brothers and sisters. Now, they are forgotten. Like our friend, poor Ida."

Janice replied, "Do you ever wonder what our former roommates Mary, Martha, Lily, or Kathrine think? I mean, do they still think of Ida or of us? Wouldn't it be fun to see each other again?"

"Hmm." Anna nodded her head in ascent.

The rest of their visit was chatting. Anna told Janice about her church blunder, how she met the nice restaurant people, and how she got Mr. and Mrs. Wong to go along with a new contract. There was little or no bitterness left in her demeanor. If there was, it was well hidden.

Janice updated Anna on what Madsen was up to and how her work stress was growing. "They forget I'm not so young anymore."

"Well, maybe you're not so young, but I consider myself a hot foxy lady!"

Janice laughed because that was the polar opposite of what she and Anna were. If anything, they were late middle-aged, buttoned-up, protestant, caring women.

§§§

In 1976, each passing day was some new growth experience for Anna, a new customer or two, or growing closer to Hilda. Time was going faster. She was sure of it. As she got more involved with her new career, there was less time to feel badly about the past, resulting in fewer episodes of anger and depression. Feeling less like an oddball, cranky old woman from an institution, she began letting the word "normal" creep back into her mind. She guessed that no one would sense she was any different from anyone else by now.

Her needlepointing continued, now with Sarah as her first student. In private, she did a profile of Hilda. Anna thought her new work had a brightness missing from older pieces, but she couldn't define why. She wondered if it was how she looked at things now versus in her institutional days.

Sarah continued to stop by as time allowed. She grew to understand the resolve and the grit of Anna Olson. Anna always got a morale boost when she came because she knew she was proving her one-time mentor wrong. Without stopping to reflect on it, Sarah and Anna became friends. Sarah asked Anna if she'd like to see either *A Star is Born* or *All The President's Men*. Anna picked the first, saying, "I don't understand all this Watergate stuff. It's over my head."

On Sunday, December 12, 1976, Anna was at St. Paul's Lutheran, listening to a brass band ensemble play Christmas music before the service started. She expected more of the splendor and beauty of the season at this church. It was part of why she formally joined by transferring her membership from Redeemer Lutheran in Grant Grove.

At the end of the service, Anna stood up, and when she turned around, three rows behind her were Sarah and Karl. Anna caught Sarah's eye, and both beamed.

"Anna, I had no idea you came to St. Paul's. Then again, we usually come to the eleven o'clock service. Are you just visiting?"

"No, I joined in July. And I come to the eight o'clock service. I like the services and have gotten comfortable here. Not that I know anybody, but still, I like it."

"Anna, excuse me for being rude. I'd like you to meet my fiancé, Karl Barnhorst."

Karl thrust out his hand, and when Anna took it, she noticed how soft and warm it was. "Anna Olson—I've heard about you. You know you are a star at our house. Sarah is so impressed with how far you've come."

"She's probably exaggerating," Anna replied. "So, when is the big day?"

"We are thinking next June, or maybe July, depending on when Karl finishes medical school. We want to get married before he starts his residency. Don't worry; you and Hilda will receive invitations, and we won't take no for an answer."

§§§

In February, Mrs. Wong and Anna watched a group of children hanging around in front of their store after school.

Some stopped at the corner carryout store to get candy or a soda; others just stopped to talk or hang out. The Wongs didn't like the children, thinking they were rude and disrespectful. Anna believed the reality was much simpler. They were simply having fun.

One day, with the temperatures hovering near zero, Anna noticed a little boy she had seen several times standing outside wearing nothing but a black hooded sweatshirt. She wondered why he didn't have a winter coat, so she got up, went out, and started walking toward him.

"Don't you have a coat to wear? It's too cold out for you. "As soon as she spoke, the boy ran down the street as fast as he could. She kept an eye out for him for the next several days, noting he now avoided the window directly in front of the laundry. When she did catch a glimpse of him, he never wore anything except that black hooded sweatshirt.

Anna tried again. This time, she waited around the corner, near the entrance to the carryout store. Once again, he ran down the street. Anna realized then that he needed a coat, and she would have to find a way to get one for him. She started by visiting her old employer, New Life Industries. Anna first talked to her old boss to assure her she was doing well and then asked about getting a coat for the little boy. "Sure thing," came the immediate reply. She told Anna to go through all the clothing bins to see if she could find a coat.

Anna found a hooded winter jacket with an arm nearly torn off. Later that evening, Hilda couldn't believe the magic Anna had worked on that jacket. Repairing several small tears plus re-attaching the sleeve of a nylon coat wasn't magic; it was the skill of a master seamstress.

After having the Wongs clean the coat, Anna waited for the little boy in the sweatshirt after school. Again, when she showed him the parka, he turned and ran down the street. Anna was mad. He wasn't getting away with simply running away this time. She quickly grabbed her purse and scarf and, with the coat in hand, set off to find the boy.

"Where does that little boy in the sweatshirt live?" Anna asked the group of children hanging around the carryout store.

"You with welfare?" one little girl asked.

"No, no, I just want to give him this coat so he has something to keep him warm."

"Oh, he lives down that way," the same little girl said, pointing east.

"What house?"

"It ain't exactly on this street. When you get to a stop sign, go up that street till you see a house with an old red car in front. It doesn't have any wheels."

Anna asked one more question. "Do you know his name?"

"Sure, that's Anthony. He's the smartest kid in the whole school."

Anna walked briskly into an African American neighborhood that most white people avoided. She was a woman on a mission and still angry at the little boy who refused her coat. Ten minutes later, she stood in front of a house where a red car rested on cement blocks in the driveway.

She had to knock twice before she saw a light turn on inside and the door open a crack.

"What do you want?" The voice was obviously that of an older woman.

"I have a coat here that I'd like to give to a little boy named Anthony. Does he live here?"

"Why do you have a coat for him anyway?"

"He comes by Wong's Laundry wearing nothing but a sweatshirt, and it's been zero or below every day for the last ten days."

"Well, step on in outta that cold. Let me find Anthony."

The older woman soon returned with Anthony in tow. "Anthony, what happened to the coat your momma bought you."

"Some kid at school stole it from me. I know who he was, too, but he's older and bigger, so I can't say anything about it."

"Look, this kind lady has another coat for you." She took the coat from Anna and continued, "Now, try this on."

The coat was too large, but Anna thought he would soon grow into it.

"Here, this nice lady has been trying to give you a coat, and you run away?"

"I didn't know what she wanted, so I ran."

"Miss, I'm sorry for the boy. He gets kind of shy sometimes. What's your name?"

"I'm Anna Olson, a seamstress at Wong's Laundry next to the school. That's how I see him almost every day. He walks by our store on his way home."

"Miss Anna, I'm Annalee Washington, but everyone calls me Grandma Washington. And this here is Anthony Grant Washington."

"Nice to meet you, Annalee."

"Won't you sit down a moment? You must be tired. That's a long walk in the cold."

"Okay, just for a minute."

Anthony sat down next to his grandmother and started to inspect the coat. "Thank you very much for getting my Anthony a coat. I'm sorry, I didn't know he was going without one. He slips out the door when I'm still in the kitchen. You got grandchildren, Miss Anna?"

"No, I never did have children." Looking at Anthony, she said, "I heard something about you from one girl who knows you."

"What'd she say?"

"She said you were the smartest kid in the whole school."

Anthony was silent.

"Anthony, tell the nice lady about you and school."

Anthony looked into his lap as he spoke. "That's what they say. I don't like to go to classes, though. They're way too boring. They've tried putting me in with older kids, but most of the time, even that is too simple. I hate it there, too, because the older boys pick on me. I start by attending classes, but after a few minutes, I do stuff that distracts the teachers and the other kids. The teacher kicks me out, and I spend most of my day in the library."

"Do you like the library," Anna asked.

"Not really. They don't have much there."

Grandma Washington said, "He's always been able to figure stuff out quickly. Sometimes, I think he knows more than most adults."

"Isn't there a school for the smarter kids in Minneapolis?"

"Sure is, but it costs a lot of money. It's a white school over on the west side. With his momma doing drugs and his dad in prison, he's got no chance to go to that school for smart kids. I can't afford it. I barely get by on a little pension and social security."

Anna nodded that she understood, and the conversation came to a stop. "It's starting to get dark. I'd better get home," she announced.

As Anna put her coat on, Anthony said, "There are a lot of kids who don't have coats."

"How do you know that?" Anna asked.

"I see them come and go from school without a coat, just like me."

"I'm sure we can find some other coats and fix them," Anna replied.

"I can sew some myself," Annalee chimed in. "Maybe I

can help you if you need an extra pair of hands."

On her long walk home, Anna was overwhelmed with her school memories, especially after her second seizure. She could identify with Anthony. Both were poor, and something about them made them different from the other children. *It's not easy being a kid and not fitting in.* When Anna got home, she checked with Hilda to see if she was okay, then headed to her apartment to let a short bout of deep depression pass.

§§§

In August 1977, a blue Pontiac pulled up in front of Hilda's house. A tall, good-looking young man wearing a formal white shirt with black buttons and a bowtie got out and bounded up the sidewalk and stairs. Anna let the young man in and asked Hilda if she were ready.

"We'll be ready in a minute," Anna explained. She went back to Hilda's bedroom and found Hilda putting on her "best summer hat."

"You look lovely," Anna proclaimed.

"Did you get our gift?" Hilda asked.

"Yes, I have it and the card."

Soon, they were off to Sarah and Karl's wedding, with Hilda in the front and Anna in the back. They discovered that their driver was both a pleasant person and a medical school friend of Karl.

"How far is this again?" Hilda asked.

"It's about sixty miles, not far."

At first, Hilda wasn't sure she wanted to attend this wedding, but she warmed to the idea once Anna found her a dress and altered it to fit perfectly. Anna was excited from the day they got the invitation in the mail because, at age sixty, she had never been to a wedding. Plus, her first and ongoing impression of Karl was good. On rare occasions,

Karl and Sarah would visit the older ladies together, taking time out of their busy schedules to see the two older women.

They entered the church, and an usher immediately seated them on the bride's side, behind the immediate family. The wedding itself was a first-class, beautiful affair. Flowers were everywhere, the attendants wore gorgeous light purple dresses, and the men wore tuxedos.

Sarah's mother and father hosted a reception at the local Holiday Inn. Sarah and Karl were gracious and charming as they went around the room, greeting their guests. When they got to Anna and Hilda, they were exceptionally kind, and Sarah told them how much she appreciated them coming. She felt a special joy looking at Anna, the woman who had come so far, "Anna, you look beautiful. I'm so proud of you." She took Anna's hands and gave them an extra squeeze before they were off to greet more guests.

§§§

In October 1977, Anna and Grandma Washington were ready to sew coats for the impending cold weather. Miss Washington asked members of her church, Nazareth Baptist, how many children needed winter coats, and within two weeks, the response was twenty-five. She also put out the word that they needed old, discarded coats. When the coats started to come in, they stored them in the church basement.

On two Saturday afternoons, Anna and Grandma Washington sorted through the coats, with Anna giving instructions—this coat needed a new zipper, that pocket was loose, or the hood needed to be sewn back together along the top seam. Anna made a pile of the most damaged and complicated repairs for herself, leaving the easier ones for Grandma Washington.

As a frigid winter set in, word of their project began to spread, and they added two more volunteers to help repair coats. Soon, Grandma Washington contacted two other African American churches to ask for donations. Of course, that also spread the word about the program, and the demand from young people in each church stimulated more growth. Anna was now a regular at New Life Industries, where they picked out and held damaged children's coats for her.

Anna and Grandma Washington sorted through more and more coats to give a growing list of volunteers to repair. On Saturday, volunteers exchanged the parkas they'd fixed during the week for another damaged one. As the project grew, someone asked, "What do you call what we're doing?" An immediate reply came from one of the volunteers. "Why this here is the Warm Coats for Children'project." The name stuck.

One especially busy Saturday, November 12, 1977, Anna was walking home at dusk. Declining a car ride, she said, "The walk will do me good." Anna noticed a large man walking past her. She hadn't been aware of him turning around and coming up behind her until he suddenly grabbed her purse, trying to jerk it from her hand. She struggled to keep the bag but collapsed when he hit her jaw with his fist, and her world went dark.

CHAPTER 5

A GRAND BARGAIN

"Anna, we got ourselves a project! I'm so excited about

this."

Janice Haggedorn

1977

Anna tried to wake up, but the urge to sleep pulled her back into its comforting arms. Later, she opened her eyes for a few minutes, and once again, sleep was too powerful. She had no idea the time or where she was, but she heard Hilda. Anna finally woke up, and sure enough, Hilda had a tight grip on her hand.

Hilda's voice was tired. "It's okay, Anna, you'll be fine. That's what the doctor said."

Anna tried to sit up, but her body screamed out in pain. Her head felt like it weighed twenty pounds. Anna tried to turn her head to see who else was in the room, but that proved too painful.

"The nurse will be back soon with some pain medication, honey. All you need to do is rest." Her voice sounded comforting, but Anna thought Hilda was griping her hand too tightly.

"Where am I?"

"You're at St. Anthony's hospital. Somebody mugged you. Don't you remember?"

"Remember what?"

"Getting hit on the head. You have a big ole black and blue welt where he hit you."

"Oh? Who hit me?"

"They don't know yet. The cops are trying to find the guy. They said a detective would talk to you when you were awake."

"Oh." That was all Anna could say before she fell back to sleep.

It took Anna twelve hours to fully awaken from the trauma. She preferred sleeping because being awake was painful. Soon, she was aware of more people in her room. As soon as Sarah arrived, she sent Hilda home in a cab, promising to look after Anna for the next few hours. Finally, Grandma Washington came, sneaking Anthony in with her.

"Miss Anna, you'll be okay soon. I'm sorry you got hurt." Anthony said, holding back tears.

Anna took his hand and told him she would do her best to recover so she could come to see him. He simply nodded and moved away from her bed. Grandma Washington told Anna she and her friends would ensure Anna returned to sewing coats. "You're too important for us to lose you. We're just starting this coat thing." She took Anthony's hand and led him out the door and down the hall, hoping to escape the wrath of a nurse.

The following two days were a whirlwind of people. The police wanted to know if she got a look at her assailant. Nurses wanted to draw blood, give her medication, or change her IV. Hilda remained worried and could barely stay calm.

With a weak smile and near tears, she said, "Anna, I can't stand to be in the house without you. You better hurry up and get better because you have so much more to learn about cooking."

Her doctor discharged Anna at the end of the third day. Sarah drove her home and explained. "Hilda said she would sleep on the couch for a few days until you can climb the stairs."

It took Anna five days to get enough strength to climb the stairs to her apartment and a few more days to start walking around the block. With Anna's recovery on schedule, a detective stopped by to tell her they had a suspect in custody. They showed Anna six pictures, asking her if she recognized any of them. "I can't be sure. It was dark."

"Why do you think it was one of these guys?"

"In this group of pictures is the man we think is our best suspect. We found your purse in this guy's trash can behind his apartment. This proves nothing, but it led us to talk to him. We've had our eyes on him for several months as a suspect in similar crimes. Please point to the one who did this to you."

"It was too dark. I didn't get a clear look at the guy."

"Let me ask you, what were you doing walking in that neighborhood?"

"Nobody told me it was illegal. And besides, I have business to do in that neighborhood." Anna's reply was sharp.

"Business? What kind of business would a lady your age have over there?"

"Winter coats. I fix old winter coats for kids that need them."

"Okay, but don't go walking there alone, especially not at night. Will you come down to the station and do a lineup for me? We'll line up six or seven men, including the person we think did this to you. You will look at them through a one-way mirror and tell us which one is your assailant."

§§§

The rest of November was a swirl of activity. Enough so that she barely had time to dwell on her assault. Dr. Karl Barnhorst, Sarah's husband, was one of her first visitors after returning to Hilda's. He asked her if it was okay for him to give her a quick checkup. Ten minutes later, he pronounced she was recovering as quickly as a woman half her age. He also told her to let Sarah know if she had dizzy spells, falls, or memory loss.

"Why get all worried about those things?"

"You had quite a blow to the head. Sometimes, we don't see any damage until weeks after the incident. On another note, I called St. Anthony's, and they agreed to give you a steep discount on the charge for your care. Let's say it's a physician's family discount."

"You mean you're claiming me as part of your family?"

"Sure, why not? I lied a bit and said you were Sarah's aunt Anna."

"Aunt Anna. I like that!" Anna's voice trailed up, and her heart warmed to the idea.

Another visitor was Margaret Pattersen. She made a brief appearance a week after Anna got home. After asking how she was doing, Margaret discussed the start of the disability advocate's lawsuit against the state of Minnesota.

"As you will recall, I talked to you about this when we had lunch in 1975. It's taken us a long time to get to this point, and there are many complicated reasons why we had to wait to file the lawsuit. We now need to talk about the important thing, will you help us? I don't need an answer today, but I would like to have lunch with you after the first of the year. In the meantime, you finish getting well."

As Anna healed, Hilda continued to dote on her, spoiling her with extra care and concern. But as the swelling in her face slowly ebbed away and the purple around her eye faded, her past sometimes reared its ugly head. The pain in her eye brought memories of being assaulted and raped by Brighton Hough. She didn't foresee there would be these lapses, these painful flashbacks. Aware of what was happening, Anna forced herself to return to her new path, where all the old pain would stay just that, her old pain.

Getting back to sewing and mending was also part of her cure. There was a pile of mending at Wong's Laundry, and on the first Saturday in December, she was back in the basement of Grandma Washington's church. Four women were getting the refurbished coats ready to deliver to their new owners. Anna and Grandma Washington sorted through a big box of donated coats, trying to pair the right jacket to one of the twelve new requests. Thankfully, they had coats on hand to fill every request they received.

Anna took in the moment. *It feels so good to be back doing something good for others.*

By late afternoon, it was time to take their coats home. "Anna, we decided you're not walking home alone anymore. One of the ladies here will drive you home. It's just too dangerous to walk in this neighborhood."

"I suppose you're right, but I hate to burden anyone. Maybe I can be sure it's still daylight when I go home."

§§§

Anna was as excited about Christmas as she had been in many years. For the first time, she was spending it with her dear friend. At first, she wouldn't visit Janice because she was worried about Hilda. But, Hilda insisted, "I'll be fine. I got by all those years before you came. Plus, I can call the neighbors if I need anything." As she got off the bus, Janice was there with a warm embrace.

The minute they entered her house, hot chocolate and a large assortment of Christmas cookies were on a plate. "My card club exchanges Christmas cookies every year. I didn't make all of these."

Sharing memories from the Big House and Bea and their apartment went long into Christmas Eve night and brought only warm memories. Both enjoyed the eleven o'clock Christmas Eve service at Janice's church. When they got home, they treated themselves to eggnog and rum.

During a late Christmas Day walk, Anna told Janice about her love for Jimmy Dale. She explained how Rhonda had taken her to see his grave and how grateful she was for the chance to feel close to him. "I would love to show you his grave. If you don't mind a ride out in the country."

"Sure, it's not like we have a full agenda for the next two days."

"That would be great, Janice. I'll treat you to dinner."

"Deal," Janice said.

On the last day of Anna's visit, she dropped a bombshell on Janice. It came after they drove by the old Helmhurst Cemetery and the weathered and worn apple orchard.

"Janice, have you made any inquiries about finding the names of people buried here?"

"Not really, but I haven't talked to that many people. So far, no one knows who to talk to about getting those names."

"Remember me mentioning finding someone to help you get access to the old records where you could match patient numbers with the spikes?"

"Yes, and that sounds great. But I'm still wondering exactly how you will do that?"

"I understand that Margaret Pattersen's group finally

filed a big lawsuit. You know, the one that demands better treatment for the residents of Minnesota's institutionalized people. Miss Pattersen wants to have lunch with me sometime after the first of the year. She wants me to commit to testifying for her in that trial. What I plan to do is barter a bit. I will testify if she can get a commitment from someone high up at the state level to help us find the names of the people buried out here."

"Wow, you play hardball, Miss Anna Olson!"

Anna smiled. "A girl's gotta do what a girl's gotta do. For my part, I will pay for a headstone for every name we find. Putting their names on the stone would be all we need to do."

Janice was shocked at Anna's offer. "How much money do you have?"

"I inherited some money when my brother sold the farm. While I was in Helmhurst, they put it into a brokerage account in my name. It grew into a nice little nest egg. I'll gladly give up part of that money to do this. That old cemetery is a part of me, you, and anyone who's ever lived here. I just can't stand to see these people forgotten. Unless we make it an important place, someday, someone will dig up all the bones and build houses on that spot."

As they talked, Janice became increasingly committed to this small gesture of respect for human life. "Anna, we got ourselves a project! I'm so excited about this."

"Janice, would you become the spokesperson for this? I'd like to stay in the background, at least for now."

"But you're the one who is paying for it," Janice replied.

"Yes, but you're the one who will be doing all the work!"

Janice and Anna talked long into the night, excited about making the world aware of those people long ignored and forgotten. Both would look back on the Christmas of 1977 as the beginning of a new chapter in their lives. On their way to the bus terminal, Anna commented, "Janice, do you realize I'm soon going to start my third year of freedom? And it feels better every day."

§§§

1978 started with a flurry of activity. On January 5, Mrs. Wong handed the phone to Anna, and there was a familiar voice on the other end of the line.

"Hello Anna, this is Margaret Pattersen. How are you feeling?"

"Fine, I don't have any more headaches, and my scrapes and bruises are nearly gone."

"Well, listen. It's time we have another piece of pie, don't you think?"

"Yeah, that would be great. It's been a while."

"Too long, I know. Do you need me to stop by and pick you up?"

"No, I can get there."

They agreed on Friday, January 13, 1978, and wished each other well.

Anna returned to her mending and immediately began worrying about how she would state her demand to Margaret. What if she said "no way" to her request? Anna decided there was no use worrying about things she couldn't control.

§§§

On January 13th, Mel's Diner was busy, and all the booths were full when Anna arrived. She sat at the counter, talking to Mary Fortis while waiting for a booth to open. Anna explained why she was meeting Margaret Pattersen.

As soon as a booth came open, Anna ordered a cup of coffee. As she drank the coffee and lit a cigarette, her mind worked on organizing and storing all their coats. She wondered, *What will we do if this continues to grow? Are there really this many poor people who need coats?*

"Anna, how nice to see you. From the looks of the cigarette and coffee, you have two of the three requirements for working in my office."

"What's the third?"

Margaret smiled as she replied, "Perseverance."

"I have plenty of that, too."

"So, you're hired!"

After ordering their food, Margaret updated Anna on the lawsuit's status. She explained, "Six parents, one from each of six state institutions for the mentally retarded are unhappy with the care their children are receiving. Each has been unsuccessful in getting the institutions to give better care. We've put all six complaints together to form what's called a class action lawsuit. That suit is slowly making its way to trial. Before going any further, I need to know if you are willing to share what you experienced in Helmhurst?"

"I've been thinking a lot about this because I knew I would have to give you an answer. And I do have one, but it comes with a requirement. You may not know this, but when people died in Helmhurst, and no family claimed the body, they buried them in a cemetery on the southeast edge of the grounds. Dead residents were dumped in graves in a cheap, pine box with only a steel stake with their resident number to mark their plot. One more thing, they got a small wooden cross, but no name was on it. Eventually, the crosses deteriorated and disappeared.

"My friend Janice, an administrative assistant at Helmhurst, and I have a mutual friend buried there. We know where she is, but no one else on God's green earth does. Janice is willing to take on the task of identifying who is in each of those graves. But she needs help from someone inside the system authorized to help get those old resident numbers on the stakes matched with a name."

Anna continued, "My proposal is this: I will testify if you get the State to agree to assign someone knowledgeable to help my friend."

At first, Margaret silently stared at Anna. "What are you going to do with the names?"

"I'm going to pay for a small headstone for each person. I want to be sure we remember everyone."

"You can afford to do that?"

"I think so. I'm not rich, but I don't need much. I know it seems like an odd thing to do, but it's important to my friend and me. Our friend was a good person and died a terrible, agonizingly slow death in the mental ward. Most of the people in that cemetery lived in hell on earth, unable to communicate, complain, or stick up for themselves. They died in a less than dignified way, and Janice and I liken the cemetery to a human waste basket."

Tears forming, Anna struggled to finish. "Janice and I refuse to let that happen. We'll fight for at least a tiny bit of respect for those people. So, that's the deal, you help us get names of dead people, and I'll testify."

Margaret Pattersen stared out into the street before giving her reply. "You've got a deal. I'll do everything I can to find you the people you need. I never knew or thought of institutions having cemeteries. Is there one in every institution?"

Anna replied, "I don't know."

Margaret leaned over, offering to shake Anna's hand. "You're one hell of a person, Anna Olson."

§§§

On February 8th, Hilda had a message for Anna when

she came home.

"You're supposed to call this number and ask for Jeanne Hall."

"Did she say what this was about?"

"Yes, she said she was with the Minneapolis Prosecutor's Office. It's about that guy who robbed you."

The next day, she called the number, and after waiting on hold for over twenty minutes, Miss Hall finally picked up the phone,

"Miss Olson? I'm sorry for the wait. It seems I'm a popular person. How about you? Have you recovered from being assaulted by Charles Johnson?"

"Yes, I'm fine."

"I'm calling to let you know I've reached an agreement with Mr. Johnson's attorney. We call it a plea agreement. Mr. Johnson has agreed to plead guilty to your assault and robbery. In exchange for his plea, we'll reduce a potential fifteen-to-twenty-five-year sentence to twelve years, with the possibility of parole after seven years. Do you have any objections to that agreement? Of course, a judge must agree to this deal."

"I don't know much about these types of things. Is this about the usual arrangement?"

"Yes, pretty much. Mr. Johnson doesn't have a previous criminal record, so he is getting a better deal than if he had prior convictions."

"Well, okay, if that's what you think is right, I don't have any objections. I don't hate the guy. Besides, I've been through worse."

"I'm sorry to hear that, Miss Olson. Thank you for your help in getting this case closed and for calling me back. For what it's worth. I think Mr. Johnson is truly sorry for what he did."

§§§

Anna had plenty of other things to keep her mind busy. It seemed every Saturday morning was more hectic than the last. More women began helping. Both the demand for and supply of old coats also grew. The inventory of coats in Nazareth Baptist's basement now took up a significant amount of space. Someone stated, "Anna, we'll need to think about finding more space if this keeps up!"

Grandma Washington and Anna said they would look for a bigger space close to their current location. Their search was short. One of the ladies noticed that a local congregation was looking for tenants. They had moved to the suburbs but wanted to keep their sanctuary and use it for outreach programs. Their basement was perfect for Warm Coats for Children.

The program spread even faster when a neighborhood paper did a piece on what Anna and Miss Washington had accomplished. The day after the news article, the number of requests almost doubled. Thankfully, the number of women volunteering also increased, allowing the program to maintain its goal of getting a restored coat to a child in need within a week of their request. The increase sometimes meant Anna would stay up until midnight sewing at Hilda's dining room table.

Anna didn't complain because she discovered the more she helped others, the fewer traumatic flashbacks. Yet, no matter how hard she tried, she had periods of depression and bouts of anxiety and fear. *You don't just walk away and forget a life you lived for over forty years.* Someone, probably Sarah, told her it would take a long time to fully adjust to her new world. Anna finally realized that statement's truth.

On the second Saturday in February, the Warm Coats for Children program began operating in a new and bigger church basement. As Anna looked at the new space and watched the coats they were moving from Nazareth slowly fill up one wall, she wondered if they should have looked for a larger space.

§§§

Hilda Brown grew to love her ever-blossoming tenant. She was proud that Anna could make a decent cake, a moist pot roast, and delicious cookies. She drilled Anna nightly on the finer points of making good Midwest food. It emphasized gravy without lumps, whipped cream from real cream, butter, meat, and potatoes.

But Hilda was most proud of Anna for how she served others. Here she was, a former institutionalized person, degraded and humiliated decade after decade. Still, Anna started a new charity helping low-income families get coats for their children.

However, what warmed Hilda's heart the most was how Anna stopped in every morning and evening to see if she was okay. At first, Hilda was annoyed, but she realized Anna cared for her and wanted her to be safe. She recalled the words Anna said three years earlier, that she wanted to be there to help her when she grew old and needed it.

On May 17th, 1978, Hilda ordered a cab and went to a small office building two miles south of her home. In the small, dark waiting room, Hilda recalled coming here to redo her will and settle her husband's estate after he died. An hour later, Hilda made a return appointment, left the office, and took a cab to the grocery store. Two weeks later, she returned to the office to sign her new will.

§§§

In June of 1978, the 4th District of Federal Circuit Court

in Minneapolis assigned a trial date for the case, known as *Gundy et al. v. Hanson*. Judge Donald Stuart would be presiding. Mary Gundy and five others, each a resident of another state hospital, were the plaintiffs. The defendant was Martha Hanson, the Director of the Minnesota Department of Welfare, who was ultimate responsible for all Minnesota custodial institutions.

A very excited Margaret Pattersen was on the phone with Anna. "We got our lawsuit assigned to a judge and have a preliminary date for our first hearing! I'm so excited! We will finally get our day in court. We're getting the chance to make things better!"

"That's great, Margaret. I wish you all the luck in the world."

"Anna, I've never told this to anyone, but I've been waiting for this day ever since my older brother, Bobby, died. He lived in a facility that housed the mentally and physically infirmed in Texas. My mom and dad thought the staff beat him until he was nearly dead. Then they sent him home to us, saying he had fallen down some stairs. I've worked hard on this case because I have the memory of my brother motivating me."

"I'm sorry to hear that. It's hard to accept that kind of treatment of innocent people."

"I bet you saw many people like my brother, didn't you, Anna?" Her voice had softened by the time she finished the sentence.

Anna paused before she spoke. "Yes, I've seen it all, Margaret. I saw a lot of people who could have been him. Over the years, there were hundreds of people beaten and neglected. I brought them their laundry. And while doing that, I saw staff do all kinds of terrible things. I thought some of the worst things were routine things like putting them in cold showers because there was no warm water. Did you know that no one cared about fixing the heating because they used to think mentally retarded people couldn't tell warm from cold?"

"Anna, getting back to your cemetery issues, I called in a favor a high-ranking person owed me, and within a week, I had his approval.

"Now comes the good news. I received the name of a historian at the University of Minnesota who occasionally consults with the Minnesota Department of Welfare. Supposedly, she knows all there is to know about the history of Minnesota's institutions. I don't know if this historian has talked to your friend yet, but she will call her and help her find the names that match the numbers."

"Wonderful. I promise to live up to my end of the bargain. Just tell me what to do. I think we're good for each other, Margaret."

"We are, but let me warn you, the next part of our lives will be difficult, especially for you. You'll relive the hell you want to put in the rear-view mirror."

§§§

On September 6, 1978, Anna asked Mrs. Wong for a break from mending. She wanted to go to Anthony's school to remind the staff that she had a group of women who fixed winter coats for needy children. *Perhaps I'll see Anthony and find out if this year was going better than last.* As she was chatting with the school secretary, the new principal, Jamelle Parker, walked into the office. She stuck out her hand and said, "Hi, Miss Olson, or may I call you Anna?"

"Anna is fine."

"Would you mind stepping into my office for a minute.?"

"No. Is there a problem?" She felt a short wave of anxiety for reasons she couldn't immediately understand.

"Oh, no, not with your coat program, that's great. You

and your seamstresses are angels. So, tell me, how did you get that idea? I mean, why did you start it?"

Anna smiled, "Anthony Washington. When it was near zero, he used to walk home from school wearing nothing but a hooded sweatshirt. Every time I tried to talk to him, Anthony ran away. With the help of one of your students, I found out where he lived and took a coat over to his house. There, I met his grandmother, a real saint, and we started working together to sew coats. It just grew from there. That's how our little program started, and now it's growing like weeds. All word of mouth, mind you."

The principal said, "That's such a great story, and I love what you're doing. But I have another problem I'd like to discuss with you. Being so academically far above the others, Anthony has outgrown this school. That causes him problems because the poor guy is so bored. I had a school psychologist evaluate him. She didn't give me any details but said he was in the genius range and needed placement elsewhere. But where?

"The only school that can meet his education needs is Westgate Academy, on the southwest side of Minneapolis. It's a private school and expensive, but they have a limited number of scholarships each year. There's one left, and they will evaluate Anthony. If he is accepted, they'll waive his tuition. But there are two problems. First, how does he get to school and back home? Second, how will he pay the one-hundred-twenty-five-dollar monthly fee for incidental expenses such as uniforms, class field trips, and science lab fees? Mrs. Washington is unable to pay the fee. I promised her I would do my best to find additional resources. I was hoping you would know someone who could help with the costs since you've been very resourceful with your program?"

"I don't know anybody, but I'll ask around. How soon do you need to find someone?"

"Next Wednesday. It's an awful lot to ask, but I feel I have to try at least. So, I'm asking everyone I know to see if I can find Anthony that money. I wouldn't want him to miss attending Minnesota's highest-rated school."

Before she left the school that morning, Anna asked if she could stop by and see Anthony if he wasn't in class. He wasn't, and the two walked out onto the playground. She opened her purse and slipped him a Milky Way candy bar. "Be careful not to get it too hot, or it will melt, and you'll have a sticky mess on your hands."

"I know that, Miss Anna. Milky Way is one of my favorite candy bars. How did you know?"

"We older people have our secret ways of knowing things."

"Really? I've never heard of a secret intelligence."

"No, I'm teasing you. I had all these choices, and I just guessed. You know, you could stop by the laundry to see me, and if I can get away, there might be more of those."

That evening, Anna was clearing the dinner table when she remembered her conversation with Jamelle Parker. "I met this interesting lady today. She's the new principal of the school that Anthony Washington attends. I think she is going to be good for that school. At least, she seems to be trying. She told me Anthony turns out to be a genius and that there was an expensive private school out in Edina that would waive his tuition fees."

Hilda said, "I don't think I've ever met a real live genius before. Then, too, I never thought kids could be geniuses. Is that right? The plural of a genius is geniuses. Or is something else?"

"I don't know, Hilda. The good news is they found him a school that can teach him. Assuming he qualifies for the one remaining scholarship, they still need to find someone who will pay the one hundred and twenty-five dollars in monthly fees. The fees pay for things like uniforms, class trips, etc. Plus, they've got to figure out how to get him from the west side of Edina to his house over in this neighborhood. I guess it's a long daily round trip."

"One hundred and twenty-five, you say. What do you think, you pay half and I'll pay half? All I need to do is to raise your rent, and the problem is solved."

The statement caught Anna off guard. "Ha, you're one funny lady, Hilda."

"No, I'm serious. We'll split the fee. You could dip into all that savings to pay your half. And I have a little rainy-day fund I could use. Okay?"

The cloud over Anna's face cleared. "Sure, I'm with you, except for the rent thing. We'll do our part to get Anthony into that school."

Jamelle Parker and Mrs. Washington couldn't believe it when Anna gave them a check for Anthony's first month's fee. Here were two older white ladies dipping into their savings to help an African American child they barely knew reach his potential. "God sent you two. You are living angels," Miss Washington said.

One last problem existed. How would Anthony, who lived in south-central Minneapolis, get to Westgate Academy, located on the outskirts of a suburb? One solution was having Anthony get up at 5 a.m. and ride city buses for two hours before walking the last two miles to the school. That option was too much for any young person. Fortunately, several days later, even this problem was solved.

The school found a pastor and his wife, who had a son Anthony's age, who also attended Westgate Academy. This family opened the door to their home and offered to have Anthony stay with them Sunday night through Friday afternoon. A church friend of Grandma Washington agreed to drive Anthony to and from the two homes.

On Monday, September 18, 1978, Anthony Washington, from a low-income neighborhood, began attending Westgate Academy, an elite private school in Edina, Minnesota.

§§§

A month later, the twenty-six women who made the Warm Coats for Children project possible met formally for the first time. Anna told them, "This week, we already have orders for fifty-six coats but only twenty-six coats on hand. We'll have to work hard to get more coats. Some of us will have to spend time beating the bush for organizations or people that will help us."

Anna continued, "Since our program is growing, I've asked Doris Patton to coordinate the coat requests. If you know someone who needs a coat, pass that information on to Doris. If you don't know who she is, she is the woman in the blue sweater. Also, Doris is the Spirit of Holiness Church AME secretary. From what I hear, she has quite a reputation as a great organizer.

"I have one final thing to say. We don't need to pass the word exclusively to churches. I went in and talked to the elementary school near Wong's Laundry and talked with the school principal and secretary about what we did. I expect we'll get a few names from them. Pass the word to any place that may encounter children in need. Now, I'll turn this over to Doris and get ready to pass out the coats we have on hand."

§§§

Janice Haggadorn was at her desk one quiet November morning when the switchboard operator put a call through to her that changed her life.

"Miss Haggadorn, I'm Martha Grady, and I work for

the University of Minnesota. I'm also a consultant to the Minnesota Department of Welfare and a historian specializing in the history of Minnesota institutions. The department has asked me to focus on a unique project. I'm not entirely clear about it, so could you please give me some background about what you and a friend of yours want to do?"

Janice was stunned. Was this Anna's doing? "Yes, well, I'll try. My friend and I once lived at Helmhurst. In 1939, when we were in our early twenties, a man raped a mutual friend. The woman never recovered. It was so bad for her that she ended up in a psychiatric ward, where she died. No one from her family came to claim her body. So, we had to bury her in a plain pine box in the Helmhurst cemetery. Like all the others, the only thing permanently identifying her grave was a steel spike with a number that I assume was her patient number.

"My friend and I strongly believe that the people there deserve a gravestone with their names. That's all we want. My friend will pay for a stone or granite marker. I promised to find a name for every steel spike."

Miss Grady said, "Fascinating. I'm not surprised to hear about the cemetery, but I assumed they stopped burying people on state grounds around 1900–1930. So, you're telling me that the practice continued. Are people still being buried there?"

"I don't think anyone has been buried there in quite a while, although I don't know."

"What you're asking for may involve a lot of work, and I'm not sure I can do it. Plus, there is the legal matter of releasing a name to a non-relative. I'll check to see if I can find where those old records might be. By the way, your friend must have connections in high places. This project already has the green light from the higher-ups in the department."

CHAPTER 6

LETTING THE DEMONS LOOSE

"What you mean is that the administration had molded you into someone too afraid to trust your abilities to get along without them."

Margaret Pattersen

1978

Gundy v. Hanson: The Plaintiffs

During the pre-trial phase, the judge ordered the two parties to try to resolve as many issues as possible. Each side was so entrenched they could only agree on one minor aspect of the lawsuit. In the first two weeks before the trial, Margaret had one meeting with Anna to tell her that although her questions should not be difficult to answer, they could be emotionally devastating. For example, there would be questions about bad events Anna witnessed happening to others and bad things that happened to her. Margaret warned

Anna that the attorneys for the state of Minnesota may try to undermine what she said by getting her to amend or change her statements.

"Anna, always remember, if you are having trouble answering a question, cross your arms, and I'll do my best to stop the question."

"You act like this will be a big deal. I've been through worse and decided to help you as much as possible. You did a good thing for me; I'll do my best for you."

"That's sweet of you, Anna, but it can be hard on witnesses. There is much at stake in this trial, and you will feel the pressure. But always remember, this is about making things better for the people you left behind at Helmhurst."

In the pre-trial phase, the sparks flew as each side presented the court with a list of witnesses they planned to call. Minnesota was adamantly opposed to Anna's testifying. They said she lacked the proper qualifications. Margaret, on the other hand, pointed out that Anna was perhaps the foremost expert on what happened inside one of the six institutions involved in the lawsuit.

Judge Donald Stuart approved each side's list of witnesses. As he overruled Minnesota's objection to Anna as a witness, he said, "I agree with Miss Pattersen. Although Anna Olson lacks a formal education, in this case, one of our main goals is to establish what conditions have and still exist inside these institutions. It seems to me Miss Olson is well qualified to discuss that."

Judge Stuart turned to Margaret, "But Miss Pattersen, given the importance of this trial, I reserve the right to disqualify Anna Olson later should I find her testimony irrelevant or inappropriate."

On December 11, 1978, Anna wore her best dress and had her hair done for the first day of witness testimony. Margaret called Anna to the stand. After being sworn in, she greeted Anna warmly.

"Good morning, Miss Olson. We are grateful for your agreeing to provide your expertise about the living conditions and treatment of the residents of Helmhurst. If you would, please state your full name and your current residence."

"I'm Anna Olson, and I live at 4132 South 23rd Street, Minneapolis 55405."

"And what is your current occupation?"

"I'm a seamstress at Wong's Laundry."

"And what other kinds of work do you do?"

"A group of women and I volunteer to repair old used winter coats for poor children."

"Is it true you started this group?"

"Yes, along with Annalee Washington."

"So, now, would you tell us please just how long you were at Helmhurst?"

"I was admitted in July of 1933 and discharged on January 7, 1975."

"Miss Olson, do you have any mental or physical disabilities?"

"No, I can think as well as anyone and am physically sound."

"Then why were you even there in the first place?"

"I was an orphan, and despite having wonderful foster parents who wanted to keep me in their home, a judge put me at Helmhurst because I had two seizures. They labeled me as an epileptic. Back then, having epilepsy was reason enough to commit someone to an institution. They also said I was feebleminded, which wasn't true. I was just a shy kid in school."

"Your Honor, if it pleases the court, allow me to define feebleminded by referring to a 1930s medical dictionary. Feebleminded meant 'deficient in intelligence.' Or 'exhibiting a marked lack of intelligent consideration or forethought.'"

After Judge Stuart made some notes, he nodded at Margaret to continue.

"Please tell the court what kind of work you did at Helmhurst."

"Most of the time I was at Helmhurst, I worked in the laundry. Mainly, I delivered laundry to the wards. But I also ran the big washers, dryers, and every other job in the laundry. Later in my stay, I began doing resident care."

"So, you spent decades in the laundry, delivering it to the places where residents lived?"

"Yes," Anna replied.

"Were you able to see what kind of care residents received?"

"I saw a slice of life, yes."

"Did you see residents busy with activities during the day?"

"No, mostly they spent all day in what was called a day room."

"And what were these rooms like?"

"They were places where residents just sat around doing nothing."

"Weren't they involved in teaching activities?"

"Nothing that I saw. No, people just sat around all day."

"So, what would the staff do on a typical day?"

"Mostly, they would sit in the office."

"Could you go into every ward?"

"No. I couldn't officially go into 6-3-E and 6-3-W. Those were the locked wards. But I eventually went to both places. And my last work assignment was 6-3-W."

"Would you please explain what those numbers and letters mean?"

"Well, the first number is the building number. The second number is the floor, and the letters are either the east or west ward. In building six on the third floor, the east ward was for men; the west ward was for women."

"When you went into these 6-3-E and 6-3-W wards, what kind of people did you see?"

"They were people who couldn't do much of anything."

"Objection, Your Honor. Miss Olson doesn't even have a high school diploma and is unqualified to discuss the abilities of the residents of these or any wards."

"Sustained. Miss Pattersen, please remember that this witness is qualified to talk only about what she saw."

"So noted, Your Honor."

"How many people were in these wards?"

"Forty or fifty in each. It was hard to count them because they moved around or were in different rooms. I recall, too, that the day activity room didn't seem big enough for them to have to spend the whole day in."

"Did these residents ever go outside for recreation?"

"No."

"Did they go to the cafeteria for meals?"

"No. We fed them right on the ward."

"Could you talk to these people?"

"No, they couldn't or didn't speak."

"Was there an odor in these wards?"

"Oh, my goodness, yes. When you go in, you nearly throw up. Some do puke."

"Please tell us what made the wards smell so bad?"

"Can I speak candidly?"

"Yes, but no profanity, please."

"The wards smelled unsanitary because it was unsanitary. People would poop on the floor or pee on the walls, and staff would let it sit there for hours."

"Didn't they clean the wards?"

"Not very often. The staff usually hosed down the floors, walls, and sometimes the dirty residents once a day. Residents often stayed in their filthy, soiled clothes until a staff member took them to the bathroom for a shower.

"Objection. It is unclear whether Miss Olson saw the residents soiling themselves or the walls and floors."

Judge Stewart asked Anna, "Did you actually see the residents do these things?"

"Yes."

"Objection overruled, Miss Olson, please proceed."

"When I worked with the women on the ward. I had to clean them up when they soiled themselves. I must have washed up poop and pee off people and the floor or walls hundreds of times. But overall, the women's ward was much cleaner. The staff were much better about regularly taking the ladies to the toilet. Accidents were cleaned up as soon as possible."

"How many staff did you see working there?"

"What do you mean? 6-3-E or 6-3-W?"

"You worked in 6-3-W, so how many staff worked there while you were on duty?"

"I'd usually work with one other person. Sometimes, we had three staff, and that was a big help. Mind you, we had about as many women as were on the men's side, between forty and fifty."

"Are you telling us there was only one staff member for every twenty residents?"

"Yes."

"All the time?"

"Objection!" an attorney for Minnesota rose and addressed the judge. "Your Honor, this witness cannot possibly know all the staffing arrangements either in this ward or for the rest of the facility."

"Sustained. Miss Pattersen, please limit your questions to those the witness can address."

Margaret Pattersen continued, "I want to switch direction for a moment. How did you come to work in the women's ward, 6-3-W?"

"The big bosses in the administration building were upset with me, so they forced me to work in 6-3-W. That's what they did, you know, how they punish the patient workers who violate their rules. They put us in terrible places to live or work."

"So, your punishment was being forced to work in a dangerous, overcrowded ward?"

"Yes. Don't forget they also forced me to live in a ward with women who couldn't do much. At least they weren't violent. Mostly they were gentle, mongoloid type women."

"Were these living and work conditions temporary?"

"No, permanent."

"What did you do to make your supervisors angry?"

Anna's facial expression turned sad, and tears started streaming down her face. "Because I had a private room. Very few, if anyone else, had that. Everyone else had to live in dorms or crowded bedrooms. See, they didn't know of or approve of my arrangement."

"How did you get a private room?"

"Well, many years before, I volunteered to help this ward supervisor by working extra evening and weekend shifts when he was short of staff. To compensate me, he gave me my own room. This took place while I was working in the laundry. And it was strictly off the record."

"Let me see if I understand this. You volunteered to help take care of other residents, which was well above what the other laundry patient workers did, and in exchange for this, he arranged for you to have your own room?"

"Correct."

"Where was this room?"

"It was right there with the other residents in 8-2-E. Building eight, second floor, east ward."

"And how long did you have this room?"

"Eleven years. They discovered it when Jimmy Dale, my supervisor, died." Anna began to cry but soon stopped herself. Margaret gave her a tissue and waited a few minutes while Anna inhaled deeply, letting the air out through her puckered lips. She was surprised at how strongly she reacted to talking about this incident. Anna always thought of herself as a strong person. But the loss of Jimmy Dale cost her the man she loved and her freedom. The mere thought of it still evoked a deep hurt to this day.

Judge Stuart interrupted with a question. "How old were you when they discovered you had your own room?"

"That was in the fall of 1968, so I was fifty-one years old."

"And the staff you worked with, how old were they?

"All different ages, but we tended to be older, and only women worked in the women's ward."

"Thank you, Miss Olson." Nodding at Margaret, he said, "Please continue."

"Now, Miss Olson, let's return to what you saw in either of these wards. How would you describe wards 6-3-E and 6-3-W?"

"These places were hell on earth—excuse my language." Anna looked sideways at the judge, who simply nodded for her to continue. "I would describe these places as chaotic. Residents wandered all day. They had nothing to do and very few places to sit. Some never wore clothes, while others wore filthy old rags. It's not how normal people live, that's for sure. Plus, they were dangerous. Sometimes, a resident would hit us from behind or bite us. There isn't a good way to describe those places. One thing I do recall is that the residents were extremely thin. Many of them looked like those people they found in the concentration camps in Poland."

"Miss Olson, I know this can get difficult, but we'll stop soon. I'd like to spend a few more minutes on your work in this 6-3-W women's ward. While you worked there, did you ever see women restrained?"

"All the time."

"Please tell the court about how you saw people restrained."

"Well, there were a lot of ways. One of the first things I saw was in another ward, a strange children's ward. Some of the kids there were kept in cribs with bars on every side, and the bars reached up to the ceilings, so they looked like cages. The children never got out except to change their sheets or to go to the toilet. Sometimes, they put adults into an isolation room. In 6-3-W, I saw this happen many times."

"These isolation rooms. How big were they?

"I'd say ten feet by ten feet. I'm not exactly sure, however."

"Why were residents put into one of those rooms?"

"When they were violent, or they refused to follow commands."

"And how long were they kept in those rooms? An hour or two or more?"

"Usually, a lot more than that. Mostly, I would say that people were in four to eight hours. I know some people were placed into a room when I was working, and they would still be there the next day."

"Objection! If Miss Olson wasn't there on the ward the entire time of the isolation, she could not possibly give an accurate estimate of how long they held other residents in these rooms."

"Sustained."

Margaret continued, "Were these isolation rooms ever part of a treatment plan?"

"I'm sorry, I don't know what a treatment plan is."

"At its simplest form, it would be a written document that spelled out exactly how the isolation room was to be used for the resident and how long they would stay in one."

"Nope, I never saw anything like that."

Margaret continued, "What other restraints did you see?"

"They tied people to water pipes, radiators, chairs, and beds."

"What did they use to tie the residents up?"

"They used leather straps or strips of cloth, ropes —you name it. Those are the main ones I remember. Oh, yes, some wore what they call straitjackets, and others had leather helmets because they spent all day banging their head against a wall."

"Were there things that you saw less frequently?"

"Some people would continually scratch themselves until their bodies were full of scabs. They would have large mittens strapped to each hand. Some people hit others. They would have their hands tied to their waists. Goodness, there was an untold number of ways they came up with to keep people from doing things."

"Miss Olson, did you ever see these residents getting medication?"

"Yes, nurses came by at least once every day."

"Did anyone ever share with you that these medications were part of a treatment plan?"

"No, like I said before, I have no idea what a treatment plan is."

"Did you ever see the residents receive any other medical care other than medication?"

"Only occasionally," Anna replied quickly.

"And what was that care for?"

"What I saw were people whose restraints caused their skin to wear away, and the area would get infected. It's only when the sore would start oozing that they finally would do something."

"And how did they treat these wounds?"

"Basic first aid, I guess you'd call it. Cleaning it up and applying some salve and putting a wrap around the wound."

"And then what happened."

"What do you mean?" Anna asked.

"I mean, did they go back to using the same restraint that caused the problem in the first place?"

"Yes."

Margaret walked back to her notes, letting the pain of willful neglect soak in, then turned around to face Anna.

"And, finally, Miss Olson, please describe the food the residents ate."

"Cold food, warm milk, sometimes they gave these people bread with mold."

"Did you see these things, or are you saying you fed these people?

She was forced to recover memories of one of the worst times in her life, and she started to cry. "I fed these people that terrible food. We dressed them in rags, and . . . I fed them moldy bread. I would stuff it in their mouths if that was the only way I could get them to eat." Anna broke down over what used to be a simple fact of institutional life.

"Your Honor, motion for a recess. I think Miss Olson needs some time to compose herself."

"Okay. Let's stop for today. I have an emergency petition to handle this afternoon. We'll pick up again tomorrow at nine a.m."

§§§

On December 12, 1978, Judge Stuart's gavel restarted the trial. "Miss Pattersen, is your witness ready to continue?"

"Yes, Your Honor."

As soon as Anna was seated, the judge reminded her she was still under oath and nodded to Margaret.

"Miss Olson, we appreciate your continuing through this challenging process. We left off with your feeding terrible food to helpless residents. I want to switch gears and ask about other things you experienced. Earlier, you said you had tried unsuccessfully to get out of Helmhurst. Please describe for the court your first attempt to leave Helmhurst?"

"You see, a friend and one of my roommates had recently been raped and badly beaten. At that time, the victim, Ida Malloy, my four other roommates, and I lived in this tiny apartment on the third floor of the administration building. I was working in the laundry at that time. We knew the guy who raped her, and I was afraid he would come after me, so I decided I wanted to get out. I went into this office, which I thought was social services, and demanded a discharge.

"I made a big mistake. I walked into the assistant superintendent's office, not social service. He was furious with me for making such a demand. He put me on tranquilizing medication and moved me to a severely overcrowded dorm. There was barely enough room to walk between our beds. It was humiliating having to live with people way below my level. These were good ladies, but they seldom spoke and were very withdrawn."

"Why did he do those things again?"

"Objection, Your Honor. This witness couldn't know what was in the mind of the assistant superintendent."

"Miss Olson, can you answer the question based on what you saw?" Judge Stewart asked.

"Your Honor, I can answer based on the exact words he said to me."

"Objection overruled; you may answer the question."

"He told me he was going to teach me a lesson. He said, 'Don't go demanding things like a discharge.' He reminded me I was a ward of the State. I had no rights. I couldn't just ask to leave."

"Did you try to leave other times?"

"Yes. Several years later, this same assistant superintendent told me he was glad I had towed the line so well and that now he had a placement for me—some laundry in Minneapolis. But to qualify, I needed to get sterilized."

"And did you get sterilized?"

"Sure, I never considered having children, and I figured that if that's what it took to get out, I would go along with it. So, yes, I did get sterilized. And soon after, he told me that before my discharge, I had to have a complete physical and that he would do the exam. He told me to go to the medical clinic at six p.m. and wait for him. That was long after it closed, by the way."

"Then what happened?"

"He tried to rape me. Here I was, all naked except for this flimsy dressing gown, and he started feeling my breasts, so I fought him off, rolled off the table, and grabbed a little knife lying on a smaller table next to the examining table. I told him if he tried to have me, I'd cut his face and anything else I could before he got his way with me. He yelled at me and left."

"What did he do to you then?"

"Nothing much. He just ensured I would never get out of Helmhurst." The sarcasm came out of Anna before she could stop herself.

"Come on, Anna, how could he do that?"

"Simple, by putting a big ole warning in my chart that I was mentally unstable and capable of harming others."

"Objection! The witness could not see this alleged warning."

Judge Stuart asked Anna, "Did you see this warning?"

She turned to look at the judge, "No, Your Honor."

"Sustained."

"Miss Olson, did the same thing happen to other women?"

The same attorney for the state of Minnesota stood again. The judge put his hand up, signaling the attorney to be quiet. "Miss Olson, can you answer this question based on your personal knowledge?"

"Yes, Your Honor. Many women had the same thing happen, and I know this because four separate women told me this guy raped them. As we talked about our experiences, none of us knew of anyone who got a discharge. We believed it was all a calculated ploy to get women sterilized. And for a dirty old man to have his way with helpless women."

"Objection, Your Honor. This could be hearsay."

"Sustained. Please strike the question and answer from the record."

Margaret Pattersen continued. "You told me once that you did leave Helmhurst without telling anyone. How did that happen?"

"There were quite a few times I walked into the little town of Helmhurst, which was right next to the institution. I went to the bank, picked up thread for my needlepointing, or bought something else I needed. I simply walked back, and no one noticed. For a few years, I had a boyfriend who worked on the Helmhurst farm."

"Anna, I need to stop you here. Perhaps, you could explain the Helmhurst farm."

"Since before I came to Helmhurst in 1933, the State had a farm next to the institution. The men who worked there did all the normal farming things. They furnished the eggs, vegetables, and meat to feed us residents. Extra products were sold to help pay the expenses of the farm."

"Okay, go ahead and finish your story."

"So, my boyfriend and I would leave Helmhurst on holiday weekends and spend the weekend with his brother, who would come pick us up and bring us back. During that time, I had a lot of freedom to move about the institution.

Later, my boyfriend asked me to run away with him. But I was too afraid. By then, I had been in the institution so long that I had missed out on how the world worked. I was sure it would end badly, so I stayed."

"What you mean is that the administration had molded you into someone too afraid to trust your abilities to get along without them."

"Yes. Later, I learned I was what is now called 'institutionalized.' And I had been there just seventeen years."

"Ladies and gentlemen, let's take a fifteen-minute break." Judge Stuart stood up and quickly walked out of the chambers.

§§§

After receiving a nod from the judge, Margaret continued, "Miss Olson, in preparing for this trial, my staff and I were discussing the issue of cruel treatment when I came across the name Trace Martin. Did you know Trace Martin?"

"Yes." The blood drained from Anna's face. The mere thought of that man pained her.

"How did you know him?"

"He taught in the Day Activity Center across the hall from mine."

"And did you ever meet Mr. Martin?"

Anna was lost, back in Helmhurst, lying at the bottom of a stairway, battered, bruised, and very sore. "Ah, do I have to answer that?"

"I'm afraid you do."

"Yes, he threatened to kill me if I ever told anyone about what he did to me." Anna tensed up, gripping the side of her chair.

"Miss Olson, I promise he won't hurt you. We will give

you police protection if he ever comes near you. He knows a court order prevents him from ever talking to anyone from Helmhurst. So, please tell the court what happened to you."

"He snuck up behind me when I was at the top of a flight of stairs. He pushed me down. I had no warning he was there, so I couldn't grab the railing. It was a hard fall face-first onto granite steps. He stood over me and laughed and said, 'Get up you old woman.' I had sore ribs, scrapes, and bruises for two months."

"Did you report this incident?"

"No, I just told the staff I slipped and fell down some stairs. Near the very end of my days at Helmhurst, I told Madsen as he was leaving my discharge meeting. Without naming Trace Martin, I said someone had pushed me down the stairs, stood over me, laughed, and said, 'Get up, you old woman.'"

"So, just to be clear, it was Trace Martin who pushed you down the stairs?"

"Yes."

"But why? Had you ever done anything to him?"

"No, I doubt he even knew my name. He was a mean person or had mental problems, one or the other."

"Objection."

Judge Stuart mumbled, "Sustained."

"You mentioned the name Madsen. Who was he?"

"I don't know what his job title was. He was the one who discharged me and said I was free to go any time I wished. The day I left Helmhurst, he gave me a pack of cigarettes."

Margaret said, "Let's get back to Trace Martin. He pushed you down the stairs. Did you see him do anything else?"

"Yes."

"Please tell us specifically what you saw?"

"One time, this guy was in Trace Martin's Day Activity

Center. He was short and slow going. I was in the bottom stairwell when he and his class went to lunch. Mr. Martin was behind the guy as they went up the stairs. He wasn't going fast enough for Martin, so he pushed him from behind, just like me, and the guy fell forward onto the steps. Then, he moved beside him, grabbed him by his hair, and dragged him the rest of the way up to the landing. The poor guy was screaming out in pain. He wanted Mr. Martin to stop, but he didn't. He kept going on about how this guy was deliberately going slow. I quickly disappeared so he wouldn't see me."

"Do you think the guy was deliberately going too slow? You know, to provoke Mr. Martin."

"No, the poor man had trouble just walking down the sidewalk. He was very uncoordinated."

"Did you see Trace Martin do anything else?"

"Yes. I saw him pick up a wheelchair-bound woman and lean her over a table. He told her that she knew how to walk but was lazy. He went on to say she would have to start walking again. The poor woman cried out in fear but soon fell off the table onto the floor, her head bouncing off the floor."

"What else did you see?"

"Not too much. I did all I could to stay away from Mr. Martin. I was so afraid of him. So were a lot of other people."

"Who else was intimidated by Mr. Martin?"

"I heard he intimidated all the staff just as he threatened me if I told anyone what he had done to me."

An attorney for the state of Minnesota objected to Anna talking about something she heard, not what she saw.

"Sustained."

"Anna, did any of Trace Martin's supervisors do anything to correct or discipline Mr. Martin for his abuse?"

"I don't know. I didn't see anything."

"Did you see Mr. Martin do anything else?"

Anna quickly added, "No, other than he was an evil man."

"Objection!"

"Sustained."

§§§

After a short break, the trial resumed with Margaret asking Anna, "Do you have seizures now?"

"Nope, I think I outgrew them."

"So, you were right when you said earlier that you didn't belong at Helmhurst. You didn't have epilepsy, nor were you feeble-minded."

"True. I could have stayed at Grant Grove just fine."

"So why do you think they kept you and people like you in the institution for so long?'

"It's obvious. The officials who ran the institutions kept us there to do the menial work. People like me cleaned the soiled laundry, mopped the floors, worked in the kitchen, and cared for the other residents. We ran the place."

"Can you think of any other example of a person who was kept at Helmhurst for a long time, although he or she didn't need to be there?"

"Yes, there were my friends, you know, women like me who could live independently if only they had the chance and some help. But I remember Albert. He was a poor guy who couldn't walk or talk, never could as far as I know. I first met him delivering laundry. When I entered his ward, I tried to have some hard candy in my apron that I'd hand out. Albert would roll his wheelchair up to me every time he saw me.

"Years later, I saw him sitting on the floor in 6-3-E with a huge sore in his mouth. Long story short, one of my friends and I got him cleaned up, and another friend got him some dental care. It was the dentist who discovered he was deaf. Like me, he could think just fine. All his life, people assumed he was retarded. All his life, everyone abused and mistreated him. I was so glad when he left for a place where he would get treated better."

"Did you or Albert ever get any services designed to help you improve, you know, so that you could function out in the community?"

"I think that would be obvious from everything I've said so far."

"Perhaps, but I want you to say it. Did you or Albert ever get programs or services designed to help you in any way?

"Objection, this witness wouldn't have first-hand knowledge of any service this Albert did or did not receive."

"Sustained."

Anna waited, not knowing if she should go on. Finally, Margaret nodded to her.

"I know I can't speak for Albert, but from my point of view, all they did to him was abuse him. I saw that with my own eyes. And no, I didn't get any services, ever."

"Anna, I mean Miss Olson, I have one final question. Were you ever raped while at Helmhurst?"

"Yes."

"Would you please tell the court about it?"

"Do you want all the details because I will never forget them?"

"No, I don't want you to go into the intimate details, just the circumstances and generally what happened."

"Well, I was in my room getting ready for bed when he slammed into me from behind, causing my head to hit the cement block walls of my room. I have no idea how he knew where I lived or how he got into the building." Anna stopped for a second as tears began to pool. She took a deep breath, realizing she was telling the real story, not the fabricated one she told everyone at Helmhurst. She stared far off into the past.

"Miss Olson, I know it's difficult, but please finish your story."

After another long pause, Anna continued. "The story I told everyone that night was that I was raped outside the building where I lived. See, I didn't want the big shots to know I had my own room. But I was in my room when he slammed me into the wall. Then, he hit me in the face with a fist and ripped off my nightgown. He screamed at me, saying he was going to kill me. I don't remember much after he hit me on the head a couple more times. The whole thing was very violent. Thankfully, my supervisor, Jimmy Dale, who was a very large man, came around, pulled him off me, lifted him up, and took him out the door. I never saw the man again."

"Miss Olson, did Helmhurst do anything to help you?"

Anna replied through deep breaths. "No, they took me to the clinic, put in a couple of stitches, some salve for the abrasions, and sent me back to my room. Those sons of bitches never did a thing to help women who were raped or abused."

"So, you're telling me that over this long period of time when you and your roommates were raped, Helmhurst didn't do anything to find who this perpetrator was?"

With water rapidly pooling and a face showing the stress of the morning's questions, Anna said, "Not a fucking thing."

Judge Stuart instructed Anna, "Language, Miss Olson. This is a courtroom."

"Sorry, Your Honor, but it hurts to talk about this."

Margaret asked, "Did anyone ever tell you why?"

The security guards told us that it was common knowledge that we inmates or feebleminded women acted like we wanted to have sex. We led men on, supposedly. So, it was all our fault."

She put her hands in her face, doubled over, and cried. The emotional control she had told herself she would show, melted into tortured sobs of pain, agony, and shame.

"That's all the questions I have for this witness for now. I reserve the right to re-direct."

Judge Stewart looked at his watch. "Does the state have any questions for this witness?"

"We do, Your Honor."

"Then we'll recess for lunch until two p.m."

Gundy v. Hanson: The Defendants

"Good afternoon, Anna, my name is Martha Mooreland. I am an attorney, and I work for the state of Minnesota. I will be asking you a few questions this afternoon. First, let me tell you I felt moved by your testimony. You have indeed been through hard times.

"My questions are mostly follow-up questions to things you've already mentioned. The first thing that struck me was that you are an orphan. You lost both your parents when you were young. Is that right?"

"Yes." Anna was quiet and reserved in her answer.

"And to be sent away to an institution was surely a shock. Getting uprooted from your home community must have felt very bad. Is that right?"

"Yes."

"I can't imagine what that must have been like. You got sent to Helmhurst, and I read in your admissions records that your first stay there was at what they called the Big House. Tell us about that place, if you will."

Anna smiled. "Oh, the Big House was this big house a former superintendent used to live in. When I was there, it was packed full of girls with epilepsy. But it was a great place to live despite being crowded."

"What made this place so great?"

"Bea Chowder was her name, but she just went by Bea. She was in charge. She loved each of us and held us to high standards. She had strict rules, but Bea wanted what was best for us. She looked out for us, and she understood us."

"You said 'overcrowded.' How many girls do you suppose there were?"

"I don't really know. Between thirty or forty."

"But still, you said it was a great place. How can that be?"

"Well, we learned to help each other. The older girls helped the younger ones. The more capable girls helped the less capable. And I made six friends there. I mean, these were lifelong friends. Most of us stayed at Helmhurst for a long time, past when we outgrew our seizures or they found medication to control them."

"It sounds like a positive place for you girls."

"Yes, it was."

"While preparing to ask you some questions, I noticed your patient files were gone between your admission to the Big House until you were transferred into a place called the Big Sky Cottage. Do you know what happened to your records, Miss Olson?"

"Objection, this is asking the witness to testify to something she could not possibly have any knowledge of."

"Sustained."

"Well, would you agree that it's unusual for about thirty-five years of residential records to vanish?"

Margaret rose, but Judge Stuart stopped her.

"Miss Mooreland. Move along. Please strike the question." Judge Stuart's tone of voice indicated he was unhappy with this line of questioning.

Martha Mooreland continued, "At least we have records

for your stay at the Big Sky Cottage. Do you remember that place?"

"I sure do. Rhonda was my staff person. She took an interest in me and made me get ready to live in the real world."

"Did you like Rhonda?"

"Yes. She had faith in me and started to mold me into a better person, one not so warped by years of institutionalization."

"So, how did you think you got on the list to be transferred to the Big Sky Cottage?"

"I think it was a mistake. Dumb luck in my favor."

Miss Mooreland changed directions. "You use the word institutionalization. It's a big word. Do you know what it means?"

"Like I've always said, I can think okay. To be institutionalized means you've grown so accustomed to living in one, you can't live outside in the real world."

Margaret Pattersen rose to her feet. "Your Honor, does counsel have any purpose for this line of questioning?"

Judge Stuart looked at Miss Mooreland, who replied, "Just getting to know Miss Olson a bit better, Your Honor. I'm ready to move forward." He nodded, and she continued. "So, Miss Olson, you worked for years in the laundry, delivering laundry to the wards. And it sounds like you got in and out of every ward in the whole place. Did you keep any records of what you saw in these places?"

Anna shot back, "What kind of records?"

"I mean notes, letters, information from or about your fellow residents?"

"No."

"Did anyone coach you about what to say in your testimony here?"

"Absolutely not. The only thing Margaret said was to

think before answering questions. Plus, she also warned me the questions would be hard, both from her and from you. And to cross my arms if I was having trouble."

Miss Mooreland smiled. "Yes, we lawyers want an escape signal for some of our witnesses. But I noticed you never crossed your arms, even when Miss Pattersen asked hard questions. Why was that?"

"I don't know. Honestly, I forgot to cross them."

"Did you prepare for testifying in any way?"

"What do you mean?"

"I mean, read papers or documents someone gave you."

"You mean someone like Margaret, don't you? No. No preparation. She only said it would be hard for me to go through this."

"Oh, why did she say that?"

"It's hard being forced to talk about bad things from my past. Especially after I promised myself that I would forget all that horrible stuff and move on to be a regular person."

"Now, I would like to ask you about a time in your testimony when you worked for the man who gave you a room in exchange for helping him out by working in his wards. Did he ever ask you to do anything else in exchange for keeping your room?"

"Like what exactly?"

"Did he ask for any other favors?"

Anna leaned back, crossed her arms, and held forth. "No, nothing. I know what you're suggesting, and I think it's disgusting. You don't know Jimmy Dale; he was a truly good man. The best man I ever knew."

"Your Honor, again, I must ask where this is going. Implying the witness gave sexual favors in return for a room, without the slightest bit of evidence behind it, is beyond ethical boundaries."

"I withdraw the question, Your Honor."

"About how many staff did you have for each resident in these units?"

"Which units?"

"The units supervised by Mr. Dale."

"Oh, that varied. On average, we had one staff member for every eight to ten residents. It never got better than that and was often more like one staff for twelve people."

"How did you arrive at these numbers?"

"Well, I'm just trying to recall what it was like working there. And I can't say I know the answer for certain. I do know that we were always short-staffed."

"It sounds like your estimates of the number of staff are just your estimates, correct?"

Anna answered quickly, "Yes.

After reviewing some notes, Martha Mooreland continued. "Now going back to your discussing these places called control rooms, or some call them time-out rooms. Were there any clocks on those wards?"

"No."

"Did you wear a watch?"

"No."

"So, would you agree when you said how long people were put into those rooms? It was your estimate, not based on any timepiece. Correct?"

"Correct. But I'm sure that people were kept in there for days. I know that."

"Thank you, Miss Olson. Aside from this Albert you helped get released, did you do anything else to help other residents?"

"My friends and I did what we could. We tried little things here and there, like getting some cookies or candy for an occasional treat. I tried to fix my residents' clothing because I'm good at sewing. But we had little extra time; it was all we could do to keep residents clean, fed, and calm.

There wasn't much time for anything else. Remember, we were patient workers, we had no authority over anything. And we were never paid."

"I have met many people who, like you, spent decades in institutions. But you are unique. You are well-spoken, you've seen a lot, and your memory is good. What I want to know is how did you keep all these skills for so long? How did you stay sane?"

"That's technically two questions, but the answer to both is needlepoint. I did this form of home craft called needlepoint. And people tell me I'm very good at it."

"So how is it that an arts and crafts activity keeps you sane and helps you retain your intellectual skills?"

"It took my mind to places far away from Helmhurst. It helped me remember those who were kind to me. It was what I did when I got down. And it always helped."

"Miss Olson, are you sure you don't know what happened to everything but your admission and medical records? I mean, a lot of your history is gone."

Margaret stood to object, but before she could speak, Anna answered.

"I don't have a clue."

Margaret asked Judge Stuart, "I move to strike that question. The witness has already answered it."

"The question will be removed," Judge Stuart said as he looked at his court reporter.

"I'm troubled by one other part of your testimony, and that was when you say you knew the guy who raped your friends. How did you know his identity?"

"Because he had a small apartment across a courtyard from my friends and my apartment. You see, our apartments were both on the third floor. Plus, we first met him when he would follow us around the administration building when we went for walks on weekends."

"But that doesn't explain how you know it was him who raped you."

"Well, we knew it was him because everyone who got raped, including me, had the same description of him."

"But did any of you actually see this man?"

"Not clearly, we were getting beaten, you know."

"Thank you, Miss Olson. Oh, I do have one more question. Did anyone give you anything in exchange for your testimony at this trial?"

"No, not me personally."

"Really, do you want to think that over?"

Once again, sitting back and crossing her arms, Anna said, "I don't know what you are hinting at."

Margaret bounded up. "Objection! Counsel is asking a leading question."

Judge Stuart directed Miss Mooreland, "Please get to the point."

"Your Honor, it's come to my attention that Miss Olson offered to testify in exchange for a Minnesota institutional historian's assistance in discovering the names of dead Helmhurst residents. As I understand it, it was a quid pro quo and deserves to be discovered by the court."

Still standing, Margaret Pattersen, now red in the face, jumped in with a reply. Looking at the judge, she explained. "It's true. Miss Olson asked for my help in finding someone to aid a friend who was looking to discover the names of people buried without identification in an old Helmhurst cemetery in exchange for her testimony. I had never heard of cemeteries on the grounds of our institutions, but Anna has a friend buried there. That friend just happens to be one of the rape victims Miss Mooreland was asking about."

Margaret continued. "Your Honor, Anna and her friend want to find the names of everyone there because Miss Olson has offered to pay for a burial stone for each person."

Judge Stuart looked at Anna. "Is that what you did, ask Miss Pattersen for help in exchange for your testimony?"

"Well, yes."

"But the only reason you did that was so you could get the names and furnish everyone with a tombstone?"

Again, Anna said, "Yes."

"What did you get out of all this?"

"Get? Nothing except I hope that someday those poor people will have the dignity of a name at least. I hope that maybe some family will know what happened to a long-lost aunt or uncle. That's all I wanted out of that deal."

"Miss Mooreland, I think perhaps you had better check out your facts before you bring up a subject. Do you have anything else?"

"No, Your Honor."

CHAPTER 7

FOSTER MOTHER

"Miss Anna, I want you to raise my little Anthony when

I'm gone."

Annalee Washington

1979

Anna spent Christmas of 1978 with Hilda. She stayed home from church during her favorite holiday. Instead, she spent all her free time sewing coats or needlepointing. Now, new and fresh images appeared on cloth—a boy, an old lady, and a group of women sewing. The details of each scene emerged in bright colors, subtle shades, and sometimes dark tones, reflecting her current emotional state.

Hilda understood her friend's duress and gave Anna all the time alone she needed. She listened patiently as her dear friend expressed hope she could right her emotional imbalance and return to the plan she started on August 17, 1975. Anna told people close to her that this date was her new date of birth.

Margaret Pattersen knew how hard Anna's testimony was and the toll it would take. She called Anna to say, "Hello" and took her to their favorite place for sandwiches and pie on Christmas Eve.

Despite her efforts to think about positive things, Anna's mind kept returning to thoughts of 6-3-W and 6-3-E. The pain seemed as agonizing today as when she worked there in 1968. Her testimony was a blur to Anna. She focused on one of the worst days of her life, May 9, 1968, when Jimmy Dale died. The losses that followed his death piled up until they nearly snuffed her spirit out. She lay on her bed as she had four years earlier, with voices, events, and emotions spinning through her mind. She struggled to focus on just one thing but couldn't.

On January 1, 1979, Sarah opened her door. "Yoo-hoo, anybody home? I come bearing cinnamon rolls."

Anna was startled but realized she needed to compose herself and talk to Sarah. "Just a minute. I need to get presentable." Five minutes later, Anna emerged from her room in her robe and found Sarah in her tiny kitchen making coffee and warming the sweet rolls in the oven.

"I understand you've had a rough patch," Sarah said as she poured the coffee.

"I have. I'm a mess again, almost as bad as when I first came out of Helmhurst. That trial was my undoing. I had to dredge up memories I swore to leave behind. Margaret's questions sucker-punched me hard. I don't know if I can carry on from this."

"Why do you think that?"

"It's obvious. Even though I try, I can't eliminate all the stuff that angers me. I know now that I'm permanently damaged goods."

"But that simply isn't true. Do you realize how many people you have helped in the short time you've been out of Helmhurst?"

"I don't think of that as such a big deal. I'm doing what I think a decent person would if they had my abilities."

"Most people with your talents wouldn't do what you do with all those coats unless they got paid. You do it because you are a caring and loving person."

"Well, I think it goes like this. I feel better when I help other people."

"So then, that's the answer to getting back on track. Get back to doing those coats! What do you think?"

"All I can do is try." Anna stared at the floor, tears forming.

"You will be fine. Believe me; you have too many people who love you and are counting on you. And here's something else to lift your spirits. I'm pregnant!"

In an instant, Anna's demeanor changed. "Sarah, that is the best news I've heard in a long, long time. When are you due?"

"The OB said it would be early in August. But then they said it could be two weeks sooner or later. I don't care as long as the baby is healthy."

"I'm so excited for you, Sarah. I've never been close to anyone who was pregnant. Can you believe that? Another thing I've missed all my life. But I'm not going to miss yours. Goodness, this is so wonderful!"

§§§

Anna gathered all her strength to get past the demon Helmhurst and back into her present life. Slowly, the ghosts that haunted her the most slipped back into her subconscious. After being absent for two days, she spent time with Hilda, who was glad to see her friend. Anna thought that Hilda seemed different but couldn't quite understand why.

"Have you been alright?" Anna asked.

"Oh, I've had some better days. I had a scare last night. I woke up, and I was numb on my left side, not completely paralyzed numb, mind you. It was a tingly, numb-like feeling. What do you think it was?"

"I don't know, but I think you need to make an appointment with your doctor," Anna replied.

Four days later, Anna accompanied Hilda to her appointment. Both were relieved when she got a good report.

The doctor surmised, "Hilda, you are getting older, but as long as you keep your salt and sugar intake down, you've got a few miles to go. Your episode was likely a TIA, a long-winded term for a ministroke. Most of the time, these episodes are harmless. But they can be symptoms of a bigger stroke down the road."

"How far down the road?" Hilda asked.

"There's no way to tell. Come see me every six months or sooner if you have problems."

Both women were relieved and began to talk about Sarah's pregnancy. "We have to give her a shower," Anna announced.

"We should probably wait to see if one of her friends will sponsor it. If they don't, we will," Hilda suggested.

Life returned to a familiar rhythm, which also helped Anna feel better about herself. But now, she worried about Hilda, who had suddenly aged. The older woman moved about less and let Anna do more cooking and cleaning. She also started getting all the groceries.

When she returned to Wong's Laundry, she was pleasantly surprised when Mr. and Mrs. Wong were glad to see her. The mending pile had grown, making Anna feel good. She remembered when she first started and how uncertain the Wongs were about her. Their partnership had paid off just as Anna predicted. The laundry business slowly grew from the time she started. Plus, Mr. and Mrs. Wong appreciated Anna's minding the store when Mrs. Wong was pregnant or had to take one of her children in for a checkup.

However, the best part of returning to her new world came the first Saturday she returned to Warm Coats for Children. She smiled when she saw the piles of coats and the long list of requests. Their message was spreading, and more churches and schools supported the women and, ultimately, the children, who received something more valuable than toys—warmth.

There was one change Anna immediately noticed. Grandma Washington wasn't there. Someone reported the sidewalks were proving too challenging for her to navigate during the cold and snow.

Anna braved the harsh Minnesota elements on February 22, 1979, and walked to see Grandma Washington. It was clear she was failing faster than Hilda. But she was still sharp mentally and spoke frankly and clearly to Anna. "You know, Miss Anna, I've never met anyone like you. A white woman willing to work so hard for poor children who are mostly black. Plus, you are a natural leader. You had one simple idea, but it was an important one—warm coats for needy children. Now, here is a group of poor mothers and grandmothers working as a team and growing every week. You realize this is all because you chose to get involved and help someone you didn't know."

After a long wait, Anna replied, "I don't know what to say. You are so kind and generous with your praise. But what about all you've done? You helped get this thing going, too."

"Yes, but I just followed your example."

She then blindsided Anna with a request. "Miss Anna, I want you to raise my little Anthony when I'm gone. There isn't anyone else in my family to do it. I don't have any brothers or sisters. They are all gone. And my daughter, she ain't able to be a mother. Plus, Anthony knows you care about him. You'll raise him up right. I know that for sure. That's how I want it to go once I'm gone."

Anna left feeling sky-high from the compliments but concerned because Grandma Washington was so frail. She thought becoming a surrogate mother for Anthony was well beyond anything she could imagine. *Was it a good thing? Yes. Would there be problems? Yes.*

A week later, Anna was shocked when one of the Warm Coat volunteers called her to say Grandma Washington had passed. Her first thought was Anthony. What would happen to him? After attending an emotional funeral for Annalee Washington, the question of Anthony's welfare returned. One of the families from Annalee and Anthony's church took him in temporarily. But they needed a longer-term answer because Hennepin County Child Services would soon step in and place him in foster care.

One of Annalee's neighbors spoke directly to Anna about the precarious position Anthony was in. "Our community has nothing too good to say about the child welfare system, so I think you should do what Annalee requested. Yes, she told me she asked you to take him in, and I agree you would do a wonderful job raising him."

Anna replied, "You realize I have no experience as a parent. I'm single, have a tiny apartment, and have been in an institution most of my life. And I'm white; doesn't that matter?"

"I think you're a godly person. We've heard a lot about you, and Annalee raved about the goodness of your soul. Those in our little community don't think the color of your skin matters."

"I don't know about the godly part. I haven't even been to church that much during my lifetime."

"The church part doesn't matter as much as how you live your life. You live the life most of us try to live but fall short. So, think about it. The boy will need a home very soon."

Hilda smiled as an animated Anna explained her

encounter at the funeral. "Ah ha, you'll finally get your family, Miss Anna Olson. You're gaining a son. That's how I see it."

"But Hilda, what do I know about raising a fourteen-year-old boy?"

"You know enough. The rest will come. You will figure it out."

"Who will take care of you?"

"You can keep your pledge to me. Anthony will stay with the people who give him boarding on school days to be close to school. He'll only be here on weekends. Besides, you two can come down here for most meals. You can take care of your elderly friend with a good boy by your side."

The next day, Anna left a message for Margaret. "It's urgent; please call me."

When Margaret called back, Anna was still excited and a bit anxious as she explained the proposal. "Oh, God, here I thought you were deep in depression after your testimony, which was wonderful. In fact, perfect. You helped more than you realize. What's going on?"

Anna replied, "One day, I was wallowing in self-pity. Then I found out about Sarah's expecting a baby. As if that weren't exciting enough, Grandma Washington passed away a few days ago. Before she passed, she asked me to raise Anthony since he has no other family other than a drug addict mother. My world is upside down in a good way."

Margaret told Anna to relax. She knew a person who could help. One week later, Anna's pro bono lawyer and the county Department of Child Welfare soon agreed that Anna would be Anthony's guardian and foster mother on a provisional basis. Anna would still have to pass a background check, personal interviews, and home inspection, all of which could take months. A week later, Anna could hardly contain her excitement when the social worker called to say that Anthony could begin staying with her until they made their final decision.

On Saturday, March 17, 1979, Grandma Washington's neighbor brought Anthony and a suitcase full of clothes, a box of books, and personal items to Anna's house. During the prior week, Anna found a used pull-out couch and hired some movers to deliver it and take the old couch out. Her new foster child would need a place to sleep on weekends and during the summer.

That evening, Anna lay awake in awe of what had happened to her life since the day she testified. *How am I going to handle all of this? I have my dear Hilda, Anthony, a job, and a growing volunteer project. Then there's my needlepointing. When am I going to have time to do it? I'm not so young anymore.* Then the adage popped into her mind. *If there is a will, there is a way.*

§§§

From the outset, the arrival of Anthony Washington in her home caused Anna's world to speed up faster than she imagined possible. With each new person under her care and supervision, Anna doubled the number of issues in her life. There was no time to be depressed about her past or angry with God for putting her through so much pain. Instead, she prayed for the strength and wisdom to be a good caretaker of all that was now hers.

Anna, Anthony, and Hilda clicked. Living with two older white women without experience raising children should have presented Anthony with problems. But it didn't. He was used to living around older people and was more mature than other fourteen-year-olds. He wasn't naïve because he understood the alternative meant the foster care system and a horrible life.

One Saturday evening, Anthony caught Anna off guard when he came up, wrapped his arms around her, and started crying. She pulled him close, stroked his hair, and said, "Go ahead, Anthony, it's alright. You need to cry." The strength of his hug and the depth of his sobs told her he had suffered more loss than he had shown. *How long has it been since this poor boy has let his emotions go? I also understand what it's like to be without parents and alone.*

Anna and Anthony often found themselves talking late into the night. He told her what his mother used to be like . . . sweet and always doting on him. Somehow, Anthony knew she still loved him even when the drugs started taking control of her life. He talked for a long time about Grandma Washington, all she taught him, and how she encouraged him to fight for what was right. His love for her was enduring.

Anthony listened with great interest to Anna's story. She told him she understood his grief because her mother and father died, leaving her an orphan. Anna talked about her foster parents and how she hoped to live with them. She, too, had people she loved and lost. Anna skipped the details of her stay at Helmhurst for both hers and Anthony's sake, nor did he ask.

As the months passed, Anthony taught her about things she never knew existed. Anna showed Anthony a form of caring he had never had. For the first time at his new school, Anthony had someone who would show up at his school events. He would grin and introduce her as his new mother, which was an odd choice of words for a boy genius who sometimes liked to tweak the sensibilities of adults.

Anna learned from his teachers that Anthony finally had a school that challenged his considerable cognitive abilities. He had a peer group of five boys and two girls who constantly pushed each other to see who could score higher on exams.

Anthony brought Anna a great sense of pride. On the

weekends, she figured out how to blend her responsibilities for Hilda with Anthony's need for something to do. She would use things such as changing sheets on Hilda's bed as a teaching moment for Anthony. He soaked up the lessons on how to clean, and Hilda still had the strength to teach him a few lessons on how to cook. Anna was so pleased watching a more energetic Hilda patiently teach Anthony to prepare a meal. Anthony was on his way to becoming a more well-rounded person.

Anna also reserved time for her and Anthony. She studied the movie options, and after checking with Sarah for age appropriateness, she offered him a choice between two current releases. Some Saturdays were spent at the downtown library and having lunch to sample different foods at a new restaurant. She forced herself to learn to play board games, and occasionally, they could get Hilda to join them in Monopoly. Anthony begged her to get Scrabble, but she knew the game and said he needed to play that game at school with his smart friends.

Hilda did not take aging gracefully. She loudly protested as Sarah and Anna told her she had to start using a walker. Sarah was adamant, "Anna is right. You know you are too heavy for Anna to help you get up. You don't want her calling your neighbors to help get you up, do you?"

"I'm not going to fall," Hilda protested.

"So, what do you call the three other times Anna has found you on the floor?"

"Okay. I'll try it."

"I'd hate to see you have to go to a nursing home with a broken hip. That will happen if you don't listen to us," Anna added.

§§§

Anna and Mrs. Wong began to share, woman-to-woman, all the things unfolding in their lives. With the recent arrival of Carrie in March 1979, Mr. and Mrs. Wong had three children. She talked about how difficult the decision was to either come back to work and leave her baby with her parents versus being a full-time mother. Anna discussed her reservations about being a foster mother and caregiver and heading up a growing charitable organization. Mrs. Wong put Anna's life in perspective.

"You are a leader, Anna. You were born that way. Look at how everything you do grows into something bigger and better. You were right. Having your services has increased our sales, now we have two stores and are considering a third. You got that boy a coat, and now you are his foster mother. You gave him one coat, and dozens of children get one every week. It's like you plant seedlings that have grown into young trees.

"Mr. Wong and I have an idea to help us both. We will advertise that we will give a ten percent discount on the first fifty dollars of dry-cleaning to anyone who brings in a coat for your program. We won't guarantee we'll do it all year long. We'll see how it goes first."

"I think it's a great idea!"

Later, Anna reflected on their conversation. She'd heard the same sentiment from Grandma Washington. She wondered what people saw in her that she didn't see in herself.

§§§

Mrs. Wong was right. Anna's leadership was becoming more evident. She felt she had to pick up the slack created by the death of her friend, and she did. She knew that her volunteers needed another meeting to address their growth. Warm Coats for Children had a potluck lunch in March of 1979. The number of coat requests was tapering off as they neared spring, and now was a good time to take a break from sewing to assess their progress and prepare a plan to meet their needs.

After the meal, the women began to organize themselves more formally. During the winter of 1978–1979, the women served two hundred and seventy-five children, a one hundred percent increase from the prior year. Anna said if that growth continued, they would again need more space. And they needed to develop a better plan for picking up donations and delivering completed coats to the children. Anna suggested that Doris Patton take that on and report back to the group during the summer.

They discussed one final topic. One of the ladies suggested that Anna take one Saturday afternoon per month to teach interested women how to sew better. She suggested that if Anna taught some of the more challenging aspects of repairing winter coats, which would increase the number of women who could fix problem jackets.

Anna was silent for a long time. She wasn't sure this was a good thing to add to her already long list of responsibilities. But she finally smiled and said, "That's a great idea. That will be an excellent move for our program!"

Through Sarah, Anna met a reporter from the *Minneapolis Tribune* who wrote a flattering article about the program. She zeroed in on Anna, with her unusual background, but who now does so much for children. The reporter even included a quote from Anna about needing more used repairable coats for the next cold season. She believed coat donations would increase with the information about the program now out in the broad metropolitan area.

Sitting in St. Paul's church one Sunday, Anna took particular interest in the story of the poor woman who gave two pieces of copper a true sacrifice. Jesus taught that hers was a greater gift than the large donations given by the rich. Looking around, Anna saw people with expensive clothing and knew that the members of this church might be a source of used coats for her program.

After the service, Anna went to the church office and asked to speak to Pastor Smith. "Pastor Smith, I'm Anna Olson, and I belong to this church."

The pastor smiled and stuck out his hand. "I know who you are. You're the coat lady!"

Anna blushed, "I am. And that's why I'd like to talk to you or someone here about having St. Paul's church support my program."

The pastor replied, "I'm not the person who does that. Let me get your number, so I can pass it along to her. I'm sure she would be happy to talk to you. Thanks so much for introducing yourself. I'm sure we'll do everything we can to help."

Anna and Doris Patton were thrilled when they finished talking to St. Paul's outreach coordinator. Yes, starting next October, she would put a notice in the church bulletin asking for coats. She said St. Paul's would arrange to get the jackets to Doris at the group's central distribution area. The church coordinator would also ask all the pastors to promote the church's participation in the charity. Anna was excited about the support this church promised. It was a big church with many influential civic and business leaders as members. Anna hoped the ripple effect would help sustain the growing need for old coats for needy children.

§§§

Since she missed seeing Janice at Christmas, Anna decided to visit her at Easter in 1979. Anthony asked to spend Easter weekend with a family from Nazareth Baptist Church whose son was about his age. The boys had been friends since kindergarten and talked about missing each other. Anna thought it was a great chance for Anthony to stay in touch with his roots.

A cool, damp April blossomed into sunshine and sixty-degree temperatures. The two women were happy to see each other and enjoyed a ham dinner put on by one of Janice's Helmhurst work friends. Later, the two sat on Janice's porch, where Anna talked about getting through a new kind of stress. Her Gundy trial testimony put her through another trying time she was sure she couldn't overcome. But Anna had people supporting her, encouraging her, and giving her loving support. There was Hilda, Sarah, and her sewing group that was also a source of comfort and encouragement. How could she not survive the hard times that landed on her doorstep? Yet the most significant change in her life was not the trial. It was becoming a foster mother.

Anna admitted, "How can it be that I'm just a foster mother, although I feel like he is my son? I worry about him, and I'm trying to teach him right from wrong. I am amazed that getting sterilized back then wasn't the end of a family life after all."

Janice listened to Anna's problems and talked about her own. She was seriously considering retiring but was under pressure to stay another year. Work followed her home, and Janice was so busy there was little time to relax. Helmhurst's problems were running her life, and she was constantly tired. Janice knew so much about how the institution worked that she had become as valuable as any highly paid professional, even though she only got a new title and a token raise. However, neither did much to change her mind that it was nearing time to retire.

Janice also heard more from her older sister and began driving to Wilmar, Minnesota, where she lived. She learned of her sister's health decline and other family news and felt her family may be coming together. She thought it funny how age and health problems make the petty grievances of the past seem trivial.

Janice had spent long hours in the cemetery making a chart of the graves' sites and a number to go with each site. Finally, with her list of patient numbers, she began looking deeper into old records to match the numbers to names. Martha Grady, the historian, gave Janice valuable suggestions for what to look for and where to look. She explained that through the years, Minnesota changed how it added numbers to patient names. Finally, she said she had arranged for a team of archeological students to study the site and survey it for any graves that might not be marked.

After visiting Ida, the women began envisioning the site, with every steel spike having a stone marker. They were reminded of the casual disregard for those buried in these sites. The scope and importance of their work began to take on a broader meaning. Their work stimulated other communities to start a movement to do the same for their dead residents.

§§§

One of Sarah's college friends organized Sarah's baby shower. Anna convinced Hilda to go despite her aches and pains. The two older women sat on the couch and smiled as Sarah's friends talked baby talk. The friends and family enjoyed watching Sarah unwrap gifts ranging from diapers to baby rattles and bibs. The younger ladies had games and refreshments, turning the whole affair into a fun event for

Sarah's mother, Anna, and Hilda.

It seemed that before she could turn around, August 10, 1979, arrived, and Anna was at the hospital greeting Julie Anna Barnhorst. Anna was thrilled they had included her name in their first child's name. For a moment, Anna began to think about her self-described new birthday and journey from a lowly resident worker in 6-3-W to standing in this maternity ward gazing at what she thought was the prettiest baby she had ever seen. *Never in my wildest dreams,* Anna thought. Sarah and Karl were thrilled with their baby girl but, at the same time, scared to death of the idea they would soon have to take care of her. Karl realized that attending medical school had nothing to do with being a parent and was humbled. A nurse calmed their fears. "People have been doing this pretty well for thousands of years. I suspect you will follow in the tradition."

August soon led to October, and the Warm Coats for Children project was now gearing up. It had begun receiving its first requests for the 1979–1980 cold weather season. Anna started to teach a group of ladies how to sew sometimes tricky areas such as re-attaching torn sleeves or closing a tear in nylon fabric. The ladies were quick to learn, and Anna soon saw the wisdom of her passing her knowledge to another generation of women. One of the women, Betty Palmer, was especially quick to learn and said she was a good seamstress. Anna agreed to have Betty come to the laundry after work to discuss what she knew and where she needed help. In the back of her mind, she was preparing for a time when she may not be able to do all the Wong's laundry.

By November 1979, Karl was finishing his residency, and the Barnhorsts were moving to the west side of Minneapolis. Karl and two of his fellow residents purchased a family practice, and the move allowed Karl to be closer to his new job. Sarah found them a recently remodeled, lovely three-bedroom home, and she soon set about decorating with baby Julie observing from her blanket.

Sarah took Anna's hand and smiled, "We won't forget you, Hilda, or Anthony. No way. You all are going to start coming to our house for Sunday dinner. Don't worry. We'll get you back home." Hilda declined the invitations, citing her age, nor did Anthony make every Sunday dinner. When he did, however, Anthony would quiz his host with anatomy and physiology questions. Or he told Karl about recent innovations in electrical engineering, his main area of interest. Anna and Sarah looked at each other and shook their heads. It wasn't long before they put Julie down for her nap and then headed to the kitchen.

§§§

At dinner, Hilda announced, "Your friend Margaret called. Said you should call back."

When Anna returned the call, she talked to Margaret's secretary. "Hi, Anna. Miss Pattersen wanted me to call you and schedule an appointment with her at your usual lunch spot, which I assume is Mel's Diner because that's always been her favorite place."

"Did she say what it was about?" Anna was understandably leery of having to give more testimony.

"No, Anna, she didn't. Now, will next Friday at noon work?"

§§§

Anna was the first to arrive because she wanted to talk to Mary Fortis. When a table came open, Anna took it and looked out the window at St. Paul's church next door. The diner had become a second home for her as she often had either Sunday breakfast or lunch here and sometimes met

Warm Coats for Children volunteers for lunch.

When Margaret finally arrived, she lit a cigarette. "You quit, Anna?"

"Trying to, at least. Hilda is relentless about it, and Anthony sounds like her echo. I'm burning up with curiosity. Why the lunch today? Are you going to involve me in another grueling inquiry?"

"No, no inquiry. You probably know from the papers that we won that Gundy lawsuit against the state of Minnesota. But they are being real asses about doing what Judge Stuart ordered them to do. It looks like we will be fighting with them every step of the way. But sometimes, that's the price of winning."

Margaret continued, "But that's not why I wanted to see you. Instead, I have something to give you." She reached into her purse and pulled out a letter. "Before we go further, I must explain how I got it." Margaret stopped, took a sip of her diet Coke and a drag from her cigarette, then continued. "I got a call from a woman who said she had a letter for you and wondered if I would deliver it. It's from your brother Peter, although his girlfriend sent it to my office. They got my name from reading the article in the Tribune about the Gundy trial and your testimony. So, I am the messenger, and here is his letter to you. As you will see, it's unopened, and you can do whatever you wish with it."

Anna was dazed. *Peter, why now?* Taking a deep breath, she looked at Margaret. "Thank you. I'm shocked. I have not had any communication with him since I was a teenager. I figured he gave up on me. Eventually, I gave up on him."

Putting her hand on Anna's, Margaret offered, "You're welcome, Anna. I hope this means something good to you."

"Well, let's find out what he wants." Anna grabbed the table knife on her right and sliced open the envelope. After reading the short letter, she put it down. "He wants to see me." Anna handed the letter over to Margaret so she could see for herself.

"I'm sure this is quite a surprise. I knew you had a brother, but I never asked about him. None of my business, but this sounds like a new beginning for you two."

"New beginning? I don't know about that. I mean, I was locked up all those years with no family to fight for me, no one to try to help me. Nothing. I get kind of worked up when I think of it."

They had nearly finished their ritual dessert when Margaret laid another bomb at Anna's feet. "I've heard what all you've done for Anthony. You were paying for his fees along with Hilda. Plus, treating him as if he were your child. And how he has taken to you is extraordinary, especially for teenagers. So, why don't you adopt him? Neither of you is too old."

"What about his mother?" Anna asked.

"Of course, his mother would have to waive her parental rights, but she hasn't shown any interest in him since she started drugs. You should know going into this, adoption is a long, complicated process. I understand you are already his guardian, which is a good start. Finding people interested in adopting a child his age is very difficult, so I think Child Welfare will consider this a good deal for Anthony.

"I think it would be a wonderful thing for both of you. If you want to do it, I have an attorney friend who will help you handle all the details."

"Oh, my god, Margaret. You are wonderful. Let me wrestle with it, and I'll ask Anthony. I never knew such a thing would be possible. You have no idea what that would mean to him . . . and me." As they stood up, Anna grabbed Margaret, put her head on her shoulder, and started to cry. The wave of emotion passed quickly, leaving Anna smiling weakly. "Oh, look, I got your blouse wet. Don't worry. I know a good dry cleaner."

As they walked away from each other in the parking lot, Anna turned to Margaret and asked, "Do you have an attorney friend for everything?"

"Pretty much, Anna. You can never have too many attorney friends." And with a wave of her hand, she was off.

§§§

After reading Peter's letter repeatedly, Anna thought she should take the high road. *What's the worst that can happen?* She sent a letter to Peter suggesting several dates, and they found one that worked.

Anna was waiting when Peter and his girlfriend walked up the sidewalk on December 9, 1979. Brother and sister had a cool, rather formal embrace. Before Peter could make an introduction, his lady friend extended her hand to introduce herself.

"Hi, I'm April, April Carter.

She walked them up the outside stairs, not stopping to introduce him to Hilda. Short of breath, Peter finally said, "Wow, you sure have a small place here, Anna."

"It's a starter. I like my landlady and my foster son, and I get by here."

"Anna, I'll come to the point. I come here today to tell you how sorry I am for all the years I abandoned you. I got no excuse, I—"

"Apology accepted, Peter. I've spent my whole life being angry with you, trying to forget you, and wondering what I did to you to make you leave me there all alone. But I've given up on all that. I'm trying to learn to forgive. I've concluded there isn't anything good to come from living in the past. I forgive you."

Peter said, "Still, I want you to know I have been trying

to understand why I didn't come to see you or try to help you. Maybe it was because I couldn't help myself. I went out to California with that girl, and she spent all my money, then took up with someone in the Hollywood scene and pushed me out. So, I returned to Minnesota, got part-time jobs, and drank a lot. Eventually, I settled into a regular blue-collar life in Redwood Falls."

Peter paused for a moment. "I don't know what was wrong with me, but I became confused after Mom and Dad died. I didn't know what to do. I felt responsible for you but didn't know how to care for you when I couldn't even care for myself. I turned to alcohol to get from day to day. I could get by on a welder's wage but never settled down. That changed when I met April. She saw something in me and helped me lead a better life. I quit drinking and finally, smoking and even went to church again. But it was all too late. I was already sick."

"How sick?"

"Bad sick, as in throat cancer that has spread to my brain."

"How long did they give you?"

"Up to six months, maybe. April and I accept it," he said as he reached for April's hand. "I am ready to go, especially since I've seen you. I just can't say how sorry I am. Please forgive me. I was so weak. I failed you in every way. I'm sorry." Peter broke down into tears, sobbing.

Anna went to him and told him once again she loved and forgave him. Peter eventually stopped crying, but he still shook his head. "Here I am, the one who should be consoling you for all you've suffered. We read the newspaper article about some terrible things that happened to you. Then someone said you started that coat program."

"Do you feel better now?" Anna still held both his hands.

"Yes, I do. I didn't know how you would treat me or if

you would even agree to see me."

"We're family, Peter, all by ourselves."

"Ya. Did I hear you say you have a foster son?"

"Yes, his name is Anthony, and he's an extraordinary kid." With that, she got up from the couch and got a picture off the wall. "Here is a picture of us. He's fourteen years old and very smart."

Peter didn't say anything, and Anna could tell he was confused about Anthony being black.

"Yes, he's black, but I really love this boy, and he has meant the world to me. Listen, can you stay for coffee?"

"Sure, if it's okay with April."

April smiled and said, "That would be nice."

Brother and sister packed a lifetime's worth of catching up into an hour, each giving the other a condensed version of events. But it felt natural to both. All the tensions, troubles, and guilt that defined their lives evaporated during that hour. As Anna walked them out to their car, she asked Peter, "Will you let me come see you someday?"

"I'm not sure I will be here long enough for you to do that."

"Let's just wait and see. I will write to you and April." Looking at April, Anna said, "Maybe you can let me know how you two are doing. And by the way, you're a saint in my book. I think you are the one who brought us together."

"Sure. And from what I've heard, you are another saint." April smiled at her observation.

"I do what I can," Anna replied.

Anna returned her attention to Peter, and they embraced. She kissed his cheek. "Take care, Peter. I love you."

§§§

After forgiving Peter, Anna didn't think much about

what it meant. That changed on January 10, 1980, when a tall woman stepped into Wong's Laundry.

"Are you Anna Olson?"

"Yes." Anna fully expected a question about her Warm Coats program.

"My name is Lilian Johnson. I am the mother of the man who robbed you. Is there someplace we can talk?"

"Not so much unless we step outside or go to the back of the store."

"The back of the store is fine. Is this a good time?"

"As good as any." Anna was wondering why this woman would want to talk to her.

Mrs. Johnson began, "I'm sorry for showing up unannounced where you work. I didn't know where you lived but knew you worked here because of the Tribune article.

"I know you are busy, so I'll get right to the point. My son's name is Charles Johnson, and he is in prison for assaulting you. He is a good person inside. We raised him up right. He had Christian values, was a good student, and had a promising future ahead of him. When he started college at the University of Minnesota, he began experimenting with drugs. Soon, he quit college and started doing part-time jobs to support his new habit.

"After a while, we told him he'd have to leave our home if he was going to stay with drugs. One thing led to another, and we lost contact with him. Finally, he took up mugging people for drug money. That led him to you and in jail.

"Now, here I am, asking you if it would be okay if he wrote you a letter? He's gotten off the drugs and joined some twelve-step addiction group. I do think he's turned his life around. But one thing he must do is to approach the people whom he wronged and ask for their forgiveness. He would like to write to you. Would that be okay?"

There was an uncomfortable silence as Anna tried to process what she had heard. "Sure, I'll read his letter. Why does he want to ask for my forgiveness?"

"He'll have to explain it all to you, but it has something to do with owning up to his mistakes."

"Why didn't you just call?"

"I was afraid you'd say 'no.' I thought if I talked to you woman to woman, you'd say 'yes.'"

Anna suggested that Charles send the letter to the laundry instead of her home. She reached out to shake hands with Mrs. Johnson. As their hands touched, Mrs. Johnson put her left hand on top and gave Anna's hand a slight squeeze.

"Thank you so much, Miss Olson. I read the article about you testifying in the trial and that story about you and your coat program. You impress me as a wonderful person, and you've been through a lot." She quickly left, leaving Anna standing at the back of Wong's Laundry, stunned and wondering anew what forgiveness meant.

§§§

For some reason, seeing Peter again brought about new creative ideas. She thought about the possibility of a quilt that told her story. Telling the world about your life using needlepoint pieces sewn into a quilt seemed far-fetched. Still, in her imagination appeared a large blanket where colorful, dark, sad, and happy scenes created her unique personal diary.

She started thinking of her life by laying out some of the several hundred needlepoint pieces from her bags. Out came the old wooden locker, where she found what she used to think were her best pieces. Now, she was startled to find they were more beautiful than she recalled. They were also disturbing because they were another reminder of the dark passages of her past.

Here was Albert. She smiled, and a small tear appeared in the corner of her eye. *God bless Albert. I hope his life is as good as mine. I'd like to see him sometime to find out how he is.*

That wasn't all. Here was Mable, Mary, and her former boyfriend, Marcus Parker. She stopped to reflect on Marcus, how she loved to be snuggled up to him after they made love. Then, Anna came across three different needlepoints of Jimmy Dale. She'd always held him close to her heart. *So strange,* she thought, *how I loved a man who would never be rich, never fashionable. But he was kind and loving—especially those with no one else to love them.*

CHAPTER 8

FORGIVENESS

"It's over, the old Helmhurst has evaporated once and for

all."

Anna Olson

1980

It didn't take long for Charles Johnson's letter to arrive. It arrived on February 6th.

> *Dear Miss Olson,*
>
> *My name is Charles Johnson, and I'm writing from Stillwater prison. My mother said it would be okay for me to send you a letter and that you would read it.*
>
> *I am currently in an addiction group with other men who are drug addicts and alcoholics but want to quit using. We have certain things we must accept in this program. Things such as admitting we will always be an addict, acknowledging that there is a greater power over us, and asking God to help us stay clean another day every morning.*
>
> *We must also confess our wrongdoings to those we've harmed and ask for their forgiveness. We don't expect it,*

mind you. We can only ask.

I have done you wrong, Miss Anna. I was so desperate to get drug money that I hit you and stole from you. I am genuinely sorry for what I did. I don't think I can ever make it up to you, but I want to try. So, please forgive me for my sins. I've asked God for His forgiveness, and by His grace alone, He has forgiven me.

I know you may not want anything to do with me, but I hope you will find a way to learn more about me and how I'm a good person. I did wrong when I assaulted you, and I am willing to pay the penalty. But that penalty alone doesn't make it right. Your forgiveness would help make my life whole again.

Thank you for reading my letter.

Charles James Johnson

My inmate number is 692758, and I'm in cell block C, second floor.

Anna stared at his inmate number for the longest time. It reminded her of the numbers stamped on the steel spikes. *Was he stripped of his name and reduced to a number? Does he suffer abuse? Was he neglected and shown no kindness by those who had the power to grant it? No mercy from the people who could have been kinder and shown understanding instead of contempt?*

Anna wondered about the similarities and differences between a prison and a state-run institution for the mentally retarded. Could Charles Johnson's prison life be like the one she lived in Helmhurst?

And here's this word forgiveness again. What does it even mean? Anna thought about the Bible verse she'd heard lately and the sermon based on the famous forgiveness passage in Matthew 6:14–15:

"For if you forgive men their trespasses, your heavenly

Father also will forgive you; but if you do not forgive men their trespasses, neither will your Father forgive your trespasses."

Anna replied to the letter the next day.

February 7, 1980
Dear Mr. Johnson,

Thank you for taking the time to write to me. It sounds like your recovery program requires you to ask for forgiveness. So, let me ask you. Are you asking because the addiction program staff tell you to do it or because you genuinely want my forgiveness?

I can't say whether I will forgive you. I know I should forgive everyone who sins against me because Jesus said it was what we must do. I have yet to come to grips with that. Before I know how to answer your request for forgiveness, I'd like to learn more about you. Maybe we could start by my telling you about my background.

I spent 41 years wrongly confined to an institution for people with mental and physical handicaps. It was, for the most part, a mean and vicious place. Once released, I got a job and started a charity giving coats to poor children. Some say I'm thriving in a world where they once said I didn't belong. I sincerely hope you will follow my example. If you are as sincere about changing yourself as you say, you, too, will need to build a new life, which is what I had to do.

You had a choice to make early on before your drug use became an addiction. And you made the wrong choice. Starting now, you get a second chance to make your life go in the right direction. I wish you luck.

I hope to hear back from you.
Anna Olson

§§§

Anna and Anthony noticed Hilda seemed to have aged significantly within the last month. There was no one thing, but she was more stooped, starting to repeat herself, and having trouble concentrating on games of rummy. Still, she knew the time, the date, and that President Jimmy Carter, a man she loved, would soon be replaced by Ronald Reagan.

"Hilda, what do you want for supper tomorrow night?"

"I don't care, just as long as it's not corned beef."

"Alright then, I say we have spaghetti. Anthony will be home for the weekend, and you know he is always hungry and loves spaghetti."

Anna wasn't discouraged by Hilda's aging. For once, she was watching someone she knew and loved die of old age. Caring for Hilda was an excellent alternative to having someone ripped away without so much as a nod or a hug. Having Anthony by her side was a plus. Somehow, his youth, intelligence, and upbeat personality strengthened her, and she realized she was gradually growing to love him as a son.

§§§

Since they usually talked by phone at least once a month, Anna was surprised by a letter she received from Janice on March 11, 1980.

Dear Anna,

I finally did it! I quit. As you know, work has been increasingly demanding. This comes at a time when I don't feel like stretching myself so thin that I barely have time to live an everyday life. I'm too old for the pressure.

I had enough years of service to retire with a full pension and health insurance five years ago. I wasn't ready then, but I am now. As state of Minnesota employees, we didn't make big salaries, but the benefits were good. So now, I will draw on those benefits and let the pressure go to someone younger and with more energy.

Before I left, I did make sure that I would still have access to the old records I'd need to continue uncovering the names of people in that cemetery. There are rumors of accelerated discharges of our residents because more community services are now available. I noticed they demolish at least one of the oldest and least safe buildings yearly. If you can believe it, Helmhurst is still shrinking. We will need to be on the lookout for any attempts to dig up the cemetery and move the bones elsewhere. I haven't heard anything specific, but this could be coming. Then what would we do? We haven't received the final approval to put headstones on those graves. So, I'm worried.

I'm feeling well and very happy with my decision. When will you have time to bring that foster son of yours by to see me? I'd love to meet him. Take care.
Love, your friend,
Janice

Anna and Anthony were on the bus to Helmhurst the Friday evening before Easter. It was nearly full of holiday travelers when they boarded, so they took the last two seats together.

Anthony said, "You know, this is my first Greyhound bus ride. These buses are much nicer than city buses. See, on these buses, you get thickly padded seats and a place to put your stuff overhead. Cool."

"Yes, it is, and they are comfortable if you don't have to go too far. Thankfully, our ride is short. It's only about forty miles with only a couple of stops."

Anthony took Anna's hand as they passed out of the last

suburb. "Can I ask you something?"

"It's, 'may I ask you something?' The correct word is 'may,' which asks permission. The word 'can' means am I able? Ha! I finally found something I knew, and you didn't."

"Sorry, *may* I call you mom? I think of you as my mother."

"I'd be honored if you called me mom or mother. It makes me proud you would say that."

Anthony continued. "When we get there, may I see where you used to live?"

"You mean like from the outside?"

"No, I mean, like, see your room and stuff like that."

"Why on earth would you ever want to see that?"

"Because I'm curious. You said you lived in an institution, but I don't know what that means. Maybe I'm too young to understand."

"I don't know, Anthony. We would have to ask permission to go in."

"Well, can we ask? Or is it, *may* we ask?"

Anna squeezed his hand gently. "I think 'may' is still appropriate in this instance. To answer your question, let me think about it."

The Easter weekend went by quickly, partly because Janice and Anthony clicked from the start. Anna was proud of him because he got along well with others, especially adults. Being cranky and uncooperative would be expected of any teen, let alone one who had lost two mother figures. Instead, Anthony was a fountain of questions, except when he had his head in a book about mathematics or the writings of ancient philosophers. When they went to Janice's church, they got many sideways glances. A black teenager with two older white women was something most of them had probably never seen.

Janice and Anna took Anthony to the old cemetery and looked at it with a more critical eye. They tried to envision it as an actual cemetery, with a fence, a nice entrance, mowed grass, and grave markers for everyone. Anthony listened as they discussed how that could become a reality and why it would be such a difficult thing to do. This was Anthony's first visit to a cemetery since his grandmother died. It brought sadness, which showed on his face and body language. He asked about the people buried here and why they didn't have a marker. He listened to the explanations, nodding his head as they spoke.

As they were leaving, Anthony asked Janice if they could drive around the Helmhurst campus. When they neared the administration building, he asked, "Mom, which building did you live in?"

"There, the one in the middle of the three that all look alike."

"Make you nervous being so close to where you have so many memories?"

"A little, but enough time has passed that I think I'm okay."

Anthony looked at Janice and asked, "Do you think we could go inside?"

"Anthony, I doubt your mom would like that," Janice replied.

"Well, I suppose there comes a time to put my anxiety in its cage for good. It's been five years, and look what's happened to me!" Anna added.

Janice stopped at the administration building to ask permission to do a short tour of the Blue Sky Cottage. She was smiling when she came out of the building. "No problem. In fact, I think you will have a pleasant surprise once we get there."

As they walked up the steps from the ground to the main floor, Anna felt her heart miss a few beats and realized she was getting tense. *Maybe this isn't a good idea.*

Rhonda Jones came across the lobby and hugged Anna. "Anna Olson! Look at you! You are beautiful! And you missed me so much that you had to return to see me. Wow, I can't believe all the things you've accomplished!"

"Rhonda, remember when you used to call me a 'crabby old lady?'"

"Yes, but you deserved the title when you were here."

"I thought of you as I was going through the worst times during my adjustment to living in Minneapolis. You know that crabby old lady followed me to Minneapolis, but thanks to friends, she gradually disappeared."

Rhonda said, "After you left, the only news we had about you came from Mr. Madsen. He said you were doing okay and mentioned that you are testifying in the Gundy trial. Wow, that's a big-time lawsuit. Then your county social worker came by and said you had a job mending. But what else have you been doing?"

"Oh, not much. After I got a job working for this small laundry, I started a charity to get warm winter coats for children who need them, which is how I met my son here, Anthony Washington." She put her arm around Anthony and gave him a brief side hug. In turn, he put his arm around her shoulder. "He's my pride and joy."

"Anthony, this is Rhonda Jones. She was mean to me and made me do all kinds of things." Anna could see the cloud come over Anthony's face. "I'm kidding! Rhonda helped put me on the path to independence. I owe her so much because she believed in me."

"Cool," Anthony replied.

"You mean you are a foster mother, too?" Rhonda asked.

Anna had a broad smile when she replied. "Who would have ever believed that the 'crabby old lady' that one day showed up on our doorstep would end up being a mother? It's like a dream come true."

Anthony looked at Anna, "Mom, where was your room?"

"Oh, right down that hall."

Looking at Rhonda, she asked, "Do you mind if I show him?"

"Not at all. The ladies who live there now are both at home for Easter. We don't expect them back until later today."

Walking down the hall, Anthony was quiet. When he saw her room with two single beds and a free-standing wardrobe, his first response was, "You said this was like moving to heaven. How can that be true? This isn't anything at all."

"Anthony, when you've lived with forty other women in a big open room, with the few personal things you had stored under the bed, this room seemed like heaven. This is wonderful after you brush your teeth, shower, and go to the bathroom without privacy. Life is relative, Anthony. Everything has a context. Hilda's little house is also like heaven to me. Our little apartment, same thing."

Anthony was quiet, listening to the lesson about life she was teaching. He was silent for the rest of the tour.

Anna wondered how she did it. Blue Sky seemed so small and unimportant to her now. But when she first came here, it was like the haven she had needed for so long. *Time alters how we think of things*, Anna thought.

Anthony was in the window seat on the bus ride back, staring out at the farm fields. Anna asked him, "What are you thinking?"

"How lucky I am that you ran after me and gave me that coat."

§§§

On April 19, 1980, Anna had a letter on the dining room table. She didn't recognize the handwriting, but when she saw the name April Carter in the return address, she knew it might contain bad news. At first, Anna set the letter aside, not wanting to deal with its contents. Later, as she slowly read it, she began to feel his loss again. Peter had left her for a second time.

April said that the end came suddenly and was peaceful. Anna's heart sank. She thought, *Why so little, why so late? We could have tried to be a family, just the two of us. Our lives may both have been much better.* Peter's death weighed on her heart for days. She thought more about him in his death than at any time in his life. She was sad, not weepy, not religious, more like remembering something lost long ago. Slowly, Anna let go of her brother and the what-ifs that went along with him.

The phone call from Lilian Johnson in July was a surprise. Anna had not anticipated ever hearing from her again.

"Good evening, Anna. Is this a good time to be calling?"

"Yes, it's fine," Anna replied.

"I have another favor to ask of you. And I wouldn't ask unless I thought it was important. Would you consider coming with me on one of my regular visits to see Charles? I've mentioned it to him, and he wants to meet you. Right now, he is struggling a little bit. Prison life is getting to him, and he has become depressed. I'm worried he might slip back into drugs. But if he saw you in person, it would help him stay focused on his sobriety."

"Me, go to where?"

"Stillwater prison, about forty miles from here."

"How does it work? I mean, what's involved with visiting a prisoner?"

"I'll be honest; it is a hassle. And you don't get any privacy. The guards don't allow touching, holding hands, or even a hug. But it's worth it, believe me. It means so much to him."

"When are you planning to go?"

"How about next Thursday? You don't need to give me an answer right now. I'll call you a few days before for your decision. I know for sure he would like to meet you. He tells me you share some common background since you were both in state institutions."

The following Thursday, Anna told the Wongs she had an afternoon appointment and wouldn't be there after lunch. When she slipped into the front seat of the Johnsons' maroon 1980 Oldsmobile Delta 88, Anna had thought she had never been in such a luxurious car.

On the short trip to Stillwater prison, Lilian told Anna about her and her husband's life. Both were from well-educated families, and both had college degrees. Mr. Johnson was an architect who worked for a large firm downtown and primarily designed office buildings. Lilian said she quit her teaching job when Charles started having drug problems. She believed if she spent more time with him, she could get him to change his ways.

"I thought I could save him from himself," she said. "I learned a hard lesson. You can't save someone. They must save themselves."

Anna replied, "I think that's true. When I was in Helmhurst, they made all my decisions for me. Now that I'm out, I've had some rough patches and learned I was responsible for my life. Which is hard to learn if you've never had a chance to think for yourself for forty-one years."

"Yes, it is. I think Charles is at that point right now. It is dawning on him that he can't blame anyone else for his drug addiction. For a while, it was our fault. Then, society was so racist that all white people hated him because he was black. Charles even blamed the people who he thought were his friends."

As they neared Stillwater, Lilian added. "My Charles also has a nickname everyone uses. You will see. It kind of suits him."

"Oh, and what would it be?"

"Big JJ."

Lilian hadn't told Anna the whole truth about what was involved in visiting someone in prison. There were questions about who they were, their relationship with the inmate, and why they wanted to see them. Then came the search of her purse and a pat down by a female guard. Finally, there was the long walk through a corridor with the doors locked behind and ahead of them. As they neared the visiting room, Anna got the chills when she heard the sounds of the institution—iron clanking against iron, occasional muffled screams, shouting, and the hum of noise emanating from the overcrowded prison. She remembered Helmhurst and, for an instant, thought, perhaps, she had been tricked into going to another institution, and they would keep her there for the rest of her life.

Anna stopped and put her right hand up against the wall for support. Thankfully, Lilian sensed her difficulty and slipped her arm under Anna's free arm, gently moving her forward. Once the brief panic attack passed, Anna was fine for the rest of her visit.

The two women emerged into a large room with rows of long tables. Each table had chairs facing each other and a piece of thick glass dividing the table in half. Lillian and Anna chose a table and sat on one side of the glass. Eventually, Charles emerged. He was well over six feet tall and carried considerable weight on a large frame. He didn't look obese; he was simply a large person. It looked like he filled a door frame.

"Honey, this is Miss Olson."

"Thank you so much," Charles said as he nodded in her direction.

"For what," Anna asked.

"Writing to me for one thing. And for coming today. Mom said you would come."

"Your mother is persuasive." Anna smiled and looked over at Lilian.

Turning his eyes to his mother, Charles said, "Hi, Mom. Yes, they feed me well, and I get some exercise." Looking back at Anna, he explained. "She asks me these questions every time she comes, so I thought I'd take a shortcut."

Small talk was difficult for both Anna and Charles. It seemed as if the victim-aggressor's chasm was too deep. So, Anna picked and prodded his past. "What was your major at the university?"

"It was going to be engineering. But I didn't like college . . . too many white fraternity boys disregarded my very existence. That was one thing. Plus, I am more of a fixer at heart.

"I finished my first year okay, but by the time I was halfway through my sophomore year, I was starting to party more. And use drugs. Perhaps, you want to know more about that?"

"About your drug use? No, that's your battle to fight. I hear it can be harder than hard, with some folks never getting back control. What I want to know more about is your life here. So far, what has living here done to you?"

Charles stared at her for a moment before answering. "Life here is just about as hard as breaking the drug habit. The physical and mental stress of withdrawal from heroin is awful. I think it's hell on earth. I have been clean for two years, three weeks, and five days, and sometimes, I still wake up sweating and with this terrible fear in my chest. The drug is so goddamn powerful it can kill you."

Lilian said, "Charles, that's not a nice way to say it."

"It's okay, Lilian. I'm not a saint," Anna inserted.

Charles started where he left off. "So here I sit, in a

prison full of drugs. They are around me every hour of every day. But I'm lucky because my cellmate is also sober and has been for five years. He's a good example of how to stay clean. Plus, I look at him with his forty years for killing a family of four while driving drunk, and my sentence doesn't seem so bad."

He sighed as if he needed a second to organize his thoughts. "Then there is prison life. If drugs don't kill you, living here can do it just as easily. I mean, there is violence everywhere. Gangs and crazy people go off the deep end and beat someone to death for no reason. There are stabbings and all kinds of impossible problems when you lock so many dangerous people up together."

"I know something about what you are going through. I spent forty years in a place where many people died. When others control your life, you lose your sense of self-worth, and that causes people to lash out. You become withdrawn and angry, and some get violent.

"You need friends to help get you through. Fortunately, when I was confined, most of the time, I knew people I could trust. Otherwise, I'm sure I wouldn't be sitting across from you today. I remember trying to be as small as possible, hoping that neither a psychotic rapist nor the administration would see me."

"I had no idea about all of that. What kind of place was this again?"

"It was an institution for epileptics, mentally retarded, and just plain slow-thinking people."

Charles pressed on. "How long was your sentence?"

"Sentence? No, don't think of it that way. Courts committed people to the Minnesota Department of Welfare's care, which for some, was a life sentence. They never got out. When you are committed to one of those places, you stay there until they agree to let you out. There was no hope for most of us. At long last, however, they realized how wrong they were and started discharging people like me. Look, I'm sorry I went into all of this. I came to see you, not go on about myself."

"Miss Anna, I want to know one thing. You don't have to answer, but have you forgiven all the people who did you wrong? It's a thing we discuss in our group. Do we have the right to ask forgiveness for what we did? Can we forgive the ones who harmed us?"

Anna chose to stay silent on the subject, and their conversation ended. Lillian and Charles turned to talking family news.

A guard told them their time was up, and Charles suddenly stopped talking. "I've got to go. Thanks so much for coming. I hope we can talk again." He stood up and walked toward the guard.

Anna was quiet on the drive home except to say, "He's a big man. I understand why everyone calls him Big JJ. In my opinion, the name fits. But I have a hunch he will be big in more than size." Burning in the back of her mind was his questions about forgiveness. How could she forgive Trace Martin, the teacher who tormented helpless residents, including her? Or Brighton Hough, the psychotic man who stalked her down and raped her and her friends, could she forgive him? She was grateful that he was dead, thanks to Jimmy Dale. But he still haunted her. Finally, there was Paul Maddox, the administrator who preyed on young women and destroyed any chance she had for parole. These were genuinely evil people. She knew what God commanded but had no idea how she would ever grant forgiveness.

§§§

Anna loved her Sunday visits with Sarah and her family.

They accepted Anna and Anthony into their home, making each person feel welcome. During her time with them, Anna concluded that Sarah and Karl loved being parents. She was most pleased with how she and little Julie bonded from the beginning. From holding Julie in her arms to get her to stop crying to playing dolls, she and Julie were often a pair.

During the summer of 1980, Karl and Sarah had two exciting prospects. The first was they were expecting their second baby in December. The second was Karl discussing starting a business with some physician acquaintances. "It'll be something completely different here in Minnesota."

"What is it?" Anthony asked.

"It's called a Health Maintenance Organization or HMO. The idea isn't unique. They have HMOs in California, but we have nothing like it here in the Midwest. In our plan, visits to your family doctor will have no fee. The idea is to keep patients healthy and to delay or avert an illness. We physicians, will monitor and approve all our patients' care. That way, we know what's going on with them. This also reduces wasteful spending on duplicated services. Our plan offers comprehensive coverage for all your medical needs for one reasonable monthly cost. That's a quick summary of it."

"Do I get this right? You sign people up to get free medical care for routine services to avoid more costly care later."

Karl laughed. "You can be our PR man, Anthony!" The hard part of all of this is the expense of getting it started. But we were lucky that two wealthy investors came along and helped with that. Pretty soon, we'll sell shares of the new company to the public. When we do, Minnesotans can get in on the bottom floor of what we think will be a profitable endeavor."

"So, what's it called?" Anna asked.

"The Minnesota Health Systems."

"So, soon you'll be out there selling stock in your company to all your patients. Will you sell me some?"

"Oh, no, Anna, we've hired a company to do that. But you're a little older. You have no business putting your money into a startup company like mine. It would be too risky. You should stay with the brokerage company you've had all these years."

Anna didn't listen. The excitement in Karl's voice and the conviction of his belief that his company would be successful led Anna to make a phone call to her brokerage company. "I'd like to know how much is in my account."

"Hold on, Miss Olson, I'll be right back."

Finally, the brokerage staff person came back on the line. "Are you still there? Well, you've done well. I see where you've withdrawn a little since 1975, but not much. As of September 9, 1980, your current account balance is one hundred twenty-seven thousand, nine hundred thirty-two dollars, and fifty-four cents. If I may ask, why do you need to know?"

"I would like you to take one hundred thousand dollars and invest it in a company called Minnesota Health Systems whenever its shares become available."

"Miss Olson, don't put so much money into one company. If it fails, you could lose it all."

Anna was silent for a long time. She knew he was right. But she trusted Karl from the very first moment she met him. There was something about him that made her feel confident.

"No, go ahead and buy the shares."

"No, Miss Olson, I think that's a bad idea. We've been your broker for over fifty years. You should stick with what we have set up for you. We have invested your money with a small amount in many different companies, plus some certificates of deposit. That way, if one goes bad, it doesn't cause you to lose most of your savings. Maybe you could put ten thousand into this company."

"I understand, but I trust the guy involved in starting it."

"I will have to talk to my boss before I do that, Miss Olson. At the very least, he will require you to sign a statement that we advised you against this and that we told you of the risk."

"Fine, but if you don't do this for me, I'll move my money to someone who will do what I ask. Damn it! It's my money!"

"We're just trying to protect you from yourself, from making an emotional or impulsive buy."

"Fine, fine. Will you do what I've asked?" Anna sounded perturbed.

"I'll call you back."

The broker called back three days later to say they would do as she asked. His firm would wait ten days from the date the stock was first available to let the share price settle before investing one hundred thousand dollars in Minnesota Health Systems.

Everyone was pleased to meet Johnny Steven Barnhorst, who arrived on December 7, 1980. Sarah had now become a full-time homemaker and a mother. She resigned from her part-time job as an advisor to Community Bound to spend full time with her children. Again, Sarah's mother came to spend a month with her and the children to help get them through the initial process of getting to know each other. The proud grandmother and honorary Aunt Anna hit it off and did all they could to make Sarah's life a bit easier. As of late, Hilda was teaching Anna baking skills, so pies, brownies, cream puffs, and cookies poured into the Barnhorst home.

§§§

In February of 1981, the Warm Coats for Children

program suffered more growing pains. Doris Patton was at the end of her ability to get the appropriate coats to the women who would clean and repair them and send them to their new owners. Anna was unsure of the next step, so she called the volunteer coordinator at St. Paul's Lutheran Church. When Paula Prescot answered the phone, she sounded pleased to hear from Anna.

"How are you, Anna?"

"Fine, thank you. And busy. We're in the midst of our busiest year yet and getting more coats to children than we ever dreamed possible."

"How many women do you have working with you?"

"I often lose track because it grows every week. We divided ourselves into subgroups based on the location of the children we serve. But I would guess over one hundred in all. Of course, we are all part-time and seasonal."

"So, what's on your mind this morning?"

"Our volunteer coordinator is at the end of her ability to put this all together. We are having problems getting suitable coats to the right group of women. In turn, this means children wait an extra week for a coat. Our coordinator, Doris, and I believe we need a full-time coordinator, someone skilled at organizing and coordinating our project. Do you have any suggestions?

Miss Prescott asked, "Do you have any money? I mean, enough to hire someone?"

"No, we only have two hundred fifty dollars, more or less."

"The only thing I can think of is to try to make an appointment with someone over at the United Way. Maybe they know of someone who would be willing to help you."

"We appreciate that very much, Miss Prescott. Do you have the number for the United Way?"

Anna felt another kind of pressure. One of the volunteers

suggested that the churches that support Warm Coats for Children would like to meet her. Anna said that she would be willing to attend a worship service at every church.

Starting on March 8, 1981, Anna, sometimes accompanied by Anthony, would attend a different African American church. She enjoyed the experience and noticed that she was often the only white person in the sanctuary. Most churches wanted her to stand and introduce herself. A member of the church asked her fellow volunteers to stand with her. Often, someone would testify to the good Anna and her group had done for children in their area. Anna came home these Sundays with a sense of pride. Her hard work was bearing fruit.

§§§

Easter was on April 19, 1981, and Anna was again back in Helmhurst with her long-time friend, this time without Anthony. The family whom he lived with when attending Westgate Academy invited him to go to Chicago to see some museums. Several neighbors had a plan to take care of Hilda while Anna and Anthony were gone. It was a significant commitment because Hilda needed help getting to the bathroom and the dining room table. Although her spirit was strong, her body was gradually leaving her dependent on others.

The opportunity to spend time with Janice was a welcome break from the daily stress of elder care, sewing coats, and the responsibility of being a mother. "I must say, Janice, I love doing all these things, but it wears me out sometimes."

"My dear friend, I hate to tell you, but you're not so young anymore. What, are you sixty-five yet?"

"Very funny. You know darn well I'm not sixty-five. Sixty-four, but not sixty-five. So how about you? Aren't you close to seventy?"

A smiling Janice replied. "No, Anna, that's someone else in your other world. I believe we're almost the same age. What else is going on in your life?"

"I still have another burden to share with you, Janice. Well, not a burden. Maybe it's better put by saying I have one last hurdle to overcome."

"I can't imagine what it would be. You seem so happy now, so full of life."

"It's still about the demons of Helmhurst. That prisoner guy, the one who robbed me, reminded me that I should forgive him and all the Helmhurst people for all the bad things they did to me. Charles asked me to forgive him for mugging me. He said we should all forgive those who harmed us because there is a passage in Matthew where Jesus says you must forgive those who hurt you. I also know that's in the Lord's Prayer. If you do that, God will forgive all your sins. That's a tall order in my book."

"Well, maybe not that tall, Anna. Have you ever thought of forgiveness as ridding yourself of the past? I heard someone explain that it was saying to those who wronged you, 'You no longer have power over me.' Even if they are long dead, they may be holding you back. You don't need any more of that, Anna. You are controlling your future now. You are loved by more and more people every day. Maybe you should do yourself a favor and cut those old sinners out of your life forever by forgiving them. In return, Jesus promises to forgive us for all our sins. Not a bad deal in my book."

Anna sat quietly, not touching her coffee. She was in a mental equivalent of a winter white-out, where she thought about but did not see the world around her. When Janice got up from the table, Anna grabbed her wrist and said, "Thank you, Janice. No one has put it like that. I will think on it tonight."

Anna woke up early and waited quietly at the kitchen table for Janice.

When Janice finally came down, she smiled as she said. "It looks like someone made a decision,"

Anna smiled coyly. "How could you tell?"

"Gee, I don't know, maybe the big smile on your face."

"I did it, Janice. I prayed last night, telling God I chose to forgive all those who hurt me, including Charles Johnson. You know what? It's over. The old Helmhurst has evaporated once and for all. I don't think I will forget everything. Forgiveness means that the sins of yesterday will no longer stain today."

§§§

"Before you head home, Anna, let's go over and look at our cemetery plans. I think there are some important things on the horizon. I suggest we go to the eight-thirty a.m. service, return for an early lunch, and stop by on our way to your bus."

At the cemetery, Anna noticed wires with yellow ribbons tied at the top of tall wooden stakes. "What's all this?"

"This is what I wanted to show you. Martha Grady, our state of Minnesota helper, came through with those University of Minnesota archeology students and their instructor. They had special ground X-ray technology that helped them find bones. They put a stake with a yellow ribbon on top of burial bones without a marker, like a steel stake. There are twelve new gravesites in all. All are on the north side of the graves with steel spikes. Perhaps the newly discovered plots were all left of a cemetery here before Helmhurst opened. There is no way to know right now."

"Wow, am I going to be out more money? I mean, if

that's what it takes, why not?"

"For now, this whole thing is out of our hands. Someone in Minneapolis must decide what to do next. Do they try to excavate one or two of these new areas, or what? Then they'll let us know whether or not we can move forward."

"According to Miss Grady, once they get into gray areas like this, someone from the legislature typically wants to get involved. One risk is they won't let us do anything."

"In other words, it gets complicated." Anna's voice had the bite of experience.

"It sure does. That's not the only thing we have to figure out. I told you about all the people Helmhurst is discharging to their home communities. If this keeps up, there is a real possibility that they will close some or all the state institutions. Indeed, there is a real fear in town that Helmhurst will close, taking all those good-paying union jobs.

Janice paused for a moment before raising the critical issue. "The big question for us is, what will they do with this cemetery?"

Anna sounded confident. "It means we need to ensure that somehow, we get control of this sacred land. It's Ida's and our history at stake here. And you know, we don't know who or where they are, but everyone here has a family that may wonder what ever happened to them. We have to speak up for all those people as well."

"We need to keep in touch about all of this, Anna. I feel that where there is a will, there is a way. Right? Isn't that what you say?"

At the bus station, a tired Anna turned to Janice and said, "I came here and unloaded a whole basket full of problems, but now a bunch more come rushing in to fill the void. It's a swap I'd make any day of the week." Janice stayed by her car until she lost sight of the bus. She marveled at all her friend had endured and what a strong person she had become.

§§§

Anna devoted all her spare time to reviewing her needlepoints. *When did I ever have time to make all of these?* But they were a lifetime accumulation of a gifted artist. From the start, she conceptualized the entire scene, from size to color and everything in between.

It became clear that they told her life's story. Again, her mind turned to a larger-than-usual quilt made totally for sharing her life with others. But as much as she knew about sewing and needlepointing, she had never quilted. She thought of all the women who were in her sewing circles. Undoubtedly, one or two of them would know how and be willing to help her get started.

Anna lay awake long into the night, thinking about the quilt pieces. What order should they take, and how do you attach them to a backing? And how much time would it take to put that quilt together? She hoped that sometime after Anthony was off to college, she would have the time needed to devote to this.

CHAPTER 9

ANTHONY WASHINGTON

Rich people get these kinds of breaks all the time. This time, I want people from the bottom rung of our society to get a break.

Representative Ronald Helmquist

1981

Anna was up early on July 23, 1981. Something vague woke her and wouldn't let her get back to sleep. She lay awake thinking about the day to come. It was supposed to be a typical day, mending at Wong's Laundry and meeting two new volunteers for her charity. If all went well, it would end with her doing some laundry for Hilda and herself after she prepared dinner. But something else kept her mind active and alert. She couldn't pinpoint what it was, so she got up, brushed her teeth, washed her face, and went downstairs to make breakfast for Hilda.

As usual, she opened the back door and entered through the porch and kitchen. "Anyone here ready to get up?" The silence was unusual. Hilda always scolded her no matter when Anna came in. "Why did you let me sleep so late?" she would often say.

But not today. When Anna entered Hilda's room, she found her on the floor beside her bed. It looked like she had tried to get up but slipped and fell to the floor. Anna stared at her for what seemed the longest time. Her mind recorded what she saw. *She is so still and at peace*. Anna calmly watched Hilda before dropping to her knees by her side. She picked up Hilda's hand and held it to her forehead. "Where will I be without you, my dear friend? You need to come back for a little longer. There are still things I'd like to share with you."

She couldn't help but think of the day Jimmy Dale died and how she held his hand and felt his spirit drift away. She didn't feel as if Hilda's soul was still in the room, but she wasn't ready to say goodbye to one of the women she credited with making her life a success. After a long time, she began thinking about what to do.

Suddenly, Anna felt the grief settle in and then the panic. *I have no clue who to call now or what to do. I'll call Sarah, and Dr. Karl will know.* But she would have to leave Hilda to get to the phone, and she wasn't ready to do that. Anna was ready to cry. She lost awareness when the tears came. But there was no relief in tears, no solace. Finally, she said, "Hilda, I've got to go call Sarah now. I'll be right back. I won't leave you."

Anna couldn't recall Sarah's phone number, but when she did, there was no answer. She looked up Dr. Karl's office number and dialed it. A tearful Anna spilled out the basics. "Tell Karl I'm all alone with Hilda, and I think she's dead," was all she could say.

"Anna, give me the phone number for where you are right now."

Anna could barely comply when the office assistant

asked for the address. "Anna, we'll take care of everything. We'll relay the message to Dr. Barnhorst and Sarah. One of them will be there soon, as will someone from the sheriff's office or the county coroner. Be sure to leave the front door open. Will you go open it now before you go back to Hilda?"

"Yes, I will."

Anna sat on the floor next to Hilda's head, gently stroking her face and pulling tiny strands of hair back from her eyes. Random thoughts passed through her mind. Each idea stood alone and vanished as soon as a new one started.

Perhaps it was five minutes, or ten, or an hour later before Anna heard the front door open.

"Hello." A long pause. "Hello. I'm Captain Smith from the Hennepin County Sheriff's Department. Where are you?"

"Here, back by the kitchen."

Captain Smith took off his hat when he reached the bedroom. He walked in, checked Hilda for a pulse, and asked Anna what she knew about what had happened.

"I don't know. I live in the apartment upstairs. I checked on Hilda earlier than usual and found her just like this."

"So, do you think she was dead when you entered the room?"

"Yes, she didn't move or do anything."

"Did you move her or try to move her?"

"No, sir, she must have tried to get up and fell. This is exactly like I found her."

"Okay, we'll help you now, and we don't have to be in a hurry. Can you just tell me a little more about who this is?"

Anna asked, "When are you going to take my friend away? And where will you take her?"

"That depends on the coroner. If he has some questions about her death, he may take her to the Hennepin County morgue. If not, you will need to pick a funeral home, and they will come to get her."

As soon as Anna finished answering Captain Smith's questions, Sarah came through the door, out of breath and looking frantic. "I'm here, Anna. I dropped the kids off at the daycare and came right over. What happened?" As Anna explained the situation, Officer Smith stepped out of the room, leaving the three women to themselves. Sarah, too, had tears in her eyes as she knelt next to Hilda.

"Oh, my dear Hilda, we will miss you so much." Then tears and grief overcame Sarah for a few minutes. She stood up and sat on the bed next to Anna.

The phone rang, and Sarah got up and answered. It was Karl who gave her instructions as to what would happen next and what they should do. "I wish you could be here, Karl, but I know you have your patients. I'll let you know what happens."

Sarah returned to the bedroom and asked Anna. "Do you know where Hilda would have left instructions for us to follow when she died? Did she tell you anything like which funeral home to call?"

Anna got up and went to a small bureau beside the dining room table. Through tears dripping from her face, she shuffled through the papers until she found the folder Hilda told her had her final wishes. It contained a list of things that were important to know. There was the deed to a cemetery plot next to her husband. A little further down was a receipt for a pre-paid funeral plan with the Dover Anderson Funeral Home. Finally, there was a letter from her attorney and a copy of her will, which Anna ignored. It was way too soon to think about all these things. Later, she would thank Hilda for thinking ahead so Anna wouldn't have to worry about her final arrangements.

The women and sheriff's deputy waited an hour before a white van pulled up outside Hilda's house. Two staff members from the coroner's office came into the bedroom.

They asked Anna and Sarah to wait in the living room as they examined Hilda's body and the room. Finally, they talked to Anna. They repeated the same questions as Captain Smith, plus a few more. After examining Hilda, one of them said, "This is a natural death, and we'll prepare a death certificate to say that. We don't need anything more from you. We need to take a few pictures, which will only take a few minutes."

§§§

On August 3, 1981, Sarah accompanied Anna to Hilda's attorney's office for the reading of her will. Her attorney said that since Hilda had no family, Anna was the only person mentioned in her will.

"Miss Olson, your friend came to see me a while back and asked me to update her will so that you would inherit her house and everything in it. If you didn't know, her husband received some help from the Red Cross during the second world war. They were always grateful, so whatever money she has in her estate when we finish her affairs will go to the Red Cross.

"Now, with your permission, I can oversee the transfer of the title and deed to you. If you have someone else to do that, that is also okay. I charge a very reasonable fee of two hundred fifty dollars. Would you like me to proceed?"

"Yes."

"Is this a surprise to you, Miss Olson?"

"I had no idea she was going to do this. Are you sure about it?"

He handed Anna her copy of the will. "I am. You may read it yourself."

"You mean I now have my very own house?"

"Again, correct."

Anna squeezed Sarah's hand, looked at her, and said,

"Did you hear that? I now own a home. Good Lord, how did all of this happen so quickly?"

In the three weeks following the reading of the will, Anna and Sarah went through Hilda's things, with Sarah advising her to think about what she wanted to keep. She cried and felt the heavy weight of depression, something she hadn't felt in a long time. The initial surprise and joy of inheriting Hilda's house soon became long, lonely nights of grief. Anna appreciated the outpouring of support from everyone around her. Karl and Sarah gave Anna a five-hundred-dollar check for her Warm Coats for Children program in memory of Hilda Brown. Cards came flooding in from people she barely knew and all the churches in her program. Anna was overwhelmed.

She was very grateful for Anthony. How did this boy, with all he's been through, turn out to be so sensitive and sweet? Anna got hugs when needed and willing ears ready to listen when she felt like sharing her thoughts and recollections of Hilda. She told Anthony, "When I was acting like a crabby old lady, Hilda told me to either change my ways or find somewhere else to live. Or go back to Helmhurst."

Anthony replied. "So she threatened you to shape up or get out. Is that what you are saying?"

"Yes, she somehow knew the right time to be stern and the right time to be understanding. She was smart in a lot of ways."

"So, how did you get this apartment?"

An hour later, Anna finished the story of her journey out of Helmhurst through Community Bound, her complex emotions, her mending job, and the expanding Warm Coats for Children program. When she finished, she commented, "You and I have been through some hard days, haven't we? Maybe that's why we get along so well."

Anthony nodded and said, "Yup."

When Anna received the deed to the house, she and Sarah had a Salvation Army truck come and take away boxes of old clothes, some of Hilda's furniture, and all items stored in the basement. Anna kept Hilda's bedroom set since it reminded her of her parents' bedroom furniture. Sarah picked out new and brighter colors for the living room. New curtains went up, and in came a new living room couch and chair. Doris Patton organized a housewarming party for Anna. Many of her sewing friends came with dish towels, lovely bath soap, hot pan holders, bread pans, freshly baked cookies, desserts, and sympathy cards. Anna was moved to tears by their kindness and hugged every woman who came.

The process of settling in also involved Anna going to her father's old wooden locker and getting out the doilies that her grandmother made in Norway. She eventually settled on two of her favorite needlepoints, had them framed, and hung them near the dining room table. The house would gradually become Anna's house, although she felt Hilda's spirit daily.

The final adjustment came when Anna moved into Hilda's old bedroom, leaving Anthony in the upstairs apartment. He lobbied Anna for this space and promised not to abuse the privilege. She agreed. Her foster son had the wisdom of people decades older. Besides, Anna figured, *He's a teenager and needs to learn to make his bed and do simple chores like scrubbing his toilet and other basic housekeeping chores. Or he'll be messy and unorganized like many young men.*

§§§

On August 11, 1981, Margaret Pattersen received a phone call from the lawyer helping Anna finish Anthony's adoption. Her friend reported that the Department of Child Welfare was just about to rule against approving the adoption.

"Why?" Margaret asked.

Her face turned red as she listened. "There are several problems. The biggest is that Anthony goes to that private school and lives with a family near the school while school is in session. Plus, all her charity work and a job. They think Anna has too much on her plate given her age."

"Have you tried to get a reversal on this?" Margaret asked.

"Of course, and then some. But Child Welfare keeps coming back with this same old thing about the Minnesota laws and the guidelines. They believe Anna should give up the other activities and move closer to the school. Or make other transportation arrangements. They want to see them live together in the same house seven days a week, week in and week out, like a conventional family."

"Have they ever mentioned Anna having been in Helmhurst for so long?"

"Not in so many words, but I can read between the lines. Yes, it is also a concern."

Margaret and her lawyer friend talked a bit longer before Margaret promised to work on it immediately.

§§§

On Saturday morning, September 5, 1981, Anna was concentrating on counting the number of volunteers who worked at the Warm Coats for Children program. She was startled when the phone rang. "Hello, this is Anna Olson."

"Miss Olson, this is Ronald Helmquist, a state representative for Minnesota's 12th district. I serve people mainly in western Hennepin County and part of two adjacent counties. You and I have something in common because we have students at Westgate Academy. As I understand it, both are in a small group of top students. We have reason to be proud, don't we?"

"We sure do."

Without missing a beat, Representative Helmquist continued, "Has Anthony mentioned anything to you about their advanced civics class?"

"No."

"This is a small class for their top students. The three oldest students in that class are required to think about a program or policy change that will help others. They are to talk directly with people who know about their subject and make an in-depth report about solving the problem.

"Anthony has chosen to explore a topic that comes from your experiences at Helmhurst. Anthony was curious about how to save the cemetery there. He learned from the teacher that I was on the House Committee on Appropriations and that, among other things, we handle all the states' property. That young man of yours is a good salesman. He convinced me to see him. He caught me off guard when he told me we have cemeteries on some of our properties. I had never heard a word about that before. So, I checked around, and yes, in fact, several of our bigger and older institutions have cemeteries.

"Anthony said he knew all about this from you and said I should talk to you."

"Well, I hope he didn't do anything disrespectful. He can be a pest if he's interested in something."

"No, no, nothing of the sort. He was very mature and polite. Would you be able to come to my office to talk about this? We are in session, so I'll have my assistant call you next Monday to set an appointment. Is that okay?"

"Sure."

"I look forward to finding out more. Stay well, Miss Olson."

"Thank you, Mr. Helmquist."

Anthony was a typical teenager who liked to sleep late

on weekends. At 11 a.m., Anna finally went upstairs to get him up. "Get downstairs, young man. We need to discuss some things."

Anna had an edge to her voice because Anthony told a stranger, a powerful one, what she and Janice were discussing.

"I understand you've taken it upon yourself to discuss our cemetery project without permission. You didn't have the right to do that. It's not your story."

"Sorry, I should have talked to you. But I thought I could help. I mean, it's not every day you get to meet an important legislator like Mr. Helmquist. And he said he thought he could help."

"That's not the point, Anthony. He may be very influential, but you need to learn that you can't always jump into the middle of someone else's problem. You should get permission first."

"I understand. I just thought I was doing the right thing."

"Maybe you are, but I want you to be careful in the future. Use common sense."

"I'm sorry, Mom."

"You're forgiven." She gave him a gentle sideways hug and started making his favorite breakfast.

§§§

It was late August 1981, and neither Anthony nor Anna could see what was coming when the headmaster's secretary called them to his office. The headmaster was Melvin King, a slightly built man who instilled fear and respect in students and faculty. "Ms. Olson, thank you for coming. I appreciate your dedication to Anthony's education." Nodding toward Anthony, he continued. "He has excelled here, as you probably know. He is one of the rare students who are ready to go to college despite his being a junior. Anthony has met all the academic requirements for graduation. However, we feel it is in his best interest to remain with his friends for at least one more year. We have the teachers with the expertise to begin giving him college-level instruction and set him on a course of self-study for the rest of this academic year.

"Young people who are as gifted as Anthony often lack social maturity. Some have a hard time fitting in with the other students. Fortunately, we think Anthony has a group of friends with whom he finds common ground."

"Anthony, what do you think?" Anna asked. "Do you think you should stay here or start college?"

"Oh, stay here. Absolutely. This is the first place where I've made friends. We smart kids assure each other that we are not totally nerdy. They are a little bit behind me grade-wise, but not by much. I like it here, Mr. King. I'd like to stay."

"What do you think, Miss Olson?"

"As he said, he wants to stay, and I don't see the need to hurry him along. For one thing, maybe you can help Anthony use this year to determine which college will be best for him."

"Good point. Anthony won't have trouble getting into the college of his choice, and they should be willing to give him a full-ride scholarship."

"What does full ride mean, Mr. King?"

"Anthony, it means they will waive all their fees for both tuition and the cost of room and board. But we also need to think of one more thing. What will your major be?"

They each left their meeting on a positive note. Mr. King was excited about keeping an extraordinary student for one more year. Anthony felt he was setting a plan for his future, and Anna was a proud mother.

§§§

On October 15, 1981, Anna and Anthony were at the state capital. She had never been there nor met with an elected representative. Anna needn't have worried. She took Anthony with her to the meeting since he was the one who got this whole thing started. They finally found Representative Helmquist's office, and the staff was friendly. The receptionist led them into the Representative's office, where his chief legislative staff person joined them.

"My name is Zachary, and I work with Representative Helmquist." He shook their hands and asked them if they needed anything. He sat at the Representative's desk. "Mr. Helmquist is finishing another committee meeting, so I'll meet with you briefly before he joins us. He hopes to be here soon. Anything we discuss, I will pass on to him.

"All we know is that Anthony says some of our institutions could lose cemeteries due to downsizing. Is that right?"

"Yes, sir," Anthony replied.

Anna joined the conversation. "That's part of the story, but much more is involved. None of the people buried there had tombstones or identification other than a steel spike with a number. My friend and I are on a mission to find the names of the people buried at Helmhurst. Ultimately, we want to give them a tombstone with their name on it. They deserve at least some small amount of dignity."

Anna continued, "But my friend Janice and I don't own the land, and apparently, you all didn't even know the cemeteries were there. So what does Minnesota intend to do with these plots when they close the institution?"

Representative Helmquist entered the room with a full smile. "Sorry, I'm late. All day long, I sit around and wait for my committee meetings to end. Boring, boring, boring. So how are you today, Miss Olson?

"I'm fine."

"Anthony?"

"I'm good, sir."

"Zachary, don't get up. I'll just sit here."

Anna started to like Mr. Helmquist at that moment. He didn't fit the traditional mold. He felt he could learn more from people if he sat close to them, without desk barriers. "Zachary, why don't you tell me what we know so far?"

"Well, sir, we're not too far along. We know we have these little cemeteries, but we don't know the names of anyone in them. All they have for identity is a steel stake with a number. Plus, from your prior visit with Anthony, we know that the University of Minnesota has done an archeological survey and discovered more graves. We don't know who is buried in them either."

Representative Helmquist asked, "Miss Olson, what is it you would like to happen here? I mean, you raise an interesting issue. What are we going to do with those cemeteries? What would you like to happen?"

"My first goal is to identify everyone buried there. In the longer term, I want the state of Minnesota to donate the cemetery to someone, or some group, who will own and maintain it. This is personal for my best friend and me. We both lived at Helmhurst, and we both know it's a horrible past. Plus, Ida Malloy, our good friend, resides in that cemetery. We hope to have the cemetery serve as a remembrance for her and all those poor people like her. They lived, died, and remained there after death, and now they are all forgotten."

Representative Helmquist responded. "Now, that's something I think we in the legislative branch can get behind. It'll take some thinking and probably some maneuvering. Anytime we get into something like this, someone always finds a way to make it complicated. So it will take time. I think I asked you before, do you know how many institutions have cemeteries?"

Anna replied. "I don't know, but I have a friend who can

probably help. Do you know Margaret Pattersen?"

"Oh, yes. Everyone around here knows who Margaret is. She's a good person and a real force. She and I get along very well because we have an agreement. 'No bullshit.'"

Anna noticed the sly smile on his face when he spoke. "She's kind of a friend of mine," Anna offered.

"Really? How did you come to know each other?"

"I testified for her in the Gundy trial."

"My goodness. Miss Olson, I'm impressed with you. How long since your discharge?"

"January 1975."

"You've done a lot in six years. You've started this growing charity, you're raising a foster child, and you've brushed shoulders with one of the big-time lawyers in Minneapolis. Wow. There are a lot of big society women who haven't done one single thing to help somebody else. And now, you want to get into the cemetery business."

Mr. Helmquist looked at his legislative aide. "So, what do you think?"

"Well, there is a history of the State granting or selling, for a minimum price, pieces of property to private non-profits. There are probably some other types of transfers, but I would need to search for those. Assuming we have some history to go on, it sounds like it should be relatively easy to put together a plan for Miss Olson. But I think we need to prepare to explain if there are any other cemeteries and, if so, what their status is. Assuming our long-term plan is to close some of these institutions, we will have to deal with all these cemeteries sooner or later, which may be the sticking point. Long-term planning is a tricky process in the legislature. I think I can get something done, but please be patient."

The aide looked at Anna. "Could you research from your end to see if other groups want to do something with these cemeteries?"

"Sure. I will ask Margaret to help us find people with similar concerns."

Representative Helmquist broke in. "Okay then. Anna, here is what we'll do. I'll get some folks together and form a working group with the Department of Welfare decision-makers and any other muckety mucks we need to involve. Hopefully, that group can cut through red tape and start transferring these cemeteries to interested parties. But we need any information you can get us as soon as possible. Okay?"

Anna nodded her head, "I understand." At that moment, she forgot she was only two weeks from the kickoff of the next Warm Coats for Children season. They already had a huge stockpile of coats that needed sorting.

§§§

Margaret Pattersen stood in the hallway outside Minnesota's House of Representatives chamber, waiting for Representative Helmquist to emerge. As a popular lobbyist, Margaret made it a point to know all the legislature members by name. She knew Mr. Helmquist when he first came to the legislature and served on the Education committee. She worked closely with him when the legislature was updating public education legislation.

Today, she had something else on her mind, which called for more than a phone call.

"Representative, may I walk with you a bit?"

Ronald Helmquist nodded. As they broke free of the logjam in the hallway, Margaret got right to the point. "We have two mutual friends who need our help."

With a sideways glance, "Oh, yes, and who might they be?"

"Anna Olson and her foster son Anthony. You may not

be aware of her efforts to adopt him. She sought and received approval to be a foster care provider and have guardianship over Anthony. So, I advised her to go all the way and adopt him."

"You're right. I had no idea about this."

"The problem is the Department of Child Services looks like they will not budge in their assessment that she doesn't meet all their requirements. He spends school days boarding with a family closer to Westgate Academy. Plus, Anna is committed to her charity, and as you know, she has a full-time job. All the things that we think are great about Anna seem to be against her adopting Anthony."

"So, what can I do to help with all of this?"

Margaret stopped walking and turned to face Representative Helmquist directly. "We both know that people with the right connections and lawyers get shit done that the average person can't do. I'm just saying that maybe it's time for the same privileges to be extended to these two wonderful souls. Maybe we can bend the rules once to make something work for two extraordinary people who've found a haven with each other. I need your help to make that happen."

"I'll do what I can."

"Thank you so much. They deserve a break."

§§§

As always, Anna made sure she was early for her November 22nd lunch appointment with Margaret Pattersen. She wanted to talk to her long-time friend, Mary Fortis. Mary told her Mel was slowing down and had begun hiring part-time help to run the grill so he could take a few days off. When Mel had a break, he poked his head out from behind the grill and smiled at Anna.

"Good Lord, you still need a ride somewhere?" Then he laughed and ducked back behind the grill.

Margaret found Anna in a booth, looking at a menu. "How long have we been hanging out here?" The voice was a deep, rich, velvety sound despite the raspy quality of a long-time smoker.

"Goodness, I think I met you in 1975 or 1976. You were softening me up to testify at the trial."

"Good memory. And look at you now, politicking at the State House. I got a call from Zachary at Representative Helmquist's office, and then five minutes later, I got your call. You are starting to circulate with some real movers and shakers, Anna Olson. Mr. Helmquist is a good guy to have on your side. He's the one who gets things done over there."

Anna blushed. "That one was my foster son's doing. He met him first and got me in the door. I think Helmquist will help Janice and me with our cemetery project."

"Exactly how many of these projects do you have going, Anna? Do I need to hire a separate staff person dedicated to helping you?" Margaret smiled before continuing. "I mean, damn, I am so proud of you. You just don't stop growing. I knew you would make a go of life outside the institution but never do all the things you're doing. That brain of yours must be in constant motion."

Anna looked over at her friend and grinned. "Yes, pretty much, but somehow it all falls into place."

After sandwiches and small talk, Anna told Margaret she needed help contacting advocacy groups, especially those associated with other State of Minnesota residential institutions. She and Janice needed to let Representative Helmquist know how many cemeteries there were and if anyone was concerned about preserving them.

Margaret replied. "I'll have my staff send the complete list of groups we know about and who are the leaders of each group. By the way, even though the Gundy trial ended in January 1979, we are still fighting with the State about how they are not complying with all the judge's orders. But things are getting better for people in the institutions. Plus, every month, I hear of another new community-based group home.

"Your help with that trial nearly cost you everything, Anna. I recognize that and will always be grateful to you. Many people should be thankful for your testimony. You helped pave the way for better care for thousands of people."

Anna said, "Change of subject, I'm still waiting for a call regarding my adoption of Anthony. It's been a long time now; is that normal?"

"I'm not sure, Anna. Did they tell you if it looked good or anything like that?"

"No, after all that paperwork and questions, interviews, etc. I haven't heard a thing. I'm starting to worry they won't approve it."

"I'll look into it, Anna." Margaret quickly broke off the lunch and reached for the check.

§§§

On November 30, 1981, Representative Ronald Helmquist seemed distracted by his thoughts. His committee meeting was bumping along as it always did. The first copy of the governor's budget for the next two years was undergoing its first legislative review. He was a member of the committee that oversaw the community services division and also served as chairman of the state's appropriations committee. That position made him very powerful because his committee allocated specific amounts of money for each division and subdivision of the Minnesota government. But today, here he was, listening to the director of human services answer questions from legislators about why her department needed to expand.

As the meeting drew to a close, Representative Helmquist wrote a quick note and signaled for a page. He whispered to the page and looked out the window at the cold gray skies and the first few snowflakes of the season. When the meeting was over, he walked directly to the director of human services. With a mantle of hardness he seldom wore, he bored down on the unsuspecting woman.

"Your department already has a serious public image problem, and I'd hate to see it worsen. But I can help you with that problem if you listen carefully. I became aware of an issue that is personal to me. My son goes to Westgate Academy with a young man named Anthony Washington. Young Mr. Washington is a genius—one of the rare minds. It just so happens he has no family, only a drug-addict mother incapable of raising him.

Plus, I've just met one of the most inspiring people we've seen in Minneapolis in a long time. Anna Olson is the woman who has started the new charity named Warm Coats for Children. Have you heard of it?"

She nodded she had.

"You may not yet get where I'm going with this, but you soon will. These two extraordinary people have somehow found a way to share a life. Miss Olson is currently Anthony's foster mother, and she is trying to adopt Anthony. That is until I find out your department, in its infinite power over the life of orphan children, is finding several ways to reject the adoption.

"Now I understand you have rules, but I'm telling you I want you to find a way to get this adoption approved without any more red-tape delay. This adoption has already been in the process for over two years. If you look closely at these two individuals, they are two of the most wonderful people you will ever meet. And they are perfect for each other.

"Rich people get these kinds of breaks all the time. This time, I want people from the bottom rung of our society to get a break. Here's the deal. You get that adoption approved, and I'll make sure you get enough money for your department to fix that public image problem you have."

§§§

Janice answered the phone and was pleasantly surprised when it was Anna.

"Good morning, my friend. What's new today?" Janice asked.

"There is one thing you won't believe. It's a long story that starts with Anthony doing a school project. It ends with a state representative organizing an effort to have the state of Minnesota sell those cemeteries to private entities."

"Hold on, are there other cemeteries?"

"Yes, but we're not quite sure how many yet. A legislative aide will talk to Martha Grady, who you already know. They are going to have her check the old records for more. So far, they know of three in addition to Helmhurst."

"They are checking with Martha Grady?" Janice wanted to be sure she understood what Anna was saying. "Wow, this is turning out to be bigger than just our cemetery, just like we thought."

"Yes, indeed. But there is one more thing. Margaret Pattersen, from the Gundy trial, will send you a list of organizations and their presidents. These are called advocacy groups, which are mainly parents. I'm sure at least some of them will want the same thing we are trying to do."

"And what am I supposed to do with this list?"

"Our idea is to contact each one and tell them that we are trying to preserve our cemetery because of Ida. We should also ask them if they have a cemetery and are interested in saving it?"

"You know that may take some time away from finding names."

"I know, Janice, but I think the names from our little cemetery can wait a while longer. How many names do you have by now?"

"I know over fifty percent of the names, and I'm starting to pick up my pace. But I agree, we need to see the big picture before we get the legislature to approve our taking over that cemetery."

"We'll probably need to form a nonprofit corporation to take possession of the land. When that is all completed, you'll be President Janice Haggedorn."

"Anna, I have no idea what you're talking about, but I feel I will as time goes on. Do you have any more announcements to lay on me?"

"Nope, that's all. How about you? Any new news from you?"

"Oh, nothing as exciting as your stuff. But I am getting new shingles put on my house next week. Does that count as big news?"

"If your roof is leaking, it's huge news. If not, not so big."

"No leaks, so it's just a humdrum boring life in Helmhurst. It will take me a while to absorb everything you've laid on me today."

"Your news and life are never boring and humdrum to me, Janice. I hope you're willing to come to the city to join me the next time I talk to Representative Helmquist. You'd like him."

§§§

1981 closed with a big surprise for Anna. The United Way of Minneapolis/St. Paul was taking Warm Coats for Children under its wing. It would be the smallest of the charities supported by the large organization. But it was a lifesaver for the charity Anna and Annalee Washington started. There was finally a paid coordinator who oversaw all aspects of the program. Anna would no longer be in charge. There was now adequate storage space, an office, and two old, donated vans for picking up and delivering coats. The program was now in a better position to keep growing. Organizations like churches, YMCAs, and schools were added as the distribution and meeting places for women to do their mending. Local volunteers ensured the coats, gloves, and winter hats got to any child who needed them.

Anna's remaining job was instructing women who wanted to learn more about the hard part of sewing winter clothes and repairing the most badly damaged coats. The new headquarters was an ideal place to meet on Saturday mornings for two hours of coffee, conversation, and sewing instructions.

Anna never left her Warm Coats for Children's roots despite its growth. She felt most comfortable with the women of those churches in the poorest part of Minneapolis who were the first to participate.

CHAPTER 10

JANICE HAGGEDORN

"She adopted me. I have a real mother!"

Anthony Washington

1982

Janice was the perfect fit for her role as head of the Helmhurst cemetery efforts. She drew on her administrative assistant skills in organizing meetings, preparing distribution information, and making day-to-day decisions. At Helmhurst, Janice had identified the names of sixty of the eighty gravesites with a steel spike. With no way to determine who was in the twelve graves without a spike or number, Janice and Anna felt their stone should read, "A Child of God."

At the end of January 1982, Anna and Janice had a chance to connect. "Oh, Anna, you wouldn't believe it. What a good day I had yesterday. I found three names in one day! The deaths are the most recent I've discovered, and they all took place in 1963."

"Other than the new names, how are we doing with our

cemetery?" Anna asked.

"Ah, yes. I think you'll be pleased. I hired an engineering firm to do a site survey that will set the exact location of our boundaries and stake them out. We need to do this so they can prepare the deed. And hey, the company agreed to do it at half price. Who said a woman can't do business?"

Anna replied, "We're one step closer, in other words."

"Yes, one step closer to having those poor souls in our care."

Soon after her conversation with Anna, Janice received Margaret's list of advocacy organizations that would either know about or be interested in preserving their cemeteries. She prepared a short letter:

Dear parents, friends, and advocates,

My name is Janice Haggedorn. My friend Anna Olson and I are former residents of Helmhurst. I started working there as a patient worker and later became a full-time employee. I stayed there until my retirement in 1980.

Miss Olson and I have formed a private nonprofit corporation, the Ida Malloy Memorial Cemetery, hoping to buy the old cemetery located at Helmhurst. We wish to preserve the memory of our friend, Ida Malloy, and everyone else buried there with nothing more than a steel spike with a patient number attached. We are also actively engaged with the state of Minnesota to connect a name to each steel spike and replace it with a small gravestone with the person's name.

We are writing because Representative Helmquist of the Minnesota legislature asked us to prepare an inventory of all individuals or organizations interested in preserving old institution-run cemeteries. Representative Helmquist shares our concern that with the current push to empty the institutions in favor of community-based alternatives, it will be easy to forget small cemeteries if or when Minnesota sells that property. If you have a graveyard associated with an institution, do you share similar concerns?

Please contact me and let me know. I hope that together, we can address this problem with greater strength.
Yours,
Janice Haggadorn and Anna Olson

Within a week, Janice received a letter from a woman in St. Cloud. Their institution appeared to be closing, and it had a cemetery about the size of Helmhurst's. She concluded by saying she didn't know about any plans regarding the cemetery. As other responses began to trickle in, Janice found herself with a small list of people interested in staying in touch. All wanted to learn more.

§§§

It was snowy and cold in January and February in Minnesota. Nonetheless, things were moving forward on two of Anna's projects. She was still slowly transferring the essentials of the Warm Coats for Children program to the new, full-time director, Doris Patton, and her two part-time employees. Anna was pleased that Doris had moved from coordinating the distribution of coats among a few small churches to a United Way director.

In early February, Representative Helmquist finally pulled the right lever of government. He told Anna the state of Minnesota was ready to divest itself of land it no longer used. He outlined the steps she needed to follow so her organization could accept possession of the Helmhurst cemetery. After listening to the first three, Anna interrupted Representative Helmquist. "I'm not sure I'm getting all of this. Would it be possible for your assistant to send the requirements to my friend Janice Haggedorn? She will know what to do."

"Good idea. I'll have him get them over to her."

By the time March arrived, the winter began to thaw. With the help of the attorney Margaret Pattersen suggested, Janice had worked out the details of the non-profit company that would buy the cemetery. Anna and Janice were getting the last-minute arrangements prepared for their upcoming purchase.

Janice took the bus to Minneapolis since she disliked driving in the city, and Anna met her at the downtown bus station. Anna hailed a cab for the ride home. She was pleased that Janice had come to Minneapolis to spend a few days seeing her world.

"Wow, Anna, I like what you've done with your house. It sounds weird to say, 'your house.'" Janice was clearly excited for her friend.

"Who would have ever guessed? Now, I'm entertaining you at *my* house. It's been a long way up for me, right?"

"It sure has. You've been in some bad places, and now you're in a good one. If anyone deserves to have their own house, it's you."

"I'll be honest; I didn't do anything to improve the house. I left that all up to Sarah. I hope we get a chance to meet up with her later because I think you will like her."

Anna took Janice to Wong's Laundry and the new headquarters of the Warm Coats for Children charity. Upon seeing the warehouse, Janice said, "This room is so big, and look at all those boxes full of coats. I was thinking back to when you were working out of a church basement."

"For sure, we're much bigger now. See those two

people hunting through the boxes? We even have paid staff members. Once they get the order filled, they put the coats in these empty crates, and a driver will deliver them first thing tomorrow morning. While there, the driver picks up the empty crates from the week before, and the process starts over again. But we're already seeing a big drop off as it gets warmer, and another season gradually comes to an end." Anna seemed genuinely proud as she discussed how far her charity had grown since she had mended the first coat for Anthony.

On Thursday, March 18, 1982, Anna and Janice met with the attorney. Janice brought several documents the attorney requested to the meeting, including the site survey. That day's first order was to establish the private, nonprofit Ida Malloy Memorial Cemetery, Inc. Janice was appointed the president, and Anna the vice president. Next came the paperwork authorizing Janice to open a bank account in the new corporation's name. Sitting in the conference room with the attorney and his assistant, they thought the paperwork would never end. When it was complete, Anna handed the attorney two certified cashier's checks. The first was for five hundred dollars for legal fees; the second was five thousand dollars for Janice to deposit in the newly formed entity's checking account.

With everything finished, there was a short break. The attorney returned to the room with a portfolio full of documents. "Anna and Janice, congratulations on your new organization. Here are three copies of the documents we just completed. One set is for the state of Minnesota to show you have a corporation eligible to receive the land. The second is for the Secretary of State's office. You will need to mail that one, and the third copy is for you. We'll need your signatures on the places my assistant has indicated." When they finished, the attorney said, "Please let me know if you need any additional help from me."

It was lunchtime when Anna said, "I have a special place to take you for lunch. They have the best pie in the world, so if you aren't too hungry, skip the lunch and go right for it."

When they stepped into Mel's Diner, they first heard, "Well, look what the cat drug in!" Anna's friend Mary Fortis stopped what she was doing and gave Anna a warm hug.

"Is that Anna?" came a booming voice from behind the grill.

"It sure is, Mel. I brought my best friend by to enjoy the best food and service in town."

Janice was impressed with everything about Mel's Diner, especially the close relationship Anna seemed to have with Mel and Mary. Anna had long ago begun to like Mel's diner for the food, but now she loved to come here because of the people.

Anna explained, "Mel and Mary are plain people, living a simple life until you look at them from the perspective of those in need. Then, you see them as unsung heroes. They make life better for the homeless, the addicts, and those unable to adjust well to life. They ask for no credit and don't brag about their giving. They set an example of what we should all strive to be."

"How did you find out about this place?" Janice asked.

"That, my dear friend, is a long story. I'll tell you all about it when we have more time."

Their first appointment at the statehouse was with Representative Ronald Helmquist. Anna planned to use this meeting to introduce him to Janice and thank him for his help in making their ownership of the cemetery possible. Anna told Representative Helmquist, "She is the person who will head up the day-to-day operation of the cemetery. She'll also advise and guide other groups wishing to take responsibility for old state cemeteries."

Anna added, "We both thank you for making our dream of owning that cemetery come true. Now, we can ensure those poor souls, including our friend, will at least have a name."

"Wow," he said. "I think this is a first, someone stopping by to thank me instead of asking for something." After Zachary took their picture, they went to their next appointment.

Their next appointment was with the Minnesota director of land management, the office responsible for purchasing and selling all the state of Minnesota properties. He knew Janice from her submitting the preliminary paperwork. It was Janice's turn to introduce Anna, and the director greeted her warmly.

"Janice, I can't believe you got all that paperwork done so well. It's almost as if you worked for the State."

"I am a retired administrative assistant. I worked at Helmhurst for over forty years, so I've done my share of forms."

"So that explains it. I understand the two of you even lived there at one time."

"Yes. But Anna was there much longer than me. Still, I taught her everything she knows." She broke out with a big smile, and all three laughed.

The director said, "Shall we sit at the conference table and review the details?"

"I'm ready," Janice said. As soon as they were seated, she handed over one set of the documents they had signed earlier at the attorney's office. That began another round of document signing, and at last, Anna handed over her final check of the day. It was for one dollar, the agreed-upon amount for the transfer of ownership from the state of Minnesota to the Ida Mallory Memorial Cemetery.

When they finished, the director thanked them for having all the documents prepared correctly and for their efforts at saving the cemetery. "Ladies, it has been fun helping you two get ownership of a tiny piece of land you hold so dear to your hearts. I commend you for doing all the hard background work and navigating the politics that made this possible. Not many people would have the ability to do what you've done.

"Now, I have a surprise for you. My assistant will take you to the governor's office. Each day, he sets aside fifteen minutes to meet with people who want to greet him, and we made a reservation for you."

When they got home, the two women tried to process their day. Meeting the governor was a pleasant surprise, but the one thing they kept returning to was that the cemetery was theirs. They started with the simple goal of finding the names of those buried in their little cemetery. Today, they bought the land, an essential step in preserving the memory of those buried there. It was all beyond their wildest dreams when they were young women burying Ida.

"Janice, I'm too tired to cook. Why don't I order delivery pizza? There's a place Anthony and I really like!"

"Sounds wonderful to me. Maybe we can watch TV and eat pizza to celebrate our accomplishments."

"Look at us," Anna said. "Two old ladies going wild celebrating a dream come true."

§§§

Anna got home late on April 18 and saw an envelope from the Minnesota Department of Human Services. It was a Friday, and Anthony would be home any minute. She quickly put the letter under her pillow, with the idea of reading it later. It had been so long since she heard anything other than, "We're working on your application, Miss Olson." She had begun to think there was a problem and that they would deny her request for adoption.

She wondered what the impact of that would be. Could she still be his guardian and serve as a foster parent? Would she and Anthony remain close?

Anna started to get ready for bed after a pleasant evening of pizza and the two sharing what all happened during the week. Finally, alone, Anna thought, *Why not just go ahead and open the letter*? So, she opened the letter which sent her spirits soaring:

Dear Miss Olson,

We are pleased to inform you that your request to adopt Anthony Washington is approved. You will soon receive a certificate of adoption, and our office will send all the required documents to the Hennepin County Recorder's office for filing.

It was true. At that moment, Anna was the happiest woman on earth. *I'm going to be an official mother. And Anthony can say he has a mother, and everyone will know. We're going to be a real family.* Anna knelt by her bed and cried tears of joy into her bedspread.

§§§

As skilled as she was in sewing and needlepointing, Anna had no experience with quilting. Yet what she still envisioned involved displaying her most precious needlepoints as pieces of a large quilt. Anna asked the women at the Warm Coats for Children to teach her how to quilt.

Six women expressed an interest in helping Anna, but only two had the expertise Anna needed. She invited Grace and Evelyn to her house to advise her if she could do what she envisioned.

"I need to tell you upfront what I want the quilt to look like when it's finished. It will be large, and I imagine, too heavy to use on a bed. On the front will be needlepoint pieces I've done throughout my life. Together, they tell my story." She showed the ladies a sampling of her needlework pieces, all on different cloth, in a kaleidoscope of colors and varying sizes.

"So, it will be like a Jacob's quilt," Grace said.

"I'm sorry, I don't understand."

"You know, like Jacob's coat of many colors. Only yours will be a quilt of many pieces."

Anna smiled. "Yeah, like that."

She shared with them how she always used the same method for making a needlepoint. First, she sketched her idea using a pencil on whatever fabric was handy. When she had time, she would return and complete the image. "The largest image is roughly twelve inches square and the smallest six inches square. But, when I trim the extra cloth off, they may be a bit smaller, and most are irregularly shaped."

Grace said, "First of all, you must lay them out, so you are certain they look like what you want when assembled. Then, you need to think about how thick you want the quilt because that will determine the batting and the backing. I'm wondering how thick it must be to help support all those needlepoint pieces. Pretty thick, I would guess."

Evelyn added, "Miss Anna, I've never seen needlepoint look like yours. They are amazing, simply amazing. How you use the colors, the shading, and the occasional thickness of your image is very artistic. It's almost like looking at three dimensions. How many pieces did you plan to use?"

Anna replied, "I'm not sure. But I'd guess it would be around one hundred. I envision it being big, say ten feet by ten feet. How long do you think that will take us to finish?"

"That depends on how many people you have working

on the quilt. Or, if you wish, to use a sewing machine," Evelyn answered.

"I don't care if we sew the backing and batting together with a machine, but I want only hand stitching for attaching the pieces."

Grace added, "Miss Anna, you ever heard of a sewing bee?"

Anna smiled and nodded. "Well, this may not be suitable for a bee, but you need at least a dedicated quilting group and a lot of patience. Something this big will take a sewing group years to complete."

§§§

On April 21, 1982, Anna received a call from Melvin King, Headmaster of the Westgate Academy.

"Miss Olson, how are you today?"

"Fine, what's happening with Anthony?"

"First, at our faculty meeting this morning, there was one hundred percent agreement that Anthony needs to graduate this spring. Our staff feels he's reached the upper limits of their expertise. They're excellent teachers, mind you, and they think it's time for him to start college.

"As you suggested at our last meeting, we used this last year to focus on a college and a major. Our guidance counselor has worked hard to develop a plan to get him started at the next level."

"Okay, I trust your judgment. Anthony's blossomed at your school. What did you come up with, and will I be able to afford it?"

"We recommend Purdue University in West Lafayette, Indiana. Why? They have an excellent engineering program. Engineering is the direction he seems to favor most right now. Of course, many young people find new interests as they learn more at the college level.

"We also favor Purdue for several other reasons. Due to his extraordinarily high ACT and SAT scores, he will get a full-ride scholarship, meaning you won't owe any tuition or room and board. Based on your household income, he also qualifies for one of several small grants that supply students with a small amount of cash for incidentals. Usually, this is two-hundred dollars per month or less.

"There is one additional reason we recommend Purdue. One of our science faculty staff graduated from there and can help with Anthony's transition."

"Miss Olson, your son is a diamond, a gem of a person. As you know, gems must be polished and cut to show their true brilliance. Attending college is exactly how he'll reach his true potential. But we feel they have the right people to look out for his well-being in and out of the classroom. They'll take care of him."

"Wow. It looks like I have a graduation party to organize."

When Anthony came home from school the following Friday, Anna was waiting for him with hamburgers, fries, and cherry pie, all his favorites. "It isn't my birthday, is it? All my favorites. Cool!"

"Somebody I know has done something special, that's what. I understand we have a lot to talk about. So, get washed up, and we'll eat in about ten minutes." That Friday evening meal lasted much longer than either of them anticipated. Anthony talked about all he had been through and what he wanted to be in the future. Mr. King told him he was a rare person whose intellect surpassed everyone else's. But that was hard for him to understand. All he recognized was that school things came easy. Other things, however, were more complicated. Talking to girls made him freeze up with tension. He didn't have any interest in sports. His fellow students often called him a "brainiac" or, more frequently, a "nerd."

"I got along well at Westgate because they had more kids like me. How will I fit in with older kids at college?"

"I don't know, Anthony. But you can't be the only brilliant young person they have ever taught. Purdue will have someone to help you through the rough spots. And I'll be there, too. Don't forget your old mom."

Anthony smiled and took her hand. "I know, I know. I'll always have you."

"When things get rough, remember that I love you and will support you in every way possible."

A grinning Anthony said, "Man, I am *really* glad you chased me down to give me that coat."

§§§

For Anna, the next few weeks were a whirlwind of activity. There were invitations to send, party decorations to buy, and food to order. Thankfully, Sarah knew just what to do. Planning events was one of her many skills. On Sunday, May 29, 1982, the basement of the Nazareth Baptist Church was ready for the big party. Anna worried about who would come. After all, it was in one of the poorest neighborhoods in Minneapolis.

The little basement was full of people from 2 p.m. to 5 p.m. Many from the Warm Coats for Children programs stopped by, plus Big JJ's parents and many people Anna met working at Wong's Laundry. Sarah and Karl helped keep the snacks, cold drinks, and cookie trays full while three-year-old Julie and one-year-old Johnny chased each other around the table. Janice greeted everyone who came and made out their name tag. Anna and Anthony moved from one group to another, trying to say hello to everyone who came. At about 4 p.m., Anna took him by the hand and led him to the front of the snack table. As they stood together, he appeared to tower over her by six inches.

"I am overwhelmed to see so many friends from every part of Anthony's and my life. We came here today for his celebration because this is the church Anthony grew up in." Anna paused for a moment before continuing. "Anthony, your grandma is up in heaven looking down at you. I'm sure she is so proud of you right now." Loud clapping and a few "Amens" floated up from the crowd.

"Here is your graduation present," she said, handing him a large envelope.

He opened it and shouted, "You did it!" He grabbed her in a full hug and wouldn't let go. Finally, he turned to the audience and announced, *"She adopted me. I have a real mother*!" Soon, somebody from the back of the room started clapping, then the whole room erupted. Everyone here knew the story of these two shipwrecked souls landing in each other's world and making a real family out of their love.

No one was prouder of Anna at that moment than Margaret Pattersen, who stood alone in the back of the room. She planted the seed in Anna's mind, and her friend did the rest. The intervention by a well-known Minnesota legislator was vital, but Anna's love for Anthony was the real reason the adoption happened. Margaret was not always known to be pleasant, but her broad smile and moist eyes signaled the warmth in her soul that day.

§§§

September came, and Anna and Anthony anxiously awaited by the front door for Sarah to pick them up for the long ride to West Lafayette, Indiana, and Purdue University. When she went down the stairs to Sarah's car, she started to worry. *He's grown up too fast, and I've had him for such a short time.*

Anna told Sarah. "I know he will be okay, but I can't stop worrying about him. Is he going to make any friends at that school? It's so big compared to the Westgate Academy."

"That sounds normal to me. True, Anthony is a bit young to go to college, but I have a feeling they'll keep an eye on him," Sarah reassured.

"Okay then, what will I do with him gone?"

"I have a feeling you'll figure something out."

Anna need not have worried. The seventeen-year-old first-year engineering student soon made a friend. He found another extraordinary student in his first-year English class. The two asked to switch roommates to share a room, and the residence hall director agreed. Their companionship helped them adjust to college life without any great difficulty.

At home, Anna settled into a routine of mending and attending birthday parties for the children and grandchildren of friends. Johnny was turning two, Julie was halfway to four, and Sarah was at her wits end some days. Anna was also delighted in watching the Wong children, who were constantly playing in the back of the laundry.

She got invitations to various celebrations from people in her sewing group. As the leaves began to fall, her sewing class picked up several new attendees because the Warm Coats for Children organization continued to expand. Her days sped by faster and faster, and occasionally, she took time out from her routines to go to Stillwater with Mrs. Johnson to see Big JJ.

On Friday, October 15, 1982, Sarah picked Anna up at 5 a.m. They had an 8:05 flight to Indianapolis, Indiana, where they rented a car and drove up to West Lafayette and Purdue University. Anthony was an excellent host, showing them the campus, where he attended classes, his dorm room, and where he ate—all places a mother wants to see for herself.

The weekend was fun for everyone, but Anna was bone-tired when she finally got home. She felt a little better about her son's welfare but still worried about everything from his safety to how he would adapt to the more demanding challenges. *I just hope he's mature enough.*

On March 17, 1983, Anna turned sixty-six and, on Karl's advice, signed up for Social Security. Her health was good, and weekly calls from Anthony eased her worries about his adjusting. College was a positive environment for him. She watched him grow both intellectually and socially with a deep sense of appreciation. The early part of his life was so hard, and now, he was happy and thriving. He even mentioned going to a movie on a double date.

Life is good, Anna thought.

CHAPTER 11

BIG JJ

"Abused while alive, forgotten in death."

Janice Haggedorn and Anna Olson

1985

Finally, his early parole became a reality. It was February 11, 1985, and Anna sat in the living room of the Johnson house, waiting for Big JJ to come through the door.

Through her occasional in-person visits and weekly letters, Anna had established a solid friendship with Charles James Johnson, the man who assaulted her. As the years passed, they discovered they shared the same institutional experiences. For example, they ate by strict schedules with a short time to eat. Day and night, there was screaming and violence. Anna and Big JJ talked about the constant fear of being attacked, beaten, or raped. Anna found it interesting that they shared very personal emotions. They shared moments of stress, secret fears, hopes, and feelings of despair. This sharing brought them close together while he was inside the prison. She sincerely hoped it would continue now that he was out.

She felt anxious about the next chapter in Big JJ's life.

She heard stories about how ex-cons had difficulty adjusting to life outside of prison. Few were successful. For example, Martin England was an ex-convict who led a life of caring and charity toward those in need. Hopefully, Big JJ would follow in a similar path.

When Big JJ finally arrived and finished greeting everyone, she took him aside.

"I have someone I think you should meet. He's a man who can help you with a big problem you will have."

"What's that?" Big JJ asked.

"Getting a job. It's hard for people like you, I mean, paroled convicts, to get a job. Employers are afraid of your background."

"I've heard the same thing, but I was somehow hoping I would be the exception to the rule."

"We'll get you through this together, but you must do your part as well."

"Which is?" Big JJ seemed offended at another insinuation.

"You have to stay straight and stay out of trouble. No hanging around with people you knew in prison."

"I think there's an echo in here. You, my mom and dad, and my parole officer all say the same things."

"Sorry about that, Charles, but we all want what's best for you."

§§§

Anthony had not lost his place at the center of Anna's life. He was still her son and reaped the benefits of a constant stream of homemade cookies, brownies, banana bread, and, on occasion, caramel corn. There was at least one letter a week, plus their weekly Sunday afternoon phone calls. He had grown up in his two years at Purdue. He was nineteen years old, and just as his old high school friends were graduating, he had completed half his bachelor's degree in electrical engineering.

From his point of view, he was no less concerned about his mother. She was older now, and he worried about her living alone in a community that was not improving. Crime gradually increased, and a few nearby homes fell into disrepair. Anna was intent on living in Hilda's house. It had become her house psychologically as much as legally. "You don't need to waste a moment worrying about me, Anthony. I'm doing just fine."

Anthony was making an impression on his professors and some off-campus mentors who watched his growth. He got straight A's except for an Art History test, where he forgot to review the Renaissance period. He tried to argue the C- up to a B, but his professor simply laughed and said, "No one is perfect, Anthony. Not even you." The comment stung, but Anthony learned he was prone to make mistakes like everyone else.

Additional aspects of Anthony emerged as he grew in other ways besides academics. He now had excellent social skills and demonstrated a concern for his fellow students. Empathy was something that professors seldom saw in young overachievers. He showed concern for those less fortunate or with lower intellectual abilities by helping them understand a difficult concept or walking them through a complex program. It didn't matter to him that they were older, more affluent, or poorer. He treated everyone the same.

Anthony returned home for the Easter break as always, but he had some news that concerned Anna. "Mom, they have a summer internship available with the Energy Select Consulting Company. It pays enough to cover the rent and living expenses, and a friend of mine also got invited. We'll share expenses and watch out for each other. What do you think? Can I accept it?"

"Where is this company located?"

"Chicago, but that's okay. They will be sure that we get housing in a safe area."

"Who promises this safety?"

"The company."

Anna turned away and remained quiet for several seconds. When she turned back to him, there were tears in her eyes. "Does this mean you won't be coming home to me anymore?"

Anthony took Anna in his arms and comforted her. "Of course not, Mom, this is my home. I will always come home to spend time with you."

"Well, you better, or there will be no more cookies for you, young man."

Anna held Anthony at arm's length and intuitively knew he was growing up sooner than his chronological age. She knew she had to let him go, that it was best for him. They spent the rest of spring break going to movies, talking long into the night, and visiting mutual friends who always asked about Anthony's well-being.

"Anthony, we both know 'you are growing up and leaving the nest,' as they say. All I ask of you is always to be safe and call me. I expect the phone calls every Sunday." Anna tried to make her statement stern but couldn't quite pull it off because his grin made her happy.

§§§

Anna watched from a distance as Big JJ, with his parents' help, began to navigate the tricky rules for those on parole. Anna did not envy him for trying to live by all the parole rules. She believed some of them were excessively restrictive and prone to easy misinterpretation. For example, Big JJ was not to associate with anyone who was a felon.

Anna asked, "How would you know if some guy you work with is a felon? You may not even know his name! That is so unfair."

Big JJ responded with an understanding of his reality. "Anna, you know as well as anyone that many rules make little sense. They want you to get out of prison and 'make it,' but they make the rules, so it's easier to fail."

For a long time, Anna feared trap doors would spring open any second and cause her to fall back into their grasp. She realized Big JJ was going through the prison version of the transition pain she endured.

"Are you ready to tackle this job thing, Charles?"

"I am."

Two days later, Anna had lunch at Mel's Diner and ate late to spend a few minutes talking to him. He nodded as she explained Big JJ's situation and said he knew a guy. He'd let her know. Two hours later, the phone woke Anna from a late nap. Mel called to say he could help, and Big JJ should be at the diner at 6 a.m. the following day.

The next day, Big JJ entered the world of day labor. He worked for a friend of Mel's who owned a small company that hired men and women by the day and paid them an hourly wage. His company supplied the muscle needed to unload an overturned eighteen-wheeler full of live chickens or dig up old sewer systems and other jobs that no one else could or was willing to do. Big JJ paid his dues by working at the bottom of the chain, but within a month, his boss noticed his punctuality and positive attitude and started hiring him every day.

He also got his driver's license, so he could now drive a van to and from work sites, another plus for his boss. Eventually, Big JJ had a crew of workers he took out and completed jobs. He somehow motivated his people to finish a job, regardless of how late in the day it was or how tired they were. He quickly got some raises and started to feel like an average person.

Driving to and from work in his parents' old car wasn't the only place he went. He regularly visited Anna, and the two would get into lengthy discussions about the stigma of being in an institution. But Anna was not the only person he saw. He often went to Eva White's apartment. Big JJ met her at a church potluck before going to prison. While he was away, she had written to him and wished him well.

Once, he told Anna, "I'm so much luckier than most cons. I have my parents, you, and a girlfriend who accepts me for who I am. That's pretty good, don't you think?"

"It sure is. You have a great start on a new life, but they will keep you under their thumb all the while you are on parole. Keep it up, my dear friend. Keep it up."

Anna was quiet for a moment. "You know, Big JJ, another bit of irony ties us together. You got out of prison ten years after I was released. The pressure is on you now. See if you can adjust to your new environment, plus do something good for others."

"Is that a challenge?" Big JJ asked. "I don't think I want any part of that contest. No one can compare to you, Anna, no one. You have done more for more people than most ever do in a lifetime. Look at all the coats you have put on children's backs! Look at all the people who are better off for having you as their friend, like me. So no, thank you. You are in the goddess category to most people who know you."

§§§

Anna met weekly with her quilting group. After they selected the material for the two essential parts of a quilt, the backing and the batting, they came up with a plan for making the large quilt. The backing and batting were cut into five-foot squares with a six-inch margin on either side. Using a specially made ruler, they marked out two hundred and twenty-five four-inch squares on each of the four pieces. Safety pins in the middle of each square initially held the backing and the batting pieces together. Machine sewing the squares vertically and horizontally around the outside of each of the two hundred and twenty-five squares required a team effort. Anna would move the material through the needle while three others held up each five-foot square. The final product was four solid white backgrounds onto which they could hand sew the individual needlepoints.

At the end of each evening, Anna always served one of her decadent desserts with vanilla ice cream. They ate their desserts while talking about quilting and sewing and sharing gossip from around the Warm Coats for Children community.

Anna wanted her quilt to be her autobiography. Each scene would highlight a different phase of her life. Before they could attach the pieces, she spent endless hours arranging them on the backing. It was her story, and she would tell all, the good, the bad, the sweet, the bitter. She included scenes of sadness and joy and those that were simply pretty. When satisfied with her overall plan, she prepared a diagram of the entire quilt on two pieces of paper taped together and assigned a number to each needlepoint.

She stitched a small number on the back of each needlepoint to ensure she would assemble the quilt according to her plan. Anna shared her final product with Anthony, who said, "Mom, let me help you. I can take this to a graphic designer I know. He can make a larger diagram that will be easier for your quilters and you to follow. Do you mind if I borrow this?"

"Okay, but you have to promise not to show it to anyone else but your friend and give it back to me."

"Promise," he said.

A month later, Anna received a long cylinder by registered mail. She couldn't figure out what it was until she opened it and rolled it out on the dining room table. It was a large 4' by 4' printed version of her chart and her small original drawing. A chill ran down her back when she saw, for the first time, the enlarged blueprint for the magic she hoped to create. Her son had come through for his mother once again. As she lay down to sleep that night, she said a prayer. "Thank you, God, for giving me such a wonderful son. Keep him safe and guide his future. In your name, I pray, amen."

Gradually, with several trial runs behind them, the women added the first scene to the batting in the bottom right of the first five-foot square. It was larger than most needlepoints. It showed a white farmhouse, a barn, and a small shed against green fields. Off to one side was what looked like a gravel road.

The women soon learned that Anna's story would begin at the bottom of the quilt's left side and unfold clockwise from the bottom toward the top. Her story continued down the right side and curled back up and into the middle.

§§§

There was an introspective side emerging from Anna. She spent more time reflecting on her Helmhurst days and how far she had come. In the ten years since her release, impossible things had happened. She wondered how and why she was living this dream. *I own a home. I have friends. I have a son! I am living the free life I desired for so long.*

She was at a loss for words to describe how she was responsible for starting a growing charity. Charity was far from her mind as Anna sat day after day in stifling heat and damp, chilly cold in the overcrowded wards of Helmhurst.

Instead, arising from those depressing days were creative inspirations, as seen in many of her needlepoints from that era. As Anna bathed in the richness of her life, putting that needlepointing into her life story, she concluded that she had it so good today because she had it so bad for all those years. Could this be good karma? Or, as Christians say, was it God's will?

While in this new stage, she did something she had never done. When she finished her bath, she wrapped herself in a towel, went into the bedroom, and dropped it. In the mirror, she saw the image of an aging woman and smiled. *I don't look too bad.* She was pleased with the woman staring back at her.

Many of the introspections led back to Anthony. He'd entered her life unexpectedly, a cold, scrawny little boy. Now, he was her son. *How did that happen?* she wondered. *More than anything, I was at the right place at the right time. I helped him, but he's helped me so much more.*

Anna wondered about her journey to this point and her sense of belonging and fulfillment. It was a journey from the back wards of Helmhurst to the bright lights of freedom, from segregation to integration. But none of her story could have happened this way without the timely intervention of women who believed in her.

Jimmy Dale would be proud of her. He would whoop, *"Ann-nuh! What took you so long?"* Anna had a smile on her face as she imagined his greased-back hair and brashness. And all these years later, she still didn't know why she loved him so much.

Sewing the older needlepoints onto the quilt, Anna remembered how she felt when she created the piece. She rediscovered her older self. It was like peeling an onion, layer upon layer of emotions and events that had come together to form that woman looking back at her in the mirror. The thing she understood least was her gift for needlepointing. *Did I inherit my talent from my mother, or was I simply a quick learner?*

§§§

On Saturday, June 1, 1985, there was a loud knock at her front door. She was still in her bathrobe when she opened the door, and there was Big JJ with two cups of coffee and a brown paper bag. He was clearly a happy man.

"Is it too early? I brought coffee and sour cream donuts."

"No, it's okay, but let me put something on first. You can take the coffee into the kitchen."

Five minutes later, she walked into the kitchen and noticed two sour cream donuts and two black coffees on the table.

Big JJ explained all his excitement. "I got a job. A *real* job!" he exclaimed. "My crew and I were cleaning out one floor of this office building, and I got to talking to this guy. He owns the maintenance company, which is responsible for the whole building. He likes the way my boys and I work. Then he asked me if I wanted a permanent job. I said, 'Sure, but I'd have to discuss it with my boss.' I told him he should know upfront that I had just gotten out of prison and was a recovering addict. He looked me in the eye and told me he had good experience hiring ex-convicts."

"When are you going to start?" Anna asked.

"It'll take about two weeks for him to complete all my paperwork."

"I'm so proud of you! I knew you could be successful."

In the following months, Anna and Big JJ had coffee and sour cream donuts at her kitchen table every Saturday morning. For an hour, they shared the events of the last week and talked about life in general. His personal life grew with the addition of a savings account and a small apartment. He always attended appointments with his parole officer. The officer smiled, watching him grow roots in the community. She felt he was one of the few who would go straight after being released from prison.

§§§

Anna was also proud of Big JJ, now a supervisor for his company. He was responsible for cleaning four floors in a large office building and had thirty people reporting to him. Like Anthony, he quickly adapted to his employer's expectations, and his employees' performance was better than that of the rest of the company.

But it wasn't the cleaning business's success that impressed Anna. It was the person he had chosen to date. Eva White was good for Big JJ. She understood addiction and that Big JJ still struggled with the desire to use drugs. Eva grew to trust him. She was less worried about his past than how they were falling in love.

Big JJ spent almost every Saturday morning talking about Eva White and how she was always on his mind. One night, as Anna prepared for bed, she stopped cold. An idea hit her, and it wouldn't leave.

The following day, she got the old pine box out of the closet, opened it, and took out a small bag. In the bag was her mother's wedding ring. She thought she would give the ring to Big JJ, who'd been talking about proposing to Eva when "the time was right."

She showed Sarah the ring and asked how she could get it cleaned and appraised. Sarah's jeweler said he had to find an expert to evaluate it correctly. Anna agreed to pay the extra cost, and when the valuation of the ring came back, Anna was stunned. Depending on the market, fifty thousand, five hundred. It had all the proper characteristics to have belonged to a queen of Norway or perhaps a royal princess. The specialist thought the ring was probably from the mid-19th century and designed by a famous Danish jeweler. Anna lay in bed wondering what to do with the ring and thought she best discuss it with Anthony.

In June of 1986, Anthony was home for a short summer break before starting the second year of his internship. She showed him the ring and told him how her father received it from a wealthy farmer. Anna smiled and recounted the story of grabbing it from her mother's dresser while leaving her home for the last time. She continued the story of the ring and how she kept it and other valuable contents in the wooden box hidden in the utility closet deep within the Helmhurst tunnels. With the ring cleaned for the first time in perhaps a hundred years, she wanted it to go to someone special. Did he want it?

"Mom, I'm not getting married, and when I do, I think I would like my future wife and me to pick out our rings. It's a beautiful ring, but I think you should give it to Big JJ."

"I'm glad I asked because I thought it wouldn't mean much to you. And Karl and Sarah can afford whatever they want as well. So Big JJ it is."

Anna didn't have to wait long for an excited Big JJ to appear at the back door with large coffees and extra donuts.

"What's the special occasion?"

"I thought you'd never ask. I'm going to get married. I asked Eva last night if she could see spending the rest of her life with me. And she said, 'Yes.' Just as quick as that, she said yes, to a druggie turned janitor like me. I plan to officially propose to her soon."

"Believe me, she knows you're much more than that. I know it, too, so hold on, I have something to show you."

When Anna returned to the kitchen, she had the ring,

now kept in an expensive box. "Here's a little something you may want to consider giving her. I'd like you to have it if you want it."

When he opened the box, his expression hardly changed, but soon, he broke into a broad grin. "Is it real?"

"What do you mean, is it real? Of course, it's real. The whole thing."

"Anna, this rock is *big*! And the setting is so fancy. Not that I know anything about this sort of thing, but it simply sparkles."

"It does, doesn't it? I had it cleaned and appraised before deciding what to do with it. I will be honest with you. I talked to Anthony about the ring, and he said I should give it to you. My only goal is to give it to someone who will treasure it. And I think Eva will."

"Oh, wow!" Big JJ said, exhaling the last bit of air in his lungs.

"The only thing is you will need to get an insurance policy that covers it. Be prepared 'cuz that policy will set you back a bit. How much? You must find that out from your insurance agent, but here is the ring's appraisal."

He looked at the appraised value and then at Anna. With tears in his eyes, he reached out and took her hands. As they disappeared into the loving grip of the big man, he simply shook his head and tried to smile but started to cry.

§§§

"Hi, Mom, what's up?" Anthony sounded more cheerful than usual.

"Not much new on my end. You know, mending, having lunches, talking, mending, then more talking. One would think I was a professional talker."

"That's because you have so many friends and people at

work. How's that quilt coming along?"

"We're making progress. We've nearly finished the first part. I'm so excited because we can start to see what it will look like. What's up with you, my dear boy? You sound happier than usual today. You got a girlfriend?"

"No girlfriend, but there is this one brilliant girl, and I enjoy helping her with her physics class. But that's not why I'm calling. I got this fantastic offer to do a one-year internship at MIT, all expenses paid after I graduate. I will earn a master's degree in industrial electrical design."

"So where is this MIT, and what does it stand for?"

"Massachusetts Institute of Technology, and it's in Cambridge, near Boston. It's a big honor to get accepted into this program. It is an extension of my work assignments with my new employer, Advanced Consulting Company."

"You mean someone will pay for you to get more schooling *and* promise you a job? You can't beat that."

"No, Mom, you can't. You know I'll be further away from Minneapolis, but they have a larger airport with more flights so that I can get home more frequently."

"You never stop creating opportunities for yourself, do you?"

"No, not if I can keep on growing. I want to be a major electrical engineering firm's CEO someday. Maybe even head up the Department of Energy for the US. Why not shoot for the moon?"

"Anthony, I'd like to see you take every opportunity that comes along. Represent your race and me proudly in whatever you choose to do. When would you start this new program?"

"August 1, 1987. So, I'll have about six weeks to be home with you after I finish up at Purdue and before I start at MIT. Won't that be fun?"

"It sure will, Anthony."

When Anna shared this latest development with her quilting group, they were pleased but had questions. These women knew Anthony as a baby and watched him grow up. They were proud of his progress and that someone from their community could be so successful.

"What kind of place is this again, Anna?"

"Some kind of college that offers technical training, I think."

"Just what will he be studying? Lord, I would think a college degree would be enough."

"I don't understand it either. It's all beyond me. Anthony explained it this way . . . his company's customers want to know the best way to upgrade or replace the equipment used to bring electricity to their customers' homes. When he is done, Anthony will work with cities, sometimes entire states."

§§§

Donuts and coffee with Big JJ on Saturday mornings always lifted Anna's spirits. The years had flown by, and her relationship with Big JJ was stronger than ever. Here was this big, strong man who was genuinely interested in her welfare. From the first signs of aching in her joints, she never had to change a furnace filter, worry about clogged gutters, or having the lawn mowed. Big JJ gladly took care of it all. He was loyal to Anna and satisfied with his new role in society.

Anna often reflected on how fortunate she was. Her son was still proving to be extraordinary. He had finished the graduate program at MIT and was now fully employed at the Advanced Consulting Company. After spending so much time in the academic world, he was ready to prove his worthiness.

Anthony made his mother very proud indeed. His first assignment was to meet with a team of people challenged with developing a plan to upgrade the city of Indianapolis's electrical grid. They struggled with where the city would purchase power as it retired its old coal-burning power plant. It didn't take Anthony long to see what was needed to establish the cheapest electricity supply. He also saw the city's need to upgrade its power transformers and other distribution equipment. As he sketched his suggestions, his peers saw a future leader emerging. His employers were delighted to see his work because it meant they had an excellent chance to win the bid to draw up the ten-year plan for upgrading the electrical system.

Anthony opened new doors for his employers. He started to turn heads with the simplicity and innovativeness of his designs. His electrical transmission and distribution work helped communities supply more reliable energy at a reasonable cost.

"Do they pay you well?" Anna asked him one day while visiting him in the Boston area.

"Very well. I make a lot of money compared to my peers. That's because I get a bonus every time one of our customers buys one of my plans."

"That's wonderful, Anthony. I'm so proud of all you have done with your life."

Anthony took his mom's hands and said, "I have you to thank for my doing well. And besides, you ain't seen nothing yet."

"Anthony," she said, "you should bottle some of this youthful ambition and open that bottle when you reach middle age and are starting to grow tired of your work."

§§§

Some things in life just naturally end. In 1989, two major parts of Anna's life came to an end. The first was at Wong's Laundry, where Betty Palmer was now a full-time second seamstress. Anna was finishing a pair of slacks when she looked at her friend of many years and, without any prior thought, said, "Betty, I think it's time for me to retire."

"Are you okay, Anna? You have never mentioned retirement before."

"Yes, I feel fine. Okay, I do find it hard to shake the aches and pains that come with each day. But it really isn't that. I just feel like I have had enough. I want to enjoy life a little bit. Go to some concerts, enjoy time with friends, and the like."

"Who else have you told about this?"

"No one. You're the first. Maybe you can talk to one of the part-time people and see if they would want to take your place. I will tell Mrs. Wong tomorrow morning."

When Anna went to Helmhurst, she watched intently as the cemetery became the sanctuary she and Janice had envisioned. The second was the Helmhurst cemetery project. In March of 1989, Anna told Janice it was time to stop looking at gravestones and decide which one fit their requirements best.

The stonemason they chose recommended granite because it would last forever. They agreed the stones could be small since they only needed the deceased person's name. Anna ended up buying ninety-four headstones. For the twelve graves where the person was unknown, the stone read, "A Child of God." Janice handed the stonemason her final list containing the names of who was buried in each of the eighty graves. Her detective work finally broke through as she found the last two names. Anna wrote a check for six thousand, four hundred thirty-nine dollars, fifty percent of the total cost.

Finally, in the spring of 1989, Janice announced the date for the dedication ceremony. Janice continued working with a local landscaper to put the finishing touches on the cemetery. She wanted Anna to be pleased because she was the first to envision saving this place as a memorial site.

Saturday, June 10, 1989, was sunny and cool. Sarah and her two children drove Anna to the dedication ceremony. When they arrived, Anna couldn't believe what she saw. There was a crowd already gathered. "I didn't think anyone would come," Anna said. As she walked closer, she got a look at the complete upgrade. The first thing to catch her eye was the off-white headstones. She thought they sparkled like oysters in a sea of jade. At last, all those stakes were changed to names.

Then, to her surprise, she saw Anthony standing beside Representative Ronald Helmquist. Those two men were key to transforming her dream into a reality, and here they were, joining the celebration of its fruition.

Anna headed directly to her son. When he saw her coming, he leaned down to hug her. She clung to him with misty eyes. "Why didn't you tell me you would be here?"

"It all worked out at the last minute. My customers in Denver canceled, freeing me up for the day. So here I am!"

Anna clung to his arm as they talked to guests who had come to participate in the dedication. Anna let Anthony do most of the talking while she reflected on her history with this spot. Here was her escape from the constant pressure of the institution. Here, she could feel at peace. And today, some of that feeling came washing back over her. She looked around and saw what she had always wanted to see. At last, everyone would remember the lives of these once-forgotten souls.

Using a portable speaker system, Janice asked everyone to take their seats. She had rows of chairs in the parking lot, looking straight into the cemetery. Facing the guests was a row of distinguished individuals. There was a member of the Developmental Disabilities community who had worked to promote cemetery preservations in other institutions. The other people were Margaret Pattersen, Representative Helmquist, Anthony, and the mayor of Helmhurst. There was also a seat for Anna, Janice, and the sister of a man buried there.

Janice opened the ceremonies by asking her pastor to say a prayer. The first speaker was Margaret Pattersen. She spoke about the power of remembering those who were victims. For the first time, she publicly described what drove her to work hard to advocate for the rights of those in the disability community. Her brother lost his life due to the cruelty of big institutions, and his memory drove her to work hard so no one else would have to die a similar death. Her closing remarks were that she wished everyone understood the long, challenging journey Anna and Janice took to make the cemetery happen.

Representative Helmquist told the amusing story about how Anthony, a high school teenager, maneuvered a meeting with him. Then Anthony skillfully planted the seed in his mind that he could help his mom by agreeing to talk to her. He closed his brief remarks by promising the legislature would do more in the future to preserve the memory of all oppressed and forgotten Minnesotans.

Anna was surprised when the woman who believed one of those buried in the cemetery was her brother spoke on behalf of the residents of Helmhurst who lost their identity when they died. The woman said it was comforting to know where his life ended. "On behalf of all those who now have a permanent marker with a name and their families, I wish to say, 'Thank you' to Anna Olson, who paid for all the gravestones you see here today. Every single one!"

After all the other guests had spoken, Janice told everyone about their friend, Ida Malloy. She said she and Anna wanted guests to know that Ida was a fun-loving, sometimes coarse, adventurous person. She had a quick temper and a speedy response to anyone needing help. Janice shared the short phrase she and Anna had used to describe the people here, "Abused while alive, forgotten in death." Janice then gave a brief timeline starting with Anna's first commitment to buy the headstones in December of 1977 and culminating today. In closing, Janice read a list of thank-you remarks naming everyone who helped make the cemetery possible.

She turned and nodded to Anthony to escort Anna to the podium, and then Janice presented her with a wreath. Anthony steadied his mother as they walked to Ida's grave, where Anna laid the wreath. They concluded the dedication with the pastor blessing the ground and giving a parting benediction.

After the ceremony, Janice invited her close friends and family to her house for refreshments. She asked Anna to follow her to the kitchen, where she thanked Anna for making their cemetery a reality. Anna told Janice she was proud of her. She had become an effective leader who put it all together. They were overwhelmed with emotions. The women's tight hug brought deep sobs of relief, sorrow, and joy. Anthony entered the kitchen but turned around and left. He knew the two women needed this moment alone.

The cemetery project was much larger and more expensive than the women envisioned. To the east, Janice put wild prairie grasses as a look back to 1933 when wild grasses were all that surrounded the rows of steel spikes and broken-down crosses. To the south, Janice planted a new apple orchard, about the same size as the old orchard but fresh with hope and beauty. It was her tribute to Anna, who often found refuge under the branches of the old orchard. Finally, to the west was the small parking lot, green grass, and hardwood trees. From her own pocket, Janice paid for a heavy-wrought iron bench and had it placed on a cement slab. She wanted a place for her and Anna to sit when they visited Ida.

CHAPTER 12

ANNA OLSON

"I believe Anna was all about forgiving without bounds

and loving without limits."

Charles James Johnson

1998

On July 10, 1998, Anna put down the receiver and stood motionless for what seemed like an eternity. The old saying about knocking someone over with a feather was appropriate. Finally, she sat down and waited for a thought, any thought. She had not seen the bad news coming.

"Anna, I have pancreatic cancer. They say it's pretty far along."

"How long do they give you?"

"Six months at the most."

"What can they do about it?"

"Anna, I want to talk to you about that. I'm considering not getting any chemo. Will you come to see me so we can talk?"

"Yes, I'll be there . . . let me look at my calendar . .

. Saturday. I'll be there on Saturday at lunchtime. I'll stop by that Norwegian place and pick up some lefse and a few things for lunch."

Several years earlier, Anthony had contracted a driving service to be on call and to drive Anna wherever she wanted. Once at Helmhurst, Anna sent her driver back to Minneapolis with instructions to pick her up Sunday afternoon at 4 p.m. Anna brought in the bag of food and a small overnight case. When Janice had tea ready, they put the food out and sat in her kitchen, eating and talking about the old days.

"What was the name of that guy you were carrying on with? You remember when we were all crowded into that little apartment where we had so much fun?"

"You mean, Marcus?"

"Yes, that handsome older guy. We were all so jealous of you. I don't think any of us had ever been with a man by that time. Only you."

Anna blushed. "He was a nice guy. Not too smart, but a nice guy. I never loved him or came close to falling in love with him. It was exciting having sex in all those terrible places. I recall him getting paroled and me staying behind. I never could get the courage to walk away from that place like he said I should."

Janice sat back and observed. "I wish we could return to those days again. Maybe the two of us could have just gone away together. But we didn't know much about the world and would have had a hard time." She reflected for a minute before continuing. "Change the subject. If you were me, would you get the chemo?"

"Did they say what they hoped to accomplish with chemo, you know, how long would it extend your life?"

"They keep saying they can't promise anything. Maybe I could keep going another six months."

"Well, if it were me, Janice, I'd skip the treatment, put

my affairs in order, and enjoy life as much as possible."

"I'm glad to hear you say that because I want my last days close to you and my family. My sister and her husband will be here with me quite a bit since we've gotten much closer over the last few years."

Anna reached over the table to take Janice's hand. "I wish I could take this on for you. If I could, I would rather die before you. I will be here, too; just give me the times you want me here or are going to be alone."

From then on, Anna spent all her free time with Janice. The women put Anthony's driving service to good use. In addition to taking her to Helmhurst, Anna had them go to Helmhurst to pick Janice up so she could spend a few days with her in Minneapolis.

Anna buried Janice in the Ida Malloy Memorial Cemetery, which had become so near and dear to her heart. Like her friend Anna, Janice had grown to love the serenity she felt each time she visited Ida. Janice left this earth on November 11, 1998, Armistice Day, leaving behind a lonely, heartbroken friend. Janice was eighty-one years old. Anna was angry with God because she didn't get much time with her after her diagnosis.

§§§

On December 5, 1999, Anna was seated in the concert auditorium on the campus of St. Olaf College. As they waited for the concert to begin, she slipped into a daydream.

"I wonder, Janice, how long have we been friends? We were teenagers when we met at the Big House in 1933, right?"

Janice said, "Yes, and this summer will mark the forty-ninth year of our friendship. Almost half a century. Wouldn't it be fun to be able to tell Bea about how we turned out?"

"Oh, my goodness, yes. I remember we had to give those 'dream speeches' about what we wanted to do with our lives. It sounds corny, but mine sort of came true. I live in Minneapolis and do mending in a laundry. I don't own a thread store, but I'm in the sewing business in a big way if you count the charity."

Anna snapped back to the current world when the woman beside her coughed. She lost Janice a year ago, and she had aged considerably. Anna still stung from the loss of her best friend and savior. Cancer took Janice from her in what seemed like a flash. It was a mere four months from diagnosis until her death, quickly by cancer standards.

During the first stage of her grieving, Anna could only deal with the loss of Janice, the person. Now, she began processing the emotional hurt, which tired her. Sarah said it was normal for her to have fatigue. "You're depressed, Anna. It's normal for people to be depressed when they've lost someone they love."

Anna tried to stop thinking about Janice. She wanted to enjoy Julie Ann Barnhorst's concert with the St. Olaf Concert Honors Choir. It was a choir known as one of the best choirs in the country. The stage was empty except for the risers, and the auditorium was slowly filling with parents and alumni.

Sarah and Karl were sitting next to her, talking with friends. *They know everyone,* Anna thought. Sarah suggested Anna dress for the occasion, so Anna wore a black wool skirt, a red blouse, and a white jacket. She sat straight, took a deep breath, and let her mind go again.

Her retirement from Wong's Laundry meant more time for Anna to enjoy life and do the things she always wanted to do. She and Janice enjoyed AAA bus tours of the Black Hills of South Dakota, the Rocky Mountains, and New York City. One winter, they even flew to California for a two-week tour.

She was eighty-two and long retired from Wong's Laundry. She recalled that, while there, she saw them grow from one little shop in south Minneapolis to a chain of ten laundries with three full time and several part-time seamstresses. They were famous for offering mending services, the only dry cleaner that still provided that service. The Wong children were entering the family business, with bigger dreams for the future.

Before she could go further down memory lane, the lights went down, and she felt Sarah take her hand. The concert began with the sopranos singing in hushed tones, "Low how a rose e're blooming."

Anna soon spotted Julie and smiled. *Julie, you are a free spirit if I ever met one.* Anna recalled holding a squirming and restless baby girl in her lap. *This child has always been on the move.*

As the program continued with some of the best choral arrangements in the country, Anna slipped back into her past, trying not to think about Janice. But it didn't work. She thought of the time Janice illegally stole her records and disposed of them by burning them in a trash barrel in her backyard. *That took so much courage on her part. She did it for me.* And later, Anna lied during her testimony in the Gundy trial, denying she knew what happened to her records. She saw it as her turn to protect Janice.

When the concert ended, Karl, Sarah, and Anna met Julie and one of her friends at a local diner for hamburgers and malts. Julie ensured she sat by Anna because she and Anna had bonded in her pre-school days when "Aunt Anna" became a regular at their home. Plus, she and her parents were at odds over what she wanted to do with her future.

"Aunt Anna," Julie said, "Did you and Mom ever get your kitchen floor redone? That old floor looks like the 1950s."

"It wasn't that old by a long shot, but yes, we replaced the old floor when your mom spruced up the house a few years ago."

"Sorry, I haven't been over to see you much. We want you to be modern, don't we, Mom?"

Sarah wasn't smiling when she replied, "Sure thing, Julie."

Anna could detect the strain between mother and daughter and recalled she didn't always see eye-to-eye with her mom. Even in high school, Julie began calling Anna to talk and share her frustrations with her mom. "She's just being your mother," Anna would reply. "Be patient. It will all be okay."

On the way back to the Barnhorsts' home, Anna sat in the back seat staring at the amber dashboard lights. Karl and Sarah discussed their feelings about their daughter and her contrarian attitude. That was a conversation she was too tired to care about. Soon, they were pulling up to their large home, where Anna would spend the night until the following day when a driver would take her home.

"You were quiet on the ride back," Sarah mentioned as she pulled back the covers for Anna.

"Oh, I was thinking about how Julie and I hit it off so well. She calls me from time to time, you know. She has called me a few times lately, but I wouldn't worry too much if I were you. A mother-daughter bond is one of the strongest on earth. She's testing her wings. You two will soon be close."

"I hope so, Anna."

"Sarah, I want to go see Janice."

"Good. I'll check my schedule and let you know."

"No, I want to go alone. I'll call the service Anthony arranged for me. They can drive me out there. No need for you to take a whole day out of your busy schedule just to do that."

"Are you sure?"

"Yes."

"And Sarah, I just want you to know that I'm ready to go. I've done the best I knew how and now, I want to be with Janice. I miss her terribly."

Sarah replied, "I think you are just going to have to wait a bit longer. We all love you here, and I think you have to spend a little more time with us. You have a big family you know."

Later that evening, when Karl and Sarah had turned out their lights, Sarah rolled over to Karl and said, "I think Anna has lost a few steps since Janice died."

Karl replied, "She and Janice were as close as sisters. I think you're right, though. Grieving has been hard for her."

§§§

September 9, 2002, Anna was the center of attention for the sizeable twenty-fifth-anniversary celebration of the Warm Coats for Children program. The charity had continued to grow and now served all of Hennepin County and a few nearby communities. There were local sewing centers where the best seamstresses came to repair coats that were too complicated to fix in volunteers' homes. The centers also served as training centers for recruits. The warehouse now required a full-time inventory manager who oversaw sorting incoming coats and the selection of a coat that matched each child's needs. A new computer program kept track of every jacket, and there were four part-time seasonal distribution managers. Finally, drivers took coats to the community centers for immediate distribution to the families requesting them.

Volunteers moved boxes of coats to the sides so the

warehouse could accommodate the celebration. Rows of chairs ran down the middle of the warehouse. Refreshment tables were placed on each side of the rows. Finally, a podium was placed at the front of the rows. The crowd was large because Anna's program impacted tens of thousands of people. In Minneapolis, she was a folk hero—the woman who came out of Helmhurst with nothing, looking for a way to understand her new life. Then, in a fairy tale twist, she met a little boy, hoping to find a mother.

The best part of the event for Anna was that Anthony came home so he could attend with her. As usual, Anna did her best to meet as many people as possible, but her efforts were hampered by her fatigue. Sarah Barnhorst served as her escort and made sure she wasn't overdoing it. Anthony was also a celebrity in the black community because he was the first person to get a coat from Anna and still represented their hopes and dreams. It went without saying they were proud of his rising to the top of his profession.

Doris Patton, director of Warm Coats for Children, opened the program by giving the background of how Anna and Annalee Washington started the program. She had slides and images highlighting the program's timeline, which Anna enjoyed. After speeches by the mayor and other elected officials, the current chairperson of the board gave her remarks. Anna felt out of place and humbled by the whole event. She begged not to be asked to provide comments, but everyone wanted to hear from her.

She stood at the podium feeling unsteady and trying to think of the words she needed to start speaking. Suddenly, Anthony was standing beside her, holding onto her arm. She looked up at his beaming face and was ready to begin. "People talk about what I have done for children, but no one knows what I got from this deal. And that's the point I want to make. By using my sewing skills, I dealt with my depression and sense of alienation. As prisoners say, 'Unless you have lost your freedom—in my case for over forty years— you don't know how hard it is to adjust to life on the outside.'

"All I know is that I received more from giving away coats than I gave. But I got a bonus, something even more important, a son." She smiled at Anthony and, for a brief second, rested her head on his shoulder. "Let me finish by saying that one way to heal whatever emotional problem you are experiencing is to give to others. Help someone out. No matter how small your act of kindness might be, it will help the recipient. Giving of yourself means receiving self-respect and healing.

"Thank you so much for throwing this big celebration."

All those close to her came to her house after the event. Eva, Big JJ, and their children, and Sarah, Karl, Johnny, and Julie Ann, were there. Anthony had arranged for a catered light dinner. Anna basked in the warm glow of having the people she loved the most all to herself. She thought of them all as her children even though she knew that wasn't technically true. Mel and Mary, plus Margaret, paid short courtesy visits. They understood this was a time for Anna to be close to those people who were now her family.

Everyone could see Anna was fading at about 7:30 p.m. So Sarah suggested they let Anna rest. When they were all gone, Anthony told Sarah, "Go ahead and get Mom ready for bed. I'll come in and talk when she is ready." He lay beside her on her bed, staring at the ceiling, and they talked for two hours. Mother and son, enjoying the chance to be alone, talking about whatever came to mind.

§§§

It seemed to Anna that she was walking a little slower each day, and the weeks passed more quickly. *It has been five years since Janice died, and I'm still here. I miss her. But I have a family for which I'm thankful. Imagine me, a person not fit to live in society, sterilized, with a loving group of people around me. I think I'm closer to my family and friends than most people are to their biological kin.*

Life was now a simple routine. Every day, her first job was to text Sarah, Big JJ, and Anthony something to the effect, `"I'm up, and I feel fine."` If, for some reason, she forgot to text by 10 a.m., one of them would be on the phone with her, wondering if she was okay.

At first, she chaffed at having to do the texts. She likened it to being on a leash. But she realized it was them caring about her. Unlike many people her age, she liked her mobile phone. She loved the pictures people sent her and the ability to text Anthony, Sarah, and Big JJ anytime she wished to ask a question or share a thought.

Then came her ritual breakfast of coffee, toast, and scrambled eggs, followed by reading the paper. And like Hilda, she fell asleep for a quick nap around 10 a.m. She enjoyed the quiet time and the ability to reflect on things that were important to her.

On Saturday morning, December 6, 2003, Anna felt different, but not in a good way. Her heart was out of rhythm. She could feel its rapid beating in her chest, followed by short periods of calm. Over and over, the cycle of fast, hard beats was followed by calm ones. It wasn't her first time feeling this, but it was more pronounced today. She heard the door open and knew it was Big JJ, so she quickly finished buttoning her blouse. Sure enough, Big JJ had the donuts and coffee ready."

"How many donuts do you think you've brought over?" Anna asked.

"I don't know, Anna, quite a few. Are you ready to switch to something else?"

"No, I still like the same old sour cream." Once again, the coffee and donuts proved to be a catalyst for pleasant conversation. But as Big JJ put their cups into the sink and cleaned up the crumbs, Anna said, "Before I forget, I have a favor to ask of you before you leave today. Would you get that wooden box in my bedroom closet? You know, the old pine box my dad brought from Norway."

"Sure. What do you want me to do with it?"

"For now, just put it on the dining room table. I'll get a towel to put underneath."

Anna opened the box, felt underneath the quilt, and came up with the old knife her dad had gotten from his grandfather. "Here, Charles, I want you to have this."

"What? You've given me so much already."

Ignoring his comment, Anna continued. "I just remembered I had this, and you are the right person to get it. It's a good-quality knife my dad got from his grandfather in Riset, Norway. I don't know of anyone else who would appreciate it. Besides, you've helped care for me for a long time."

"Naw, stop talking like that. This is so nice. I will always treasure it. Not to change the subject, are you feeling okay this morning? You look tired."

"I am. My heart is out of sync, and I think I need to go lay down for a bit."

Big JJ helped Anna get under the bedspread. As he turned to leave, she grabbed his arm. "I love you, Charles. I'm ready, you know. I'm ready to be with Janice. Would you call Anthony and Sarah for me and tell them I love them, too?"

Before he could reply, she was asleep. He immediately texted Anthony and Sarah. `"I don't think she is doing well. She returned to bed and was out like a light within seconds. She said that her` heart is out of sync."

Although Dr. Karl Barnhorst had retired, he canceled his morning workout, picked up Sarah, and drove to Anna's house. Big JJ stayed with Anna, sitting by her side and holding her hand. She was not responsive to his questions and struggled to breathe.

Karl examined Anna, and he, too, failed to get any response. He called Anthony, "Karl here, and I have some bad news for you. I think the time we have all been dreading has come. Your mom isn't doing well. She could go at any time. I think you need to get here as fast as you can.

"You have a choice. I can call St. Ann's and then transport her there. They can help her live a little longer, but she won't have a quality of life. The second option is to leave her here, and I can have a friend come to examine her and, if necessary, give her some comfort medication."

"Karl, I don't think that's even a choice. Mom would want to die at home, and she signed all the forms waiving any measures to prolong her life. Go ahead and have someone examine her and order some comfort medication in case we need it. Plus, if we need a nurse, order that as well. Is Sarah and Big JJ there with you?"

"Yes, they're here."

"Keep me posted on how she's doing. I'll be there as soon as I can. Hopefully, tonight."

The next day was Sunday, and everyone was in the living room, including Anthony, who arrived about one a.m. Anna remained in the bedroom, lost to the current world as she slipped further away from those she loved.

My mom loved all kinds of people, Anthony thought. *Look how Big JJ, Sarah, and their families are all here, enjoying the support we can give each other.* Anthony looked at everyone in the room and smiled, "You know, I am amazed at how she brought us all together. She created a family where none existed. I think that's very powerful, don't you?" Everyone nodded as Sarah got up and hugged Anthony.

During that day, they each took one-hour shifts at Anna's bedside, holding her hand. Around dinner time, they decided to order pizza. About an hour after they finished eating, Karl re-evaluated Anna. "Maybe we should all gather around. She is very close now." Big JJ suggested they hold hands and say the Lord's Prayer. They waited, talking softly, sharing small bits and pieces of their experiences with Anna, and saying prayers. With heavy hearts, they listened as she struggled to breathe. The gurgling from deep inside her chest continued until she grew quiet.

Karl listened to her chest and nodded that she was gone.

Anthony kissed his mother's forehead and pronounced, "She's with Jesus and Janice now."

Karl stood up and suggested they all leave the room so Anthony could spend time with his mother. On his way out of the room, he stopped, put his hand on Anthony's shoulder, and said, "Let me know when you want me to make the call."

§§§

December 22, 2003, was crystal clear and a minus one degree. The storm from the night before had moved off to the east, leaving the city covered in a fresh blanket of snow. In addition to preparing for Christmas services, St. Paul's church staff were hard at work preparing for what they anticipated to be an overflow turnout for Anna Olson's funeral. They readied the basement as an overflow room with a large screen showing a live video of the funeral upstairs. On either side of the lectern and pulpit, the traditional sea of poinsettias spilled down the two steps to the main floor.

Pastor James Truman was the St. Paul's pastor who knew

Anna best. At Anna's request, he worked with Rev. Charlene Bond from Nazareth Baptist Church to include that church in the service. They worked out all the details for a joint ecumenical funeral.

The pastors stood at the back of the church, surveying the packed pews. They noticed the ushers were moving latecomers to the basement, where they could watch via the video feed. Already seated were people close to Anna and her family. Mr. and Mrs. Wong, the first people to arrive, sat just behind the family. Many of the people who were close to Anna sat near the Wongs. They included Margaret Pattersen, Mary Fortis and Martin England, Representative Helmquist, Doris Patton and her oldest son, and many others who came into Anna's life.

As soon as the family assembled for the funeral procession that would go down the main aisle, Pastor Truman began the service from behind the congregation.

"Blessed be the God and Father of our Lord Jesus Christ, the source of all mercy, and the God of all consolation. He comforts us in all our sorrows so that we can comfort others in their sorrows with the consolation we ourselves have received from God."

The congregation responded: "Thanks be to God."

He paused a moment before nodding to Pastor Bond, and the two led Anna's coffin down the middle aisle to the front of the church. Anthony, Sarah, Karl, and their children Julie and Johnny followed the casket, as did Big JJ, Eva, and their three children. Soon, everyone noticed the quilt covering her coffin. They had never seen such a large and colorful blanket cover a casket.

The audience listened closely to the fifteen Nazareth Baptist Church choir members who sang "On Christ the Solid Rock I Stand" as an African American spiritual. Their emotional goodbye to Anna brought tears to many.

Julie Ann Barnhorst read from Ecclesiastes 3. *"For everything there is a season, and a time for every matter under heaven: a time to be born, and a time to die."*

Sarah came to the lectern to give the first testimonial to Anna's life.

"Like you, I am overwhelmed with sadness today." She stopped for a moment to take a deep breath. "I am sad that Anna is gone, and I'm sad because her journey through life was so difficult. She endured suffering the likes of which I hope no one today will experience. I'm going to tell you about the side of Anna you may not know. Perhaps it will help you appreciate her other strengths.

"Anna was born on a small family farm near Redwood Falls. She had one older brother. In her early teens, tragedy struck her family when her father died in a freak snowstorm, and then her mother died of influenza. She was confined to Helmhurst by court order in 1933 because she was an orphan and had two seizures. The judge felt Helmhurst would give Anna the proper care for her seizures plus a formal education. Although her confinement was ill-advised, some good came from her early years at Helmhurst. For example, she met Janice Haggedorn, who remained a lifelong friend.

"But Anna always believed she didn't belong in an institution and never stopped struggling to be released. At one point, she learned she could get out of Helmhurst if only she would agree to be sterilized." Sarah stopped again and wiped away a tear from her cheek. "She agreed, but with the procedure completed, she learned that the opportunity for a discharge no longer existed. Researchers later discovered that administrators used this ruse to sterilize thousands of people, primarily women, in the United States.

"But as the decades passed, she experienced even more hardship. The psychotic son of the institution's chief

Psychologist raped her. Shortly after, the man who sheltered her by giving her a private room died. She told me once that he was the only man she truly loved.

"Now, she was alone. Her world deteriorated until she became an unpaid aide in a 'hell on earth' women's ward in Helmhurst. Plus, she lived with people with much lower cognitive abilities. Her spirits reached an all-time low.

"Anna's lifelong friend, Janice Haggadorn, finally found a way to help Anna out of her miserable life. Janice, now an administrative assistant, broke some rules and secretly added Anna's name to a list of candidates for discharge. Finally, the path was open for a release.

"And that's when I met Anna. She came to my Community Bound program tangled up with emotions. My staff and I soon realized she was intellectually normal and ready to learn something she always maintained while in Helmhurst. Unfortunately, she left Helmhurst with decades of trauma weighing her down." Sarah stepped back, bowed her head, and tried to compose herself. She stood there, looking vulnerable and alone, so Johnny came to her side and put his arm around his mother's shoulder. She straightened up and continued.

"But Anna had more character and grit than we all thought. She struggled with adjusting to her new life and was making progress. She dedicated herself to leaving her trauma and anger in the past. At this point, Anna re-subjected herself to all the horrors from her Helmhurst days by agreeing to be a witness in what became known as the Gundy trial. At that trial, she talked about all the terrible things she saw and experienced. Sharing her horrible experiences opened the way for the court to have a firsthand look at the life of a person who lived in institutions like Helmhurst. She demonstrated that those who lived there and other places like it did not have the same Constitutional guarantees everyone else enjoyed. Somehow, she overcame all that pain, anger, and trauma and gave us a powerful example of how to give to others.

"Anna was the strongest person I've ever met." With tears streaming down her face, Johnny helped her return to her seat between her husband and Julie.

The second lesson, Isaiah 61:1, was read by a member of Nazareth Baptist Church and one of the women who helped Anna with her quilt.

"The Spirit of the Lord God is upon me, because the Lord has anointed me to bring good tidings to the afflicted; he has sent me to bind up the brokenhearted, to proclaim liberty to the captives, and the opening of the prison to those who are bound;"

"My name is Charles Johnson. You may know me better by my nickname, Big JJ. I stand in front of you as a drug addict and a convict. I'm the man who assaulted Anna for the small amount of money in her purse. I admitted to my crime and accepted my punishment of seven years at Stillwater. Those seven years were a nightmare, but interestingly, they served as a bridge between Anna and me.

"As a recovering addict, I am thankful for my sobriety daily and attend a weekly support group. I am pleased that I am the old man of the group, with 8,850 days of sobriety.

"Here is how I think of Anna. Imagine if there were a person who forgave you for leaving her unconscious and lying on the frozen sidewalk. Imagine someone who wrote to you each week you were in prison, encouraging you. Try to think of how many people you know would come to visit you in prison when you are depressed or discouraged. I met a person who did those things, Anna Olson.

"We bonded, the older white lady and a young black convict. You wouldn't understand such a bond unless you did seven years in prison or forty-one years in an institution where you did not belong. Anna helped me, and in some ways, I think I helped her.

"We shared everyday experiences and emotions. For example, in both places, there was always background noise, such as screaming from someone being beaten or terrorized by a ghost in their head. We both lived with the constant presence of danger, where a fight or a staff person might harm you at any moment. It wears on you.

"But besides our institutional background, Anna and I shared something else . . . sour cream donuts. Every Saturday morning, I would bring coffee and sour cream donuts to her house at eight a.m. sharp. We'd talk for no more than an hour before she was off to sew coats. But that hour was a great time to share what we'd been doing during the prior week, what we were looking forward to, and sometimes, flashbacks to the bad old days. It was a time for us to be honest about our feelings.

"She challenged me to do something to help others as she had done. I told her there was no way I could live up to her legendary kindness. There was no way I could start another Warm Coats for Children service. Only Anna had the compassion needed to create that charity. But I promised her I would learn the practice of doing small things that benefit others. And to be sympathetic to the plight of anyone less fortunate whenever possible.

"I am one of the lucky ones. I had two loving parents, a wonderful, accepting wife, and Anna Olson, to help me get by. I will miss Anna. She was a part of me, and I will dedicate the rest of my life to living up to the example she set. I believe Anna was all about forgiving without bounds and loving without limits."

Big JJ walked toward where he and Eva sat. She got up, went to him, put her arm through his, and walked him back to their pew.

A soloist from St. Paul's Lutheran sang "Ave Maria," one of Anna's favorite songs. Its melody drifted out over Anna's casket and those in attendance. Tears moistened the eyes of those who knew that Anna loved the song.

Anthony Washington walked to the lectern and took notes from his suit coat. "Thank you all for joining us in remembering my mother. I'm very grateful for your outpouring of love and support for me, my brother, and my sister. I know that sounds strange, but Sarah and Charles and their families were as much a part of Anna's family as I was. We have all grown close, and yes, that's another of Anna's accomplishments. We thank Pastor Truman and Reverand Bond for creating a funeral service for my mother that includes two churches. My mother is looking down on this service, and she has a big smile on her face. Watching her church and mine work together to make this beautiful service is a dream come true for her, and I know it is for me.

"Like Charles or Big JJ, as we all affectionately call him, said, I, too, am one of the lucky ones. For some reason, Anna noticed me hanging out in front of Wong's Laundry, wearing only a sweatshirt when the temperature was well below zero. In her mind, I should have been wearing a coat. But someone stole my coat at school, and I was too shy to tell my grandmother because I knew she couldn't afford to buy me a new one.

"Later on, Anna told me she was upset with me since I ran down the street every time she tried to talk to me. Well, finally, she chased me down. She found my house, met my grandmother, gave me a coat, and the idea for Warm Coats was born. Anna and my grandmother Annalee Washington became friends. Their charity work was infectious. Soon, other women got involved, as even more people stepped forward, saying they needed a coat.

"Anna's charity didn't stop with coats. She found out I could go to Westgate Academy on a scholarship if only they could find a way to pay the one hundred and twenty-five dollars per month in fees. Again, Anna stepped forward. She and her landlord, Hilda, paid my fees so I could attend Westgate. That school opened the world of knowledge to me.

"To say that Anna was my mother is miraculous. Just as she was opening her heart to support me financially, she agreed to take me on as a foster child when my Grandma Washington died. It was an impossible dream come true for a poor, scrawny child bouncing between my mother's druggie life and my grandmother's house. It's like God reached down and put Anna Olson before me." Anthony stopped, wiped away some tears, and took a breath.

"I don't want you to think of me as vain or self-aggrandizing, but I will soon be the first black and youngest CEO of a major energy consulting firm. That was made possible by my mother, her friend Hilda, and the encouragement of my church. I'm so thankful and appreciative of your ongoing support.

"Now, on to another topic. Anna probably knew the ladies of Nazareth Baptist Church best. They all became friends when they were the first volunteers for the coat project. But you probably don't know, there were some prolific quilters in that group. Those quilters taught Anna to quilt and helped her make this astounding piece you see on her coffin today. That is no ordinary quilt. Instead of writing in a journal, Anna recorded the significant events in her life through needlepoint. Anna made those needlepoints into that quilt.

"How can that be, you ask? Needlepoints are flowers and plants and trees and cottages in the woods. As you will someday see, her needlepoints are vivid and detailed scenes of things that happened in her life. You can see shadows on a brow and the whiskers on a grizzled man sitting on the floor. I'm not overstating the fact when I say they are breathtaking. There are nearly one hundred separate scenes or needlepoints that Anna and the ladies from Nazareth Baptist assembled through endless hours of stitching. They spent years making the quilt. The scenes on that quilt prove that she was a genius of an artist. Yet, she wanted to keep that part of her life secret for some reason.

"I'm pleased to tell you that we will share her secret gift someday. I've donated the quilt to the Minnesota Museum of Art for mounting preservation and display. I believe it is something you will want to be sure to see. I know . . . it's just a quilt. But once you see it, it will affect you, move you.

"As I now have to say goodbye to my beloved mother, I think of her as humble. She stayed with her principles of love, forgiveness, and doing good for others. She lived a Christian life. And we are all the better for her touching us."

Anthony bowed his head and walked toward his seat, stopping by her casket to put his hand on the coffin. He put his forehead on the top of the quilt and said whispered, "I love you, Mom." With that, a member of the Nazareth choir got up, came to him, and consoled him as he cried. When he was ready, she led him to his seat.

Reverend Charlene Bond stood up and sang the first few lines of "Amazing Grace." She then gave a short sermon on how God works through people some call "the least of these."

"Consider Anna Olson, forced to endure suffering and shame because some people saw her as unfit for society. God raised her up to be a queen among the faithful and the poor. He gave her the kindness and mercy to reach out to those who hurt her. And God also gave her the ability to forgive. It was hard for Anna to realize that she needed to forgive the people who did her all that harm. But she did as God commanded, and now she is there with Him. She is there enjoying eternal love and peace forever." Reverend Bond concluded by reading Psalm 23, with a piano playing softly.

Pastor Smith led worshipers from two churches in a traditional Lutheran funeral service. He brought the service to a close by placing his hand on the coffin and reciting this commendation, *"Into your hands, O merciful Savior, we commend your servant, Anna Olson. Acknowledge, we humbly beseech you, a sheep of your own fold, a lamb of your own flock, a sinner of your own redeeming. Receive her into the arms of your mercy, into the blessed rest of everlasting peace, and into the glorious company of the saints in light."*

After the service, the mourners spilled out onto the sidewalk but didn't disperse. Most stopped and waited out of respect while the pallbearers placed her coffin, minus the quilt, into the hearse.

§§§

Five days after her funeral, two dozen people stood beside the open gravesite in the Ida Malloy Memorial Cemetery. Anna's final wish was now a reality. She specified in her will her desire to be buried here, with the mostly forgotten people. It was because thoughts of poor Ida sneaked in and out of her mind all the rest of her life. Unlike many, who eventually forget an old friend, Anna held Ida close. Anna had always wished she could have done more to help her friend, who suffered so much. Perhaps this was the foundation for her charity and kindness late in life. At least she could help somebody else. That's how Anna Olson survived trauma.

But equally important was Janice, her best friend, the person she was closest to in the world. She wanted to be next to Janice, who was already waiting for her friend. Bundled against the cold, Pastor Truman began with a prayer and conducted the short graveside service. Before they dispersed, Anthony had a few things to say.

"Some of you find it odd that we're miles from her Minneapolis home and people she knew. I think, though, she has returned home. She often came to this place when she needed refuge from the madness inside the institution. She has returned to the place that shaped her and set the course of her life. Finally, we can share in the love the three young women had for each other. Plus, the dignity of a name for the rest of the poor souls buried here.

"Anna brought us together. Now, we must love each other the way she taught us. Be kind, charitable, and humble." Anthony smiled. "My preaching is over. Please join our family at Davidson's Restaurant here in Helmhurst for brunch."

CHAPTER 13

THE QUILT

"Ballard. His full name was Albert Tommy Ballard."

Susan Halterman

2004

It took nearly a year and a half to establish the debut for Anna's quilt. Polly Morgenstern, the artistic director of the Minnesota Museum of Art, had several steps to complete before previewing the piece. In August of 2004, technicians from the Smithsonian started preparing the quilt for viewing in a gallery. They sewed rows of loops using heavy thread. The rows of thread were twelve inches apart, making ten horizontal and ten vertical rows.

They carefully threaded a small fiberglass rod through each row, and where the fiberglass rods intersected, special clips held them together. Then, they placed the quilt on a custom-made hardwood backing and inserted it in a ten-foot square vacuum-sealed frame. When placed upright, the viewer had an unobstructed vision of Anna's masterpiece.

With the quilt ready for display, the next decision was to determine when and how to show an additional thirty-eight pieces of Anna's most outstanding needlepoints. The overwhelming answer was that they be displayed with the quilt but in separate rooms.

The Anna Olson Trust moved forward with three plans regarding the quilt's future. They accepted Minnesota Press's proposal for publishing a table book showing high-resolution pictures of each quilt piece and an explanation with each photo. Their second decision was to authorize well-respected biographer Charles Grant to write Anna's biography.

Finally, Art Tours, Inc. was selected to manage all aspects of showing the quilt in different cities. After one year in Minneapolis, the quilt would spend six months at the Museum of Modern Art in New York, the Art Institute of Chicago, the National Gallery in Washington, DC, and the Los Angeles County Museum of Art. The quilt would finally return to Minneapolis by the fall of 2009.

The art museum began renovating the display rooms to best display the quilt and the accompanying examples of Anna's needlepoint. Meanwhile, Miss Morgenstern started to spread the word about the quilt. She invited people from the media, quilting groups, art collectors, and disability rights advocates to private viewings and asked them to provide their thoughts. The early comments were not as positive as Polly Morgenstern had hoped. It was soon apparent that the quilt was a complex display of talent and required several viewings to comprehend all it represented.

As 2004 edged into 2005, praise for Anna's quilt increased. Polly became more confident that the world would accept the quilt as a treasure. Gradually, the media began to do a few news articles on Anna and her quilt. The arts and crafts community hailed it as a breakthrough into the relatively new medium of needlepoint as art. For reference purposes, they pointed to well-known pieces of needlepoint art that emerged in the 1970s. Those pieces, however, paled in comparison to Anna's masterpiece. The disability community marveled at how Anna had captured so much of the institutional life in which many of their people lived.

§§§

"The Quilt," as it came to be known, was a success. The news media eventually provided extensive coverage. Art critics used phrases such as *"A must see!"* or *"A new art form is born!"* Anna's quilt was *"An instant classic!"* and she, a *"Genius!"* Requests for interviews with Anthony were numerous, and his assistant worked with him to be sure everyone got an interview, even if it was late at night.

With the publication of Charles Grant's book *Bad Genes, Genius Genes*, several pieces of the quilt began to stand out. The first was a haunting piece that featured a close-up of a woman's face. Anthony named it *Ida* because Anna had told him it was a portrait of Ida Malloy. With hollow eyes, pale, sunken cheeks, and her hair a tangled mess of red, it was a portrait of suffering. The discussion in the art community was about how Anna had stitched an emotionally revealing piece. The picture of her needlepoint of Ida made its way to the top of the many stories Anna told in the quilt.

Another needlepoint, called *Albert*, also caught the public's eye. It displayed a man on the floor, reaching up. Anna had captured a poignant interaction between the man and a woman leaning over him. A final piece called *Family* brought a strong reaction. It showed an older white woman and a tall, young, black man staring straight ahead. This piece was oval, with a background that quickly faded away, bringing the subjects closer to the viewer. Critics were especially interested in the relationship between the two. They sat close to each other, and if one looked at the details, one could see they were holding hands. There was no doubt it was Anna and Anthony.

§§§

On May 9, 2005, the quilt and companion pieces selected for the gallery were less than a month away from the June 1 grand opening. A gray-haired woman repeatedly knocked on the door to the offices of The Minnesota Museum of Art. Finally, a janitor approached to see what she wanted. He listened to her explain why she was there and said she could accompany him. He took her to his small workroom and called someone. Finally, after about twenty minutes, he smiled and said, "Come with me."

"Miss Morgenstern, this is Miss Susan Halterman from Green Bay, Wisconsin. She would like to talk to you for just a moment."

Polly nodded, and the janitor stepped aside so Miss Halterman could enter. "I'm sorry to barge in on you. I know the quilt will not be open to the public for several weeks, but I'm leaving for home today, and it would mean the world if I could see the quilt for myself. For just a few minutes."

"I get the feeling there is more to this than that," Polly said.

"There is. You know that piece with the older man sitting on the floor with his arm up? Well, I am sure it's my Uncle Albert. After his discharge from Helmhurst, he eventually came to live with my mother and our family. Oh, he would brag about Anna. Using sign language, he told us how kind she was. He said Miss Olson enlisted help from a friend, and they got him to the dentist. They also got him clothes to wear and a wheelchair. As far as he was concerned, she was responsible for saving his life."

"That's a powerful story. I love hearing it. Of course, you can see the quilt."

"Thank you, Miss Morgenstern, and God Bless."

A few minutes later, Susan Halterman stood looking at the quilt with Polly Morgenstern in the shadows. Tears were streaming down her face as she saw in person the image of her uncle Albert, a discarded and despised human, being tended to by Anna Olson.

Susan turned away from the quilt and started walking out the door. She looked at Polly and said, "Ballard. His full name was Albert Tommy Ballard."

AUTHOR'S NOTES

The story of Anna Olson's life may not have come about had it not been for my good friend Ric Zaharia. Without his encouragement, guidance, and input, her journey through life would not be as historically accurate as it is.

I am also blessed to have the unwavering support of my family and neighbors. For *American Dream*, Donna Jackson read a late draft of the book and suggested changes that made the book read better. I am also in debt to my nephew, Kevin Nielsen, who gave me valuable insights into the behavior of people recently discharged from mental health institutions.

A fictitious trial in *American Dream* played a central role in shaping Anna's life. The trial draws from an actual lawsuit, *Welch v Likens*. In 1972, Patricia Welch, a resident of Cambridge State Hospital, and residents from five other state institutions sued the State of Minnesota for failure to provide services guaranteed by the US Constitution. Three of these services were the reason for the specific questions attorney Margaret Pattersen asked Anna in *American Dream*. After a two-week trial, the judge ruled in favor of the six residents, ushering in a new and better era of care for developmentally disabled citizens of Minnesota.

Anna left the Glacial Ridge Training Center, a part of Wilmar State Hospital, in the early stages of what was later called deinstitutionalization. Her release to a transitional program was factual, although the way I described it in

American Dream was fictitious.

While doing research for this book, I learned that one of the most significant adjustments people like Anna had to make was adapting to freedom. Almost all long-term residents of institutions experienced some level of post-traumatic stress after being discharged. Anna was no exception. She had flashbacks, periods of withdrawal, anger. Plus, she was ambivalent about her hatred toward the people who harmed her for decades.

Now that you've finished reading *American Dream,* perhaps you will agree that two of the most powerful scenes come at the end. I thought Anna's burial at Helmhurst was a fitting end to her life. Her son Anthony did an excellent job of explaining why. The second scene is at the very end when Susan turns away from the quilt and tells the museum curator Albert's last name. As you may recall, Anna was concerned that everyone buried at Helmhurst had a name. Even though he wasn't in that cemetery, Anna would have liked to join you in learning Albert's.

§§§

The most significant person in my life is my wife, Cheryl. She was, once again, with me throughout this book, reading, and editing line by line. She keenly sees a missed verb or when something is unclear. She sometimes made good observations about the storyline. For example, Cheryl is the one who suggested, early in our work, that I bury Anna at Helmhurst. I now believe that scene is the most poignant part of *American Dream.*

I owe all three books to Cheryl's never-ending love and encouragement. Not every spouse would be so supportive of their mate's daily disappearance into the office and sitting in front of a computer screen for hours on end.

Anna's story is now complete, but is it my last book? Right now, I would say, "Yes". But one never knows. A writing friend once told me that the urge to write is like a curse that never goes away. I think he might be right.

ABOUT THE AUTHOR

Kirby Nielsen lives in Delaware, Ohio. He has written three novels and numerous short stories. His research and subject matter are eugenics in America from 1900–1970.

After receiving his Master of Arts in Applied Behavior Analysis from Drake University, Mr. Nielsen became the director of professional services at the Wilmar State Hospital in Wilmar, Minnesota. There, he began a career that provided him with a rich background for his stories.

Although historical, Mr. Nielsen hopes his work will raise red flags in America so we may avoid the horrible mistake of adopting eugenics as a legitimate science. It is crucial work since eugenics and its ugly ramifications are beginning to reappear in some parts of American society.

ABOUT YO PRODUCTIONS

Yo Productions, LLC was founded by *Essence* bestselling author, Yolonda Tonette Sanders, Ph.D., in 2008. Initially, Yolonda started the company to produce a stage adaptation of her first book, *Soul Matters.* Over the years, Yo Productions has grown into a multi-faceted organization.

As a literary services provider, Yo Productions specializes in proofreading, editing, ghostwriting, and consulting, among other things, to address individual client needs. As a theatrical entertainment provider, Yo Productions aims to produce thought-provoking, dramatic performances that reach people from all walks of life. The company's motto, "Performance with Purpose," stems from the founder's desire to create and produce works that have meaning far beyond simply entertaining audiences. As a publishing consultant, Yo Productions helps authors navigate through their entire publishing process from the conception of a book idea to the publication of their work.

In addition to overseeing Yo Productions, Yolonda is also certified in emotional intelligence training, specifically using the EQ-i 2.0 and EQ 360 assessments. She has a Doctor of Philosophy in Organizational Leadership and enjoys using her skills and knowledge to assist others in achieving their organizational and personal goals.

Visit www.yoproductions.net to learn more or scan the following QR code.